MW01233046

Snowbound

Other novels by Patrick J. O'Brian include:

The Fallen
Reaper: Book One of the West Baden Murders Trilogy
The Brotherhood
Retribution: Book Two of the West Baden Murders Trilogy
Stolen Time
Sins of the Father: Book Three of the West Baden Murders Trilogy
Six Days
Dysfunction
The Sleeping Phoenix

Snowbound

Book Four in the West Baden Murders Series

A Novel

Patrick J. O'Brian

iUniverse, Inc.

New York Lincoln Shanghai

Snowbound

Book Four in the West Baden Murders Series

Copyright © 2006 by Patrick J. O'Brian

iUniverse books may be ordered through booksellers or by contacting:

iUniverse
2021 Pine Lake Road, Suite 100
Lincoln, NE 68512
www.iuniverse.com
1-800-Authors (1-800-288-4677)

This is a work of fiction. All of the characters, names, incidents, organizations, and dialogue in this novel are either the products of the author's imagination or are used fictitiously.

ISBN-13: 978-0-595-42136-7 (pbk)
ISBN-13: 978-0-595-86476-8 (ebk)
ISBN-10: 0-595-42136-9 (pbk)
ISBN-10: 0-595-86476-7 (ebk)

Printed in the United States of America

This is for all of the volunteers who
have kept the West Baden Springs Hotel
looking beautiful all these years. I appreciate
you all putting up with me, and want you
all to know we don't take the hard work
you do in the garden, giving tours,
and behind the scenes for granted. Thank
you all very much!

Thanks to Brad Wiemer, Carol Pyle,
Mark Adams, Nannette Bell,
Joy Winslow, Shane Buis, Jeff Lane,
and Sandi Woodward, for their insight
and contributions.

Thanks to Dave Blackford, Chi Baldwin,
Bob Fergison, Bruce Steward, Mike Ritchie,
John Craiger, Melissa Epping, and Rob
Fedorchak for their assistance on the cover.

Special thanks to Kendrick
Shadoan at KLS Digital for creating
the cover, handling photography, and
doing a great job as always.

Visit www.klsdigital.com

Another special thanks to Amy Burke
for the cover's background photo and
for the author photo.

Visit www.smalltownphotos.com

Forward

Factual History of West Baden Springs

1855   Dr. John A. Lane builds and opens the Mile Lick Inn a mile from French Lick, Indiana. He renames the inn to West Baden after Weisbaden, Germany and renames the hotel the West Baden Hotel.

1888   Indiana banker Lee Wiley Sinclair gains controlling interest in the hotel, changing its name to the West Baden Springs Hotel. The hotel is transformed into a world-class resort, adding an opera house, bicycle and pony track, casino, and a regulation-size baseball diamond. Local mineral water is touted as a cure for many ailments.

1901   On June 14 a fire breaks out at the hotel, consuming the entire wood-frame building. Sinclair vows to rebuild a better hotel that is fire-proof within the year. West Virginia architect Harrison Albright designs and builds a freestanding 200-foot dome at a cost of $414,000. Construction begins on October 15.

1902   Sinclair moves into his apartment at the hotel on the one-year anniversary of the fire. The hotel receives its first guests on September 15.

1916   Sinclair passed away on September 7 and lay in state in the Grand Atrium before his burial in Salem, Indiana. His daughter Lillian and son-in-law Charles Rexford inherit the hotel.

1917   The couple makes significant changes to the hotel including:
Refacing the fireplace in the atrium.
Adding a sunken garden with a fountain centerpiece.
The Seal Fountain is moved from the atrium to the driveway in front of the hotel.
A veranda is constructed that wraps around one-quarter of the building.
Brick spring houses replace the old wooden structures.
Over 12-million small tiles are placed as the new atrium flooring.
Benches, statues, trees, and urns are placed throughout the atrium for decoration.

1918   The hotel is leased by the government, serving as a military hospital during World War I.

1919   The hospital is closed, allowing the hotel to reopen for regular business once more.

1923   After her divorce from Rexford is final, Lillian sells the hotel to Ed Ballard for one-million dollars. Ballard is an entrepreneur known for his ties with circuses and gambling. Half the money repays the debt the Rexfords owed Ballard for hotel renovations, while the other half allows Lillian and her new husband to live out their dreams.

1929   The stock market crashes on October 29, leaving the hotel virtually empty within four days as the country entered the Great Depression.

1932   Poor economy forces Ballard to close the hotel on June 30.

1934   Ballard sells the hotel to the Jesuits for one dollar. The Catholic sect uses the hotel as a seminary called West Baden College. They remove many of the hotel's elaborate decorations, opting for plain adornments.

1964   Sometime in June the Jesuits closed the campus, moving to Chicago, Illinois.

1966   On November 2, the hotel is purchased at auction by the Whitings from Midland, Michigan.

1967   The Whitings donate the grounds to Northwood Institute for use as an Indiana campus.

1974   The building is listed on the National Register of Historic Places.

1983   Rising maintenance costs and several other factors force Northwood Institute to close their Indiana campus. The hotel has remained vacant since that time.

1987   The hotel is named a National Historic Landmark.

1991   An ice buildup and construction flaws cause a portion of the exterior wall to collapse.

1992   The Historic Landmarks Foundation of Indiana spends $200,000 for emergency repairs to repair and structurally stabilize the building.

1996   Historic Landmarks purchases the grounds for $250,000 which came from an anonymous donor.

Forward II

Where the Trilogy Picked Up

In 1998, I took my first tour of the grounds on a weekend when I had nothing else better to do. Though my parents had visited the grounds when they were in disrepair, I passed on the opportunity.

Regrettably.

My first look at the hotel's atrium awed me, and I still had the rest of the tour to finish. With the flash from my camera popping every several seconds, likely annoying those around me, I grew fascinated with the building in a heartbeat.

Immediately wheels spun inside my mind, telling me I had to write a novel centered around the West Baden Springs Hotel. Being a horror movie buff, this was my first attempt at a mystery novel with horror elements.

Centered around a professional firefighter who works part-time helping to restore WBS, he discovers the gruesome murder of his wife may be pinned on him by local detectives. Making matters worse, more murders happen around the hotel, which makes him the prime suspect in everyone's eyes.

The primary mystery behind the murders stems from the hotel's factual past, which helped me create several colorful characters. Toward the end of *Reaper*, my first hotel novel, I decided to follow it up with a tale of revenge, keeping the same core characters.

While in the early stages of writing *Retribution* it became painfully clear the characters needed even more development, so the trilogy was born with a major plot twist at the end of the second installment.

Everything ended on a happy note, closing the chapter of the hotel's restoration era … at least fictionally.

In the real world, Bill and Gayle Cook have done an exceptional job stabilizing and renovating the grounds. I commend them on the beautiful work they and their teams have done restoring the building and garden to their previous splendor.

Orange County residents voted, though not overwhelmingly, to allow gambling in their county, which allowed the Cook Group to take bids from other companies. What looked like a sure thing with the corporation voted to lead the project ended in disaster when that group filed for bankruptcy.

Luckily the Bill Cook chose to finish the renovation himself, creating another chapter in the legacy of WBS. Now, with the atrium, the ground floor, and the grounds completely finished, work has begun on model rooms. Next, the remaining five floors will see finished rooms, allowing the building to function as a hotel for the first time in decades.

Perhaps even by the time this book is complete and printed, which brings me to the reason for a fourth book.

While the trilogy focused on the restoration era, the new book, and any following it, will deal with current events in Orange County. They will allude to the events in the trilogy, but more importantly, the hotel's true past will be involved in solving any mysteries divulged by the characters.

Please keep in mind the events mentioned in this book from the restoration era through the present refer to my original trilogy, which is why the aforementioned time line stops abruptly in 1996. This is by no means an effort to diminish the rest of the hotel's history, or the hard work of the Historic Landmarks employees, but rather my way of keeping the continuity from the trilogy carrying into this new project.

Hopefully you've enjoyed the trilogy because this new chapter in the West Baden saga will revisit the past while bringing up new questions. It is meant to be a great read for newcomers to the series, yet highly rewarding for those who have experienced the trilogy.

1

Jana Privett's life read like a harlequin novel with bittersweet twists and turns, but no happy romantic ending.

Over the course of the past year, she had ended a sham of a marriage, lost her job at a tax firm, and redefined herself as an independent woman.

Despite losing custody of her only child to her unfaithful husband before he moved to Georgia, Jana refused to lay down and die. She found new work with an understanding boss soon after the settlement. She literally had to blow the dust off her real estate license after being hired by a firm that dealt almost exclusively with upscale properties.

Working in a more private sector, Jana loved the absence of squabbling over commission, and the competition conventional real estate sales brought. She had quickly gained confidence about selling upscale property, including the grounds she currently stood upon.

Jana felt more than a little strange standing in the parking lot outside the West Baden Springs Hotel grounds in Southern Indiana. After all, the hotel a short walk up a red brick drive had a sordid past. Though rich in history, its floors had seen their share of spilled blood.

By all rights she had permission to enter the grounds at her leisure from the man who owned them, but it seemed prudent to learn something about the hotel's history.

When Paul Clouse asked her firm to sell the grounds she jumped at the chance to make a big sale for a major client. Of course the hotel had a checkered history, but mostly from rumors that circulated after Clouse survived several attempts on his life.

She recalled his trouble centering around the Halloween season several years in a row. Ironically, today was October 30th, but she felt safe considering the hotel and Clouse had led quiet lives the past several years.

Around her, people either sat on several benches, or paced along the brick lot beside the ticket booth. After buying a ticket, Jana was given a white bordered sticker with a "12" printed on it in black marker. The numeral indicated she was part of the noon tour, meant to keep her from trying to take the tour twice.

Taking a moment to observe the dozen or so people taking the tour with her, Jana noticed most of them appeared to be older couples. A glance at their license plates indicated most of them visited from other parts of Indiana. One Illinois plate caught her eye, but she focused more on the tour, wondering how her new boss convinced Clouse to let their firm find the hotel new ownership.

Jana's position didn't allow her to ask too many questions of her boss because she was still his newest hire. Being a former resident of Orange County gave her an edge over her colleagues when Bryan Bell made his decision about who would show the property.

Some of the agents wanted no part of the assignment, considering the hotel's reported history.

Especially the murders.

She had one month to prepare herself for the first investment firms and casino companies wanting to make their bids on the property, so Jana simply focused on the task at hand.

Working with Bell, she formulated several ideas how to do more than simply show the hotel like a realtor might run prospective buyers through a regular home.

"We're ready to go," she heard a man's voice say, causing everyone to look up like dogs being called inside for dinner.

Following her fellow tourists toward a man wearing a green shirt and tan baseball cap with West Baden Springs emblems on them,

Jana stole a look at his name tag. She learned her tour guide's name was Max as the older man motioned for the group to walk behind him.

Most of the tour guides at the hotel were retired, or worked jobs allowing them to dedicate time to giving tours. Jana guessed Max to be a retired man from the gray hair protruding from the ball cap. His skin looked somewhat weathered from years of outdoor activity, but Jana figured him to be in his mid-sixties.

He carried a large binder of some sort, which appeared to contain photos and documents in protective plastic sleeves.

Thunder rolled in the distance as gray clouds overtook the sunny sky several miles away, ominously rolling in their direction. Jana couldn't recall the last time Southern Indiana had a rainy Halloween, but the forecast called for wet weather into early November.

"We should probably get started," Max said in his deep voice. "We should be inside by the time the rain hits."

Everyone huddled close together as they passed under the arch at the front of the grand hotel. Once through the opening they spread out along one of the brick paths leading up to the building. Two brick paths once served as drives up to the hotel, their red coloration unblemished by years of sunlight.

"Today we're going to take a trip back in time. Imagine if you will that visitors a hundred years ago visited these grounds for simple pleasures. The West Baden Springs Hotel was a pleasure resort known as far away as Europe. As many as fourteen trains per day might have stopped in the valley, bringing visitors to any number of pleasure resorts in the area."

Between the two drives a thick column containing a variety of garden plants and Victorian-style lamps led up to the hotel. Jana noticed the lamps all had small dedication plaques attached about eye-level on their green posts.

Keeping his back to the hotel and his eyes on the tourists, Max began speaking about halfway up the path, continuing to walk backwards as he did so.

"Back in 1887, when the railroad came to West Baden and French Lick, Lee Wiley Sinclair, a textile mill owner and banker, stepped off the train finding opportunity abound. He saw the future of big business, and knew there was money to be made through tourism. He wanted to make significant changes to the hotel as a new shareholder, but the other investors bucked the idea."

Max drew a crooked smile, pausing for effect. His eyes grazed over each member of the tour, drawing each of them into his story.

"He showed them by buying enough stocks to gain controlling interest of the hotel, and eventually changed the name to the West Baden Springs Hotel."

Stopping just short of the hotel itself, Max pointed to his left, still facing the guests on his tour.

"On your right is the old golf course," he began, prompting everyone to look to a mammoth yard beside them.

A few trees and some sort of small gazebo were the only objects blocking their view to the highway in the distance.

"Boxer Joe Lewis often came to the valley to train for his fights," Max commented, leading them a bit further down the path, glancing toward the ominous sky in the distance before continuing. "To your left, we have the footbridge that led to the Number 7 Spring, also known as Sprudel."

Max paused for everyone to look as he pointed toward the bridge, then led them down some brick steps into the sunken garden.

Jana looked around the garden, still colorful from the summer season, undisturbed by any fall frosts. A sudden breeze beat down some of the taller plants, bringing a cool chill along with it. She folded her arms, returning her attention to Max's presentation.

"Across the garden we have Hygeia, otherwise known as the Number 1 Spring in the day," Max said, pointing across the grounds to a beige structure about the size of a residential garage.

"Why did they have names *and* numbers?" one of the tourists inquired.

"It's believed the springs were all given odd numbers here because the French Lick Springs Resort had springs with even numbers. The two hotels were rivals in the early 1900's with businessman Thomas Taggart owning the resort down the road."

Max took them over to Apollo, another of the named springs, leading them to the edge of the intricate concrete monument that once served as a source of mineral water.

"All of the springs were capped when the Jesuits took over the grounds," Max explained, "but when renovation began in 1996 the springs were permanently sealed with concrete to keep them from bubbling up and disrupting the foundation of any buildings."

Thunder grumbled and clapped in the distance, growing closer. And louder.

"Let's head across the garden," Max suggested.

He stopped at the fountain centered in the sunken garden, talking about the original fountain being removed from the grounds years prior. Likely destroyed in the process, the fountain needed replacing because the garden appeared empty without it to the renovation crews.

Jana noticed concrete turtles and frogs spitting water streams at one another from rings inside the design element. Water continued to spurt upward from the centerpiece, surprising her that they left the fountain running so late in the season.

Max explained a bit more about the fountain to them, then led the group toward the small building he had identified as Hygeia. He led the way through the spring building's two doors, pausing until everyone squeezed inside behind him. Jana discovered relatively new concrete flooring where the spring had been capped, with stained glass windows and a single light fixture above.

Outside, the spring building had acquired foliage in the form of vines and plants along either of its lengthy sides, but inside Jana heard an echo from Max when he next spoke within the confined space.

"This is one of two remaining springs on the grounds. You've seen the walkway and bridge that led to the Sprudel Spring. That spring was capped with rocks and concrete blocks during the Jesuit era, and subsequently torn down sometime during Northwood Institute's tenure."

Max went on to explain some of the eras of the hotel, including its service as a hospital, the Jesuit era after the stock market crash, and the Northwood Institute days when it served as a college. He spoke briefly about dollar amounts and the parties involved with each transaction.

"If we time this right, we can be inside the hotel by the time the thunderstorm reaches us," Max commented. "You're on your own after the tours ends."

Everyone chuckled, including Jana, who suppressed urges to use her authorization to walk the grounds at her leisure.

She knew the tours were restricted, failing to cover every area of the grounds. If she planned to sell the hotel she needed to know the building and the grounds like her own house. Grand ideas raced through her mind about how to present the property as the perfect business opportunity when the time came.

Bell actively sought investors who might want the property, thinking he already had five potential buyers, so Jana needed to formulate a plan somewhat quickly.

"I'd be remiss if I didn't give you a look at the old bowling alley and the cemetery," Max noted aloud, leading them toward a building with a front that looked like an old city hall.

Colored the same yellow as a freshly baked cake, the building had writing inscribed within several bricks used to construct the facility that identified it.

"This is the old bowling and billiards pavilion," Max said, allowing people to peek through the front windows as they passed by. "Used for storage during the renovation, this building now sits empty until new ownership decides what to use it for."

He led the way toward a cemetery visible across the brick road that served as an employee and volunteer entrance. It too was brick like the main walk from the highway to the hotel's front entrance. No traffic passed by, but Max kept them at the edge of the garden, allowing only a distant view.

Jana took in the battered white crosses behind a series of winding brick steps with trimmed shrubs acting as borders. Perfectly mowed, the area sat partway up a hill with a full grove of trees behind it. She seemed to recall that the virtual forest behind the hotel grounds once served as a golf course for entertaining guests.

Some of the graves stood to the right side of the shrubs leading the way up, but Jana noticed something strange about one of the plots, finding Max staring at it as well. He quickly regained his composure, turning to usher the group toward the hotel.

"What is it?" she decided to ask him before he said a word.

"Nothing that concerns you, dear," he commented, forcing a thin smile.

Jana turned to look once again as he rounded the group up, saying something about them needing to beat the rain inside.

To the side of one tombstone, whiter than the others, sat a mound of dirt. She immediately recalled something about Clouse's trouble beginning when a Jesuit body was found inside the hotel basement after being dug up. This mound looked far too large to be the work of an animal.

It appeared deliberately dug, since part of the grave looked disturbed, but Jana had little time to take in the view as Max called for the rest of the group to join him.

She initially decided to exercise her right to roam the grounds, but when she saw Max lag behind the group to call in something on the portable radio he plucked from his belt, Jana changed her mind.

As she rejoined the group, her mind wandered to Paul Clouse and the rumors about his troubles with the property. Perhaps the stories were more than just urban legends after all.

2

Jana still couldn't believe she was invited to dinner with Paul Clouse to discuss her plans about how to present the hotel to potential buyers.

Her concerns about the disturbed grave reached his ears, through security at the hotel, giving her an opening to address security at the grounds when she invited out-of-state groups. Bell had already extended invitations to four groups, promising them details by the end of the week, which brought Jana face to face with the hotel's owner.

Seated at a corner booth in the back of the restaurant, Jana had a view of the entire place, including the maitre d' near the front door. A look at her watch indicated Clouse was fashionably late, causing her to wonder if he might cancel. The few wealthy clients she met through Bell seemed extremely full of themselves, caring little about anyone's time except their own.

Pleasant smells of grilled beef and some sort of garlic seasoning entered her nostrils, making her wish she was ready to order. She occasionally looked to the door, having expectations of how Clouse might look after seeing only newspaper clippings of the man from years past.

When a tall, slender man approached her in blue jeans, a tan flannel shirt, and a cautious grin, she thought for certain a lumberjack was about to ask her out.

"Jana?" he asked, surprising her enough that she had to quickly withdraw the stunned look crossing her face.

"Mr. Clouse?" she stammered, half expecting the man to show up in a tuxedo or suit of some sort, especially since the restaurant came just short of requiring ties and sport coats.

Apparently inheriting riches did little to change Clouse's lifestyle.

"I apologize," he said, taking a seat across from her. "I've been running errands all day, and there was no time to change."

He didn't even give her time to stand or shake hands. She was about to offer a handshake when their waitress approached, then the notion completely left her mind.

"I'm *so* sorry I didn't realize it was you."

"Don't worry about it," he said, waving off the mistake airily.

A few minutes later the two had placed their drink and dinner orders. Jana felt guilty about ordering a seafood platter, but he insisted she order whatever she wanted. She ordered a glass of domestic red wine while Clouse ordered an import beer with a name that escaped her.

She studied the man now named one of the wealthiest men in America by several magazines. Perhaps he chose to lay low, or maybe his fortune failed to change Clouse, but Jana noticed he probably hadn't shaved in a day or two. His brown hair appeared well-kept, combed to one side, and the thick mustache he always sported in photos remained present.

His blue eyes occasionally met hers, but Jana fought to remind herself this was a business dinner. Flirting with a handsome billionaire served her in no way, except to put her career in harm's way.

Besides, he was happily married with a son and a stepdaughter.

"I looked over your proposal to woo prospective buyers and it looks good," Clouse said before sipping from his complimentary glass of ice water.

"Thank you."

"Using the old mansion for lodging is a very nice touch."

Jana nodded again, feeling her cheeks warm as she blushed. Being complimented by the owner came completely unexpected to her, but she quickly disguised her girlish feelings, deciding she needed answers to a few questions.

Their waitress returned, setting their drinks down before whisking herself away like the wind. Jana wondered how the woman learned the art of virtually being a ghost when passing by, ensuring she didn't interrupt conversations.

"I know Bryan doesn't want me prying, but I have to ask why you would want to sell the property."

Clouse nodded, taking a swig from his beer this time.

"If you don't want to answer, I understand," she added quickly.

"No, no," he insisted. "It's fine. There are no taboo questions with me, Jana. I'm an old farm boy at heart and nothing is ever going to change that."

He paused, thinking of how to formulate his answer.

"As much as I love the hotel, it just holds a lot of bad memories for me," he answered finally. "I'm sure you heard about the murders there."

She nodded, putting forth a compassionate appearance.

"I lost a lot of friends," he continued. "Two of my best friends in fact. I just don't have the ambition to carry out the casino plans, but the county desperately needs the revenue. *Someone* should take advantage of the opportunity, but it won't be me."

Jana could hardly blame him. He already had money, so he planned to do the right thing by letting others profit by allowing the hotel to become what it was meant to be.

And once had been.

"I absolutely love the place, but as long as I'm affiliated with it I think it'll be cursed," he confessed.

Clearing her throat, Jana let him know she had a question based on part of his statement.

"Is something wrong?" he asked.

"The grave disturbance last month. Is that something we need to be worried about?"

Clouse sat silently a moment, cupping his chin with his hands.

"I don't think so. Nothing was removed, so I think it was some sort of prank."

"It was Martin Smith's grave."

Clouse smirked uneasily, obviously already knowing that information.

"I'm aware of what it was, Miss Privett. The fact that Martin Smith's body was exhumed and moved to that hill was a travesty."

"Wasn't that a legal battle of some sort?"

"Yes. And one I lost at that."

Jana seemed to recall some strange circumstances about Smith's death, or his two deaths that the newspapers hinted about. She decided not to press the issue, considering Clouse seemed somewhat testy about her probing into the sore parts of his past. Despite his earlier statement, perhaps there were some forbidden questions.

"To answer your concern, I don't anticipate any trouble with security on the grounds. We still have off-duty state police working there around the clock, so one of them will be there whenever you have guests."

"So you approve of my ideas as a whole?"

"I think they're fine. Having the guests stay at the mansion is a good idea because it would save me selling it separately if they liked the idea of a package deal."

"Bryan thought the same thing. He went to college at the hotel when it was Northwood, but he lives just north of Bloomington now."

Clouse nodded as she spoke, indicating he actually listened to what she had to say. She really expected a man in his position to be more callous and unconcerned with the lives of other people. Perhaps money didn't change people after all.

"Is there anything I should know about the mansion?" Jana asked, receiving a curious look. "I mean does the building have any history behind it?"

"Smith built it shortly before renovation started," Clouse answered. "He wanted to live near the grounds to monitor the construction himself. I found out later why he was so consumed with seeing daily progress. He kept to himself, but he observed what Dave Landamere and I dug up when we searched, because the items were important to him."

"Have you ever stayed there before?"

"At the mansion? No. My wife said it gave her the creeps the one time she went through it to inventory Smith's belongings."

A road ran along the far side of the hotel grounds, giving access to another road for employees and volunteers on the grounds. An access code moved a gate aside for people to drive through, but the road also ran further up a hill. The second golf course and a Catholic church once comprised much of the hill, but they were long since gone.

Jana recalled her one visit to the mansion just one week prior. Every piece of furniture had some form of plastic or cloth covering it. Though the mansion remained in perfect condition because of climate control, it reminded her of old monster movies where white cloth and cobwebs overwhelmed the central settings.

"I'll have a crew go through and clean the place before we entertain overnight guests," Jana informed him.

Their waitress stopped by, informing them their meals would soon be ready. Clouse thanked her, then returned his attention to Jana.

"I think Bryan knows my terms better than anyone. When the hotel finds a new owner, I don't want to be a deal stopper. My family doesn't need VIP treatment, we don't need our own personal room, and *if* I ever make my way to West Baden it will be as a regular person. I relinquish all rights and privileges to the hotel when I sign on the dotted line."

"It shouldn't take long with the number of investment firms Bryan has invited."

"I'm hoping to have it out of the way pretty soon. The courts have tied my hands long enough over Smith's estate. With everything legally in my possession, I'm ready to move on with my life and cut some loose ends."

"I see. Anything special you want me to know about before people begin arriving?"

Clouse sat back, thinking a moment.

"Whatever the public thinks happened a few years back, and whatever *you* think happened, is irrelevant. We need to put a positive spin on the grounds. Stick to the facts you know about. The history, the good times, and the future are what people want to hear about."

He paused again, a hurt look crossing his face, then vanishing when she blinked. Whatever memories haunted the man he kept to himself, refusing to burden those around him.

"Think you can put a positive spin on all of this?" he asked, looking her in the eyes.

"Probably," Jana said, putting forth her best business face. "It's been a few years, so public fears should be subsided. I won't lie to people, but I will skirt around the facts. People want a casino in this county. They want revenue. I'm not going to let them down, and I'm not going to let you down either."

Raising his beer glass, Clouse waited until Jana tapped it with her wine glass.

"I'd say we'll both be happy if this goes off without a hitch," he said before taking a drink.

Jana put forth a smile, secretly wondering if selling the hotel was an opportunity for advancement or a death sentence.

3

Cloudy skies fixed themselves over the West Baden Springs Hotel as Dan Duncan walked along the brick path between the front gate and the hotel itself. A special pass got him past the volunteers at the front gate after tours concluded for the day.

He prayed he wasn't too late for an opportunity to purchase the hotel with his investment group. More than anyone else in the group, Duncan's bloodline connected him with the grounds, making their two-day tour of the hotel personal to say the least.

Now splitting his time between Nashville, Tennessee and a residence just outside Salem, Indiana, Duncan owned riches passed down from three generations. His great-grandfather helped bring the railroad to West Baden, investing heavily in the market, and in local construction at the time.

Andrew Duncan made his millions, invested it wisely, and died before his fiftieth birthday. His son escaped the Great Depression with minimal financial casualties, leaving the family inheritance intact for future generations.

Duncan picked up his walk, heading toward the hotel. So far as he knew no one else from his group had arrived, leaving him some private time with the old grounds. After all, their official tour was the next day, but he wanted to arrive a day early to reminisce.

It took a great deal of figurative arm twisting to convince his investment partners to simply *look* at the grounds. Getting a majority vote to buy the hotel and the grounds was the next battle, but he planned to win on both fronts.

Approaching the sunken garden, Duncan looked over the flower tops, observing the two remaining springs, along with the old bowling pavilion behind them. Where others saw history and local ties, he found possibility. He knew the current owner of the French Lick Springs Resort down the road wanted to sell, despite the possibility of a casino drawing unlimited cash.

In need of upgrades and repairs, the resort needed several million dollars to make it a realistic luxury hotel. The owner seemed content to leave it running for convention business and tourism, but Duncan's insider sources told him the man wanted to sell if the right offer came along.

Buying both hotels assured the group control of the grounds on which a casino could be built and run efficiently. Duncan worked during his teenage years for his father, then took over several family businesses. No stranger to management, he knew casino ownership was significantly different from his own experience, but figured the group members had solid contacts who ran hotels and casinos.

Ordinarily Duncan rode his motorcycle everywhere until roads became slick or icy. Because of impending snowy weather, he brought his truck with a trailer attached to the hitch. On the trailer he hauled his new Harley-Davidson Road King, which he rode from the resort down the road, leaving his truck behind.

Because of the cold conditions Duncan wore full leather chaps and a thick black leather riding jacket. He left his skullcap and gloves with his bike at the entrance, not planning to stay long. His stomach grumbled because he had only eaten once since leaving Tennessee shortly after dawn.

Duncan had celebrated the new year in Tennessee the week prior, drinking far more than usual. It took him several days to recover, but what he recalled of the lavish party he attended made his misery somewhat worth the sickness and suffering.

He strolled into the garden, thinking back to the photos of his great-grandfather around the hotel. Most of them showed Andrew Duncan posed with friends or clients atop what was known as the Water Wagon in the day.

In the early days, the hotel had numerous forms of entertainment aside from the bowling and billiards hall. An opera house stood near the pavilion, a bicycle and pony track was located a short walk from there, and an indoor pool was erected beside the grand building. Usually some sort of show or convention kept guests busy, and some came to West Baden simply to partake in the mineral water, which they believed had healing powers.

From what Duncan knew, the Water Wagon was built and owned by a man hired by the hotel to take water from one station to another along the hotel grounds. Constructed entirely of wood, the wagon looked like a giant keg laid horizontally along an axle, which served as the wagon, drawn by a single horse.

Many a photo opportunity occurred on or beside the wagon. Everything from couples to groups of a dozen men had been captured on film during the hotel's heyday with the wagon. Duncan suspected photographs served as a form of entertainment on the hotel grounds, if not just another way for the ownership to line their pockets with extra funds.

Just a month over fifty-years-old, Duncan definitely felt his age, especially when he rode his motorcycle on long trips. He had never been married, had no children, and no significant other at the moment. His longest relationship went sour the year prior, after his girlfriend decided she wanted to see other people, officially breaking up after eight years.

They were off and on, living together sometimes, though usually just getting together for trips or events like normal couples. Duncan kept expecting her to call during the first few months, but when she didn't, he gave up completely, throwing himself into his work.

Around that time, he heard rumors about the West Baden hotels possibly coming up for sale after the casino bill passed. Something sounded right about leaving Tennessee for a fresh start, so he convinced Red Sanders to look at the hotel with the group.

He knew some of the investment group members remained skeptical about the building's potential versus the investment, but Red and his brother, Keith, created the Lone Star Investment Corporation. Their mission was simply to make sound investments, and though Duncan was biased in this particular scenario, he felt the hotel was a sound buy.

Split between Tennessee and Texas, the group typically worked as two separate teams, but this time they came together for an out-of-state venture. Red lived in Tennessee, making his millions from a prospering trucking business. Keith owned a dozen ranches in Texas, gaining his initial wealth from oil and cattle.

While Red had an interest in the hotel, several other group members remained skeptical about Duncan's idea. Some didn't trust Duncan, while a few thought the hotel needed too much work before becoming operational.

Putting any negative thoughts aside, Duncan moved toward the hotel, looking up to the top level.

"Needs work my ass," he commented.

After taking several extended tours, he knew Clouse had fully finished the hotel, but tragic events prevented it from opening several years prior. The atrium, the basement, and every room was fully restored, but Duncan wondered if his fellow investors would approve of the changes Clouse made.

Deciding the weather made it too cold to stand still, he walked toward the hotel itself, wanting a look inside before anyone else from his group arrived. He doubted many of them wanted to spend a night inside anything except the mansion, meaning he might be the only one in town at the moment. Some of them were pampered, not accustomed to working with anything except their minds.

Duncan looked at his hands, noticing callouses and rough skin. He worked, but he also found time to play around. Taking his time as he walked up the steps to the secondary entrance, he looked behind him, watching the garden fade as twilight engulfed it.

Turning around, he bumped into someone who had silently made his way behind the millionaire.

"Sorry about that," the man immediately stated as Duncan noticed the gun at his hip. "I'm Brent Guthrie, one of the state police who'll be watching over your group this weekend."

Duncan let a quirky grin escape his lips.

"So you know who I am?"

Guthrie appeared at least as old as Duncan, so the investor wondered if he might be a retired state trooper.

"They radio everything back to me, so I heard a member of the latest group to tour the grounds was on his way in."

"Latest?"

"Two other groups have already done overnight stays."

Duncan supposed the idea was competitive bids, which meant he had two hurdles to clear. Not only did he have to convince his group to seek the property, but he had to make certain they presented the nicest package to Clouse for his approval.

"You might find some of the locals unfriendly, since some of them didn't like the casino bill passing," Guthrie noted.

Duncan grunted to himself, knowing how religious the county remained. Despite having some of the worst employment figures in the entire state, Orange County seemed to put religious teachings above financial improvement.

"Some of them will tell you stories about screams and moans up the hill there," the trooper said, nodding toward the wooded area behind the hotel. "They say late at night you sometimes hear things going on up there."

Duncan grinned, though uncomfortably. Guthrie didn't seem entirely convinced something *wasn't* happening in the hills.

"Were you here when all of that stuff happened a few years ago?" he asked.

"Yeah. For all of it."

Since the trooper wasn't forthcoming, Duncan didn't push the issue.

"I doubt you'll have to worry much about the locals with this wintery front coming through tomorrow. You may want to get your tour in early."

"I can't believe we're getting snow here at all," Duncan commented. "I grew up around here, and it seemed every year we got an inch of snow maybe once or twice a year. And never at Christmas."

"I'd say you're going to more than make up for it this time around. Every so often we get a front that dumps a load on us, and this is one of those rare times."

Duncan thought Guthrie seemed a bit too cheerful about a snowstorm heading their way. He couldn't imagine worse possible circumstances for an overnight stay on the grounds. If his group had a bad experience, they might never vote to purchase the property. Bad weather would prohibit viewing some of the hotel's greatest assets, which placed a sour feeling in the pit of Duncan's stomach.

"Where you staying tonight?" Guthrie inquired.

"Down the road at the resort."

Giving a nod, the trooper seemed ready to lock up for the night as he began looking around. Most of the tourists had departed, leaving only volunteers and staff inside the building.

"Can I get a quick look around before you lock up?"

"Sure. We have someone here around the clock, so take your time."

Duncan followed him inside, immediately seeing the grand atrium beyond the hallway. It teased him because the entrance obscured its full beauty, which he was unable to see until he stepped into the opening, seeing six stories of rooms looming above him. Literally a round atrium, it held several balconies from particular rooms, topped off by a drum and chandelier in the center of the roof.

From one end to the other was practically the length of a football field, and everything seemed to echo when less than a handful of people made any kind of noise within its confines.

He said nothing, but Duncan remained awed, as always, by the spectacle before him. He wondered how his great-grandfather felt about the grounds, considering the man visited the hotel almost daily to chat with friends and business partners.

Just looking at the atrium brought a tingle to Duncan's spine because he knew of the hotel's good history. He wanted to usher in a new, better era for the hotel to erase any ill-will toward the place from local residents. A sense of family pride urged him to purchase the grounds, no matter the cost in money or time.

If meeting Clouse in person became necessary to secure his wish, Duncan planned to make it so. Looking to his left, he thought he saw a shadow inside the old barber shop across the floor from the corner of his eye. By the time his blue eyes focused on the barber shop the shadow was gone.

Or never existed.

He stared harder, seeing no movement over the next few seconds.

Grunting to himself, he decided to get back to the resort. He planned to monitor the weather through the Weather Channel by the hour, praying against the impending snow.

4

The front door made an eerie creaking sound when Maria Richards entered the mansion up the road from the hotel grounds.

Contracted to clean the house the day before the next batch of tourists visited, she still wondered why they chose her, a relative newcomer to the cleaning business, over more popular professional cleaners. One of her competitors had cleaned the house the previous two times, which she heard about through local gossip.

Tired from a full day of work, she hated cleaning the mansion after dark, but she wasn't about to disappoint her regular clients for a one-time job. Besides, there was no one around to criticize her, and no one staying in the large building until the next day.

Most of her equipment remained inside her van because Maria wanted to analyze exactly what needed cleaning the most. Since people had stayed there as recently as two weeks prior, she doubted the dust buildup was extensive.

Unfamiliar with the building, Maria stepped inside before closing the creaky metal door. Surprised none of the three sets of deadbolt locks were in use, she looked around the mansion's main lobby. Two sets of rooms on her left appeared to be living and entertaining space while two rooms on her right were possibly bedrooms or kitchens. The lobby ahead of her appeared more like a mammoth foyer the size of a sports field.

Before her, the main staircase, constructed completely from hardwood and stained to a shimmering caramel finish, stood as wide as most cars were long. It led to a second floor with a wraparound balcony and at least eight more rooms she readily counted.

"Wow," she muttered, wondering where to begin.

During her conversation with Jana Privett she learned about a full restaurant-style cooking area in the basement, complete with dumbwaiter, industrial stoves and refrigerators, a large aluminum preparation table, and at least three sets of cooking wares and utensils.

Maria's instructions made it clear that the bedrooms and living areas needed her full attention. Vacuuming, dusting, and if necessary, carpet shampooing were among the chores she needed to have completed by the next morning.

From outside, the mansion appeared to have three stories, but the stairs stopped at the second landing. She wondered what the third level held, or if it might simply be an aesthetic feature built to enhance the building's luxurious appearance.

Starting her own business less than a year after her divorce took courage, but there were times she doubted it would work out. Her ex-husband's money and the business knowledge he instilled upon her before sleeping around, allowed her enough success to keep the business open.

Only now were larger clients beginning to seek her services, apparently sensing she was a mainstay in the West Baden area.

Knowing she had a long night ahead of her, Maria took a peek in each of the downstairs rooms, finding them loaded with expensive furniture and decorations. Why no one resided in such a house escaped her, but her jaw remained agape throughout most of the personal tour.

Upstairs provided even more surprises because she found twelve separate bedrooms, each with its own full bathroom and walk-in closet. They looked practically immaculate already, so Maria wondered exactly why she was hired to clean the place. Shrugging as she left the last bedroom, she supposed rich people had outlandish standards, so one hair out of place might throw them into a tizzy.

What impressed her the most was how each bedroom contained a different theme, complete with various colors and accent pieces. The place seemed meant for entertaining and lavish parties, yet it remained vacant. Evidence of covered furniture and cobwebs disappeared with the previous cleaning jobs, leaving Maria the much simpler task of dusting.

Prepared to fetch her cleaning tools from the van, she started down the elegant stairway, watching the carpet that ran from top to bottom. Containing a red, black, and charcoal dotted pattern that virtually entranced her, Maria only looked up as she neared the bottom stair.

Her eyes widened at the sight of a man clad in a black robe blocking the front door. No face emerged from beneath the shrouded hood because some sort of dark mask covered it. Slowly, the face lifted from some deep stare at the floor, but what chilled Maria to the bone was the gleam from a sharpened knife in his right hand.

Shrieking, she turned to dash up the stairs, knowing the entire second floor wrapped around the staircase railings, meaning she couldn't be cornered.

In an instant, the man clad in black gave pursuit, grabbing her ankle halfway up the stairs. She fell forward, instinctively kicking him in the face before he had a chance to use the knife on her. He fell back several steps, allowing her to reach the top of the stairs without injury.

Maria stared down, seeing him dart up the stairs with barely a moment's hesitation. She had no doubt a man was chasing her, because he was tall, with a grip like that of a gorilla. Making her way around the banister atop the stairs, Maria watched him join her on the second floor, deciding that entering any of the rooms meant certain death.

She had to lure him away from the stairs before attempting any kind of escape, but any rational thoughts were drowned out by the thumping of her heart. Absolutely terrified of the urban legends concerning the hotel, she suspected they held some merit, because no one she knew would play such a sick joke on her.

"What do you want?" she demanded loudly, trying to stall for time as she carefully walked, touching the railing with shaky fingers.

In response, he slowly rotated the knife with his right hand, indicating he wanted to twist it once it plunged through her soft skin.

She waited until he began making his way around the railing before dashing in the opposite direction. Like a cheetah, he gained ground on his prey with amazing speed and skill. Knowing there was no way to outrun him, she turned to backhand his face, which felt soft beneath the mask. The move registered no pain or sound from her attacker, so she launched a foot into his groin.

He doubled over, giving her time to dash down the stairs toward freedom.

Reaching the bottom stair, Maria stumbled, but kept her balance long enough to use the door as a backstop. She twisted and yanked the doorknob to no avail because the deadbolts were all locked.

"Damn it," she muttered, ducking just quickly enough to avoid the blade that clanked harmlessly against the door.

Her informal tour of the mansion had informed Maria of several other exits and the location of the catering area in the basement. Though she hadn't visited the industrial kitchen, she decided it might be the safest area for her because it would likely offer some cover.

She dashed toward the kitchen, finding nothing in her path to throw down as a form of hindrance for her pursuer, and no time to lock the door at the kitchen entrance. Once inside, however, Maria discovered the basement door. She yanked it open, expecting to be knifed from behind at any moment, but managed to close it behind her. Her assailant entered the main doorway too late to attack her as she shut him out.

A stairway led down to the basement with occasional bulbs to light the way. Maria didn't question why the bulbs were on, simply thankful not to be in complete darkness. She reached the bottom step, desperately looking around for cover, despite hearing no one behind her.

It appeared very much like she envisioned it based on Jana Privett's description and the floor plans Maria had viewed before taking the job. Along one of the other walls she heard a strange clunking noise, like something being dragged by a chain.

She cursed under her breath, suspecting the dumbwaiter was being lowered toward her.

But why?

Hesitantly drawing closer to the contraption, Maria found a small elevator that had an up button only fixed upon the wall. She never saw an elevator on the second floor, meaning it likely went exclusively to the third floor.

Was there some sort of grand dining room or ballroom up there? She couldn't picture guests being ushered through the basement toward the dining area. No, she thought, something far more sinister or dark waited for her on the other end of that elevator shaft.

Slowly backing away from the single elevator door, Maria chose to risk confronting the killer instead of trapping herself on the third floor. As she made her way around the stainless steel work table, she heard footsteps hurriedly marching down the main stairs, instantly changing her mind for her.

"Shit."

Returning to the elevator in a run just short of a sprint, she pushed the elevator button several times in desperation. As she waited, listening to her nervous breathing, Maria looked around her, finding several covered tables nearby. An idea came to her, so she peeked around the corner, but no one was visible.

Her plans changed in a blink.

Swallowing hard, she decided to approach the main stairwell, wanting nothing to do with the elevator. Suddenly it felt as though the entire mansion was possessed entirely by some form of evil. The person chasing her was somehow a minion of the building, tied in with whatever secret it harbored.

Listening intently, Maria drew closer to the stairs, hearing a creak from the end of the table that reached her ears too late for an appropriate reaction.

As she turned to run for the elevator, her attacker sprung from behind the table's end, dashing after her with ill intent. Knowing she couldn't outrun him, Maria snatched a wooden rolling pin from the table, swinging it at his head while she spun around.

Instead of connecting, however, the rolling pin missed completely as the cloaked attacker ducked, scooping Maria into his arms as the makeshift weapon fell from her hand.

"No!" she screamed, resisting with kicks and flailing arms. "No!"

Suspecting her life was about to end, she continued to fight as he carried her in a modified bear hug toward the elevator. Now her suspicions of the third floor felt verified, but she wanted nothing to do with its mystery.

As the elevator door opened with a ding, Maria fought against her attacker's grip in futility. He carried her inside the elevator car as she let out a bloodcurdling scream that ceased when the door sealed behind them, swallowing them whole.

Jana woke up early the next morning, making the trip to French Lick hours before the arranged time of noon when she planned to meet the investment group.

With the impending snow, her plans had changed slightly. Putting off the tour of the West Baden Springs grounds could no longer wait until after lunch and an initial meeting. She felt as though she might be cheating the group of the tour's full effect by altering the itinerary given to the other groups.

Carrying a personal planner with her, Jana entered the French Lick Springs Resort expecting to meet at least a few of the investment group members. She stepped inside the main lobby, finding very few guests up and about.

A look at her watch revealed it was barely past eight o'clock, but even if she failed to locate anyone from the group, Jana had plenty of things to accomplish by noon.

Including a rewrite of her planned tour and lodging schedule.

A look at the group's website gave her short biographies and photos of each member, since it felt somewhat inappropriate asking Red Sanders for additional information. His secretary had already forwarded paperwork about the group's mission and formal accomplishments. The additional materials simply gave her an opportunity to familiarize herself with the members before they arrived.

In business, nothing felt more embarrassing than not knowing the people one met by name. Clients tended to want special treatment, and in her business, bad first impressions usually meant a failed property closing.

Walking through the lobby, Jana made her way to the restaurant housed within the resort where a buffet breakfast was being served. Doing her best not to appear snoopy, Jana's gaze panned from one end of the seating area to the other.

Despite a packed dining area, she found two of her guests seated in the far corner. They sat across from one another, speaking casually with their plates in front of them. Thinking she might be interrupting as she drew closer, Jana noticed napkins and silverware atop their plates, indicating they were finished eating.

"Excuse me," she said as she approached, drawing their attention immediately.

Both were easily recognizable from her dossiers. Dan Duncan was the only man in the group with blond hair, though it had grayed around his temples. He obviously ate well, because he sported a small pot belly. Based on the black leather jacket behind him and the sunglasses perched atop his head, he rode motorcycles. The weathered skin on his face acted as evidence that the man worked and played hard, despite having money.

Dennis "Red" Sanders sat to Jana's right side. With a full head of rustic hair and blue eyes, he failed to challenge her memory because he too was unique within the arriving group. She assumed his nickname came from his hair color, but knew very little about the man. His funds came from owning a trucking company, which she heard his older brother helped him start.

She recalled his listed age being forty-nine, a few years younger than his brother, but he looked years younger to her.

"I'm hoping you're Jana," Red stated. "We're not used to having stalkers."

They all chuckled a moment, lightening the mood.

She shook hands with both of them quickly before Duncan motioned for her to sit down.

"I hope I'm not imposing," she said. "I just wanted to see if any of you had arrived before we started the tour this afternoon."

"We're looking forward to it," Duncan said, though a look at Red's face didn't reveal quite the same enthusiasm.

"Dan here prodded us into coming down here," he admitted. "The rest of us are reserving judgment until we see the place, and the possibilities."

Jana grinned, understanding their hesitation.

"The property *will* sell," she assured them. "It's just a matter of who wants it most, and their ability to maintain the historic integrity."

"I'm very much for that," Duncan said sincerely. "My great-grandfather frequented the hotel during its prime, so I guess you could say I have a link to it."

"So I've heard," Jana said, much more knowledgeable about the hotel's history than before she took the assignment to sell the property.

Red continued to look doubtful about something, despite his friend's eagerness.

"I've done some research," he said. "This is the second poorest county in Indiana as far as tax base and average wages. How do you expect a casino to draw in enough cash flow to stay afloat?"

A strange look crossed his face.

"No pun intended," he added, since the casino design would have to be a large river boat.

Indiana legislature made certain any gambling facilities never touched base on Indiana soil. What started as a river boat concept along the state's rivers and lakes was adapted for Orange County and a few other needy areas.

"There are no guarantees," Jana stated, "but if you look at Corydon and New Albany, their tax bases more than doubled the first year their casinos opened. If you open the casino, you bring new jobs and hope to this area."

"There is such a thing as flooding the market," Red argued. "There isn't much else around here besides the historical value. I just can't see why people would come here over the established places near bigger cities."

Duncan stepped in, seeing Jana wasn't getting through to his friend.

"There is a lot of convention business in the area, Red. You more or less said it yourself, there's nothing else to do around here."

"But we don't have a *major* highway anywhere close, and there's a lot of negative publicity from the Bible beaters around here. There could be a lot of heat over this project."

"Are you even giving this a realistic chance?" Duncan asked a loaded question.

"I'm here for *you*, Dan. This is your thing, and I'm going to give it a thorough look, but above all else, I'm a businessman. If I'm asking this many questions, just imagine what Keith is going to say when he gets here."

"Why don't you ask him yourself?" Jana heard someone ask in a Southern drawl just over her shoulder.

Everyone turned to see an older man in his early fifties standing behind her. Dressed in slacks, cowboy boots, and a bolo tie, Keith Sanders looked very much like Jana expected a successful Texas rancher to look. The little bit of his dark hair Jana noticed beneath his black Stetson had grayed, including the mustache he sported. She continued to study the man as Red stood to give his older brother a hug.

She doubted they saw one another much, living in different states, so this trip was probably an excuse for them to get together.

Keith appeared even more rugged than Duncan, likely spending afternoons and weekends on horseback, or working his ranch. His face had a few wrinkles, but he remained slender, showing no signs of his age slowing him down.

"About time you got here, you old coot," Red told his brother.

"Goddamn airport security and their *random* searches got me this time."

He looked down as though seeing Jana for the first time.

"Oh, sorry about my language," he quickly apologized, taking Jana's hand before gently planting a kiss on it.

He put forth a crooked grin that seemed boyish for such a distinguished man.

Jana thought true gentlemen were extinct, but Keith's charms caused her to rethink her preconceived notions. He seemed genuine, like a cowboy hero out of the old westerns her father watched on weekends when she was growing up.

"Thank you, Mr. Sanders," she said, standing up because everyone else already had.

Keith looked surprised she knew his name until Jana introduced herself with a formal handshake.

"Pleasure, Miss Privett," he said after discovering her identity. "It is 'Miss' isn't it?"

She nodded, feeling her face blush.

"Ignore my brother's Southern charm," Red spoke up. "He's on his way to a blissful union this spring."

"Not *that* blissful," his older brother noted gruffly, almost under his breath.

"And to a bride barely old enough to be his daughter," Red added, aside to Jana, drawing a scornful stare from his brother.

Neither of the previous visiting groups were so open, or so friendly. Comparatively speaking, they were bland and extremely formal. Jana had yet to meet half of the Star Investments group, yet she felt at home with them already. She especially liked Duncan's personal interest in the property, but wondered if he fought an uphill battle, convincing his group the hotel was a profitable purchase.

She decided to check on the grounds, and the mansion, before meeting the entire group at noon. Staffing on the grounds was minimal, with only a state trooper providing security and two people from a catering service providing dinner for the group in the hotel's sixth floor suite.

While Red and Duncan remained behind to leave a tip, Jana and Keith walked toward the lobby.

"My brother likes to speak out of turn," Keith assured her as they left the dining area.

"It's okay," she replied. "Really."

"I just don't want you to get the wrong idea. I'm not some pervert who hits on every woman I meet."

Jana smiled, though uneasily.

"I wasn't worried about it."

Keith didn't look reassured, but put forth a strong front as his brother and Duncan caught up with them.

"I've got a few things to prepare," Jana informed the trio. "I'll see you all at noon?"

All three nodded.

Jana approached the front entrance to walk outside, seeing an unusual sight through the glass doors before she even touched them. What looked like sheets of snow fell from the sky, limiting her line of sight to about twenty yards outside. So far, the moist ground refused to accept a white lining, but as the temperature dropped, and far more precipitation fell, it would yield to a snowy blanket.

Her hesitation allowed Duncan to approach her without the brothers.

"I stayed up half the night watching the weather reports," he confessed. "I was afraid of this."

"So was I, but the grounds still look beautiful with snow. And the inside doesn't look any different."

Duncan's concern showed.

"This is my one shot at convincing my group this is a good idea. It's the first time I've ever asked them to invest in one of *my* ideas, so it's a big deal."

Jana couldn't find the words to comfort him. It seemed as though he might be hinting around for some help, but Jana had no tips to offer. She knew competition for the hotel was destined to be fierce, and his group already sounded skeptical about viewing the grounds, much less buying them.

"I know you're just selling the place, and you probably think we're all rich snobs, but I actually live around here most of the year. There's nothing that would make me happier than running this place."

Grinning to himself, Duncan seemed to recollect something as he stared outside almost blankly.

"When I was a kid, I used to visit the hotel with my father. He told me about our family's link to West Baden, so when the grounds closed for good, I sometimes snuck in for a look. Every time I saw that atrium it just took my breath away, and I dreamed of owning the building one day."

Jana looked at him, wondering how many people daydreamed the near impossible notion of owning the property.

"See, I understand the old days," Duncan continued. "I don't want to own it for selfish reasons, like making more money, or being a big shot. I watched the building decay, then start falling to the ground. It upset me to see it fall from grace like that, so my dream has been to restore it and see it reopened like it used to be."

Now she understood his plight, feeling his pain through what sorrowful expressions he let slip past his macho biker facade.

Jana knew the West Baden Springs Hotel hadn't functioned as a hotel in nearly a century. The Great Depression decimated its appeal to the wealthy, taking with it the county's ability to expand.

"There aren't many hints I can give you," Jana admitted after some silent reflection. "Paul Clouse makes the final decision about who gets the place. No one else has shown as much devotion as you have to this project, and I think he'll really appreciate that."

Duncan's face began glowing as she spoke the words. He seemed relieved, if not holding back refrained ecstacy, that Clouse shared his values for the hotel.

"I really have to get some things prepared," Jana said, inching toward the grand entrance. "I'll see you at noon."

Duncan nodded, still walking on air after her encouraging words.

"Drive safely out there," he said.

"I will."

Jana stepped outside, immediately finding her overcoat covered by fluffy snowflakes. If the forecast proved accurate, she would have to leave early, or risk being stuck on the grounds overnight. She owed it to the group to give them the full tour, even if that meant spending the night away from her cat.

One thing seemed certain.

The day ahead would certainly be etched in her memory for years to come.

6

A warm, sunny atmosphere surrounded the grounds as Dave McCully walked in front of a large domed building. He walked in what he considered the front yard, but as he looked to his left, he noticed several men standing behind a man about to tee off during a round of golf.

Curious, he wondered why anyone chose to place a golf course in front of a building, in plain view from the road. Continuing to stroll, he rounded the front of the building, finding a set of stairs that led to a veranda where women in what he termed Victorian dresses drank tea.

They sat on wooden chairs, rocking easily as they enjoyed the beautiful weather. To his left, he spied a footbridge and a sunken garden, solving the mystery of where he was standing.

But not when.

McCully had seen brochures and photos of the West Baden Springs Hotel, but why he stood in the middle of a working hotel, obviously decades before he was born, eluded him. Having out-of-body experiences was nothing new, but traveling through space and time without provocation felt odd.

And a bit scary.

While most people only encounter strange new experiences through dreams, McCully had experienced visions since a very young age. They didn't come often, but usually delivered some sort of purpose or meaning to him.

Sometimes his visions came through dreams, but most of the time contact with people or objects provoked his mind to jump into another time and place. McCully had seen the past, present, and future with his visions, realizing the public viewed his psychic powers or "ability" as abnormal and strange. He remained very self-conscious and secretive about the visions, frustrated because he had no one to confide in when it grew too weird for him.

Twice in his life he had tried explaining the sensation to a close friend, and both times he lost a friendship. Those around him always seemed to know something wasn't quite right, but they said very little. He heard rumors about his sexual preference being questioned, or about him being a recluse, which commonly irritated him.

While some people considered them a gift, he regarded his visions as a curse.

Walking along, he went unnoticed by the guests patronizing the hotel. The visions never allowed him to interact with others. Like a ghost, he typically made his way around to whatever intrigued him most about the scene. No one ever saw him, so he tended to overhear strange conversations, or observe private rituals without interruption.

"Why am I here?" he asked himself, since no one else would hear.

Everything around him looked lush and green, but the air felt comfortable, leading him to believe the season was late spring. Visions allowed him to actively partake in the environment, as though his senses received stimuli from whatever setting he visualized. McCully suspected his mind just simulated the sensations, but he had no proof either way.

The grounds appeared busy compared to the photos he had viewed on the internet and the package the sellers sent his group. He noticed three springs right away, a bicycle and horse track, a mowed baseball diamond, and as he walked toward the building's rear, a large church with stained-glass windows.

"Wow," he murmured, his eyes following the winding steps up the hill until they finally landed at the front door.

He knew the church had been torn down at some point, but one gaze upon the beautiful structure had him questioning the logic of whomever made that decision. An extension of the golf course, or a completely different course, remained hidden from him over the hill's crest, but he heard chatter, and the occasional "Fore!" being yelled.

When he looked to his right, he spied three men standing beside a back door that apparently led to the dining room inside. He drew closer, unable to hear their conversation. It appeared as though two of them were trying to convince the third man of something.

McCully instantly felt connected somehow to the third man, who spoke to the two men with animated hands, one of which clasped a cigar between two fingers.

Sensing this particular man was the reason for his vision, McCully slowly approached the trio, as though expecting to be seen any moment.

He observed the man, noticing he wore a felt fedora hat, rather than a derby or cap. Dressed in a full suit with a tie, the man had shined two-tone shoes, giving the impression he wasn't just a regular guest at the hotel. If memory served McCully correctly, his attire seemed indicative of the 1920s.

Regardless of how he looked, he seemed important.

"I can't go through with it," McCully heard the man say before a hand smacked his arm, bringing him back to the real world.

With sleepy eyes, McCully regained his senses slowly as greenish colors blurred past the window beside him. He quickly remembered letting his agent take over the driving duty after they passed Louisville.

A country singer and songwriter from Nashville, Tennessee, McCully had enjoyed moderate success, mostly through his songs being picked up by major recording artists. In turn, he joined Lone Star Investments after Frank Oswalt, his agent, talked him into making the 'smartest decision of his life' a few years prior.

"We there yet?" McCully asked between yawns.

"About ten minutes out."

A closer examination of his surroundings revealed more white than green along the state highway. As Oswalt rolled up his window, a pungent sweet odor crossed McCully's nose, which he readily recognized as pipe tobacco.

"You been smoking in my car?"

"Why, no," Oswalt answered with feigned hurt, since he knew he was caught.

"I'm going to write a song about a close friend dying of cancer."

His agent hesitated a moment, clearing his throat, before replying.

"And I'll probably go buy a new car with my cut after it goes to number one."

McCully chuckled to himself.

"You're too much."

Studying his surroundings, McCully looked from the road to Oswalt, who appeared a bit fatigued. Though he complained about making trips, Oswalt needed a few days away from work every so often. He led a frantic life dealing with music superstars and blossoming rookies. McCully hoped the man made enough money to retire early, though he would miss having Oswalt's representation.

And having to find a new agent.

A few years over fifty, Oswalt moved a little bit slower, but he appeared healthy most of the time. He had rough nights with little sleep, so dark bags under his eyes weren't uncommon. His dark hair remained parted to one side, and he had grown in a full peppered goatee the past few weeks.

A moment of silence passed before the agent spoke again.

"Is Dan off his noggin by dragging us up here?"

"Hard telling. He's pretty passionate about the area, but I don't think he's the type to jump into a bad investment."

"There's already too many casinos sprouting up in the area," Oswalt complained. "We may be the ones to flood the market to the point of extinction."

McCully wondered if there *was* such a thing as a flooded market so far as casinos were concerned.

He stared at the pasty snowflakes attaching themselves to his side window. Most were large enough that he could see their distinct patterns before they melted or floated away.

"You're not fixin' to fall asleep on me again, are you?" Oswalt asked in his raspy voice.

"Nope. I'm ready to see this place for myself."

Their relationship had grown beyond a simple agent and songwriter capacity. If not for some key choices on McCully's part, the two might never have enjoyed a working relationship.

McCully found himself in the music business at an early age, working local gigs with his father, brother, and two other band members. George McCully redefined bluegrass music the way a select few brokers altered the course of the stock market. Among true bluegrass followers, George McCully was a household name.

Following in his father's footsteps, and learning from the man directly most of the time, young David learned to play a banjo because the instrument's sound fascinated him from an early age. When he turned fourteen, he played several local shows with his father when the Midnight Run's banjo player fell ill.

Midnight Run was one of many bands George McCully played in, or founded, during his years of bluegrass music. Dave lost track of how many bands his father played with until George found some commercial success in 1989 with Union Crossing, the last band he joined before forming a new band that brought along both of his sons.

While Dave enjoyed the success of being in a mainstream bluegrass band, he devoted much of his spare time to writing songs. Some were perfect for the bluegrass genre, while others seemed too deep in country roots for George to use on his albums.

"Try selling them in Nashville," his father told him one time at a family picnic. "That's just the kind of thing those kids are playing these days."

His father never criticized his playing, or his song writing. It seemed to sadden him when things blossomed for his son, not because he envied Dave, but because he knew their time together was growing shorter.

The elder McCully had recently parted ways with his last agent when he suggested Dave take his songs to Nashville. It just so happened Frank Oswalt was an agent with connections in Music City, and the George McCully Band's emergence as a bluegrass mainstay brought them into his stable.

Dave's hidden talent for writing songs didn't remain secret for long.

Within two years, recording artists landed three of his songs in the Billboard charts, two of which cracked the Top Twenty. Suddenly his writing became a focus for him because he was very much in demand.

While he never officially left his father's band, he took time off to write more music and eventually record a solo album that followed a mainstream country sound, rather than bluegrass.

He played guitar, rather than the banjo, on the album, showing another dimension to his talent base. The album enjoyed moderate success, mostly from his father's faithful followers, and a few people who saw the one music video he made that ended up on CMT for several weeks.

Oswalt regularly found buyers for his songs, from rookie singers making their first album to veteran performers wanting something different to resurrect their careers. McCully wrote about life experiences, things he knew about from Tennessee, and the wonders of his country that caught his eye while on various tours.

He seldom wrote love songs, because he had never experienced marriage, or a relationship that lasted beyond eight months. Being on the road made relationships nearly impossible unless a performer found just the right person.

McCully envied his father for finding such a woman in his mother so easily.

Now in their sixties, the couple had recently celebrated their 41st wedding anniversary.

"Quit daydreaming," Oswalt said, drawing his attention once again. "There it is."

Following the pointed finger of his agent, McCully saw a mammoth dome in the distance, partially obscured by tall trees and the translucent curtain of falling snow.

"Wow," McCully couldn't help but mutter.

"We're a little bit early, Dave. Want a bite to eat before we meet up with the others?"

"Sure."

Oswalt continued past the hotel on the highway, slowing slightly as they passed upon McCully's request, so he could see the grand hotel a little better. Even the second look failed to satiate his desire to see the building up close and inside. His tours had landed him in all kinds of historic and interesting locations, but this building intrigued him.

Able to place some of the now missing buildings from his vision, McCully felt like a kid being promised a trip to the toy store. He could barely contain himself as they passed the grounds, because he wanted to know more about what awaited him inside.

And why he had a vision about the place that occurred almost a hundred years ago.

While most people harkened back to their childhood with fond memories, his mind clung to images of the unknown. Most of his visions foretold of terrible occurrences, sometimes even violent encounters he found himself unable to forget.

He reflected often in the family scrapbook his mother made him for happier times. One picture of him sitting on his father's lap as a toddler, holding a banjo, often brought a grin to his face. It was black and white, and they looked like poor cabin folks with his father in bib overalls and him wearing blue jeans with two distinct patches in plaid patterns.

McCully grinned with delight in the photo as his tiny fingers strummed the banjo. His hair looked like it had been combed with salad tongs pulling up, down, and to the sides in random order.

Memories like that never stayed in his mind. He needed photographs and family videos to remember such things. He blamed it on all of the visions running through his mind, filling his head like a computer hard drive. Apparently his brain deleted the oldest files first, because he never remembered much about his childhood until he viewed his personal collection.

To some, his life would seem lavish and virtually perfect, but McCully felt a void that came from being alone. He found it impossible to talk about his *abilities* to other people, and functioning in society felt awkward, because he never knew when a vision might strike.

People might misinterpret him as having a seizure, doing more harm than good for him. At the very least, medical personnel might come to persuade him to ride with them to the hospital for a checkup.

"I didn't have a seizure, I had a psychic vision that transported my mind to another time and place," never seemed the logical or sane thing to tell them. The few times it had occurred in public, he simply signed the release form and answered their competency questions.

Luckily the media never ran any stories about the incidents, but McCully supposed they had far more high profile celebrities to bash in the tabloids.

Sitting back, he enjoyed the rest of the ride, hoping his mind stayed at rest during the overnight stay.

7

Glenn Turner had found most of his visit to West Baden uninviting so far.

Choosing to avoid flying to Indiana from Tennessee was the one choice he made that seemed wise. He made good time, reaching the hotel's front gate in six hours, finding no one awaiting his arrival, including his fellow group members.

Cursing under his breath, he parked his Mercedes in the front lot long enough to pull out a map. He quickly realized he was less than half a mile from a nearby access road that passed the hotel's southwest corner on the way up a hill toward the mansion.

Somewhat tired from the drive, he decided to see if anyone might have dropped by the mansion ahead of schedule. Putting the map down, he turned his car around toward Highway 56 once again.

Because of a business meeting the night before, Turner chose to turn in early, waking at three in the morning. He left after a quick shower, bringing only a light suitcase with him. After hearing a weather report that predicted heavy snow in Southern Indiana and parts of Kentucky, he decided to stop only once for gas and a meal.

Now twisting his neck in an attempt to stretch it before it grew any more stiff, Turner followed the road up to the mansion. He drove slowly, taking in the view of the grounds. The hotel appeared miles away, with several buildings and the large garden between the road and the dome.

He drew closer to the mansion, spying the large gate to his right. Fortunately the wrought iron partitions were open, but he saw no vehicles parked near the mansion.

"Just my luck," he commented sourly as he pulled his car into the crescent-shaped driveway, caddy corner to the building.

A larger paved area remained further to the side for multiple vehicle parking. He stood from the car, finding his legs behaving like stiff rubber. They ached, feeling somewhat numb from being cramped inside a car for hours on end.

A few years away from middle-age, Turner knew what to expect from his body as he grew older. The past several years had provided hints about the progression of his body's slow deterioration as it aged.

He knew tired legs would eventually be the least of his worries.

While blood pulsated inside his legs, Turner simply stood by his car momentarily, taking in the view.

Though built in modern times, the mansion had a gothic feel about it. Most of the exterior was gray stone, giving it the feel of several French cathedrals Turner had seen in books. Somewhat of a classic building buff, he admired any building with good craftsmanship and attention to details.

He drew closer to the mansion, eyeing the intricate details carved into the stone facade of the mansion, as though it was indeed a church, rather than a residence. One look at the robed figures carved into the building gave Turner the impression they were biblical figures of some sort. His knowledge of the Bible was limited to church sermons from his childhood, and what tidbits he learned from game shows.

Spaced evenly across the front of the building, almost discreetly, the carvings reminded Turner of the Stations of the Cross found in Catholic churches. He wondered if the Jesuits, who inhabited the hotel for the better part of three decades, somehow served as inspiration for the artwork.

Deciding he had all evening to ponder the custom artwork, Turner stepped to the front door, expecting the knob to resist as he turned it.

It didn't.

Stepping inside, Turner looked around, seeing no luggage, and no indication anyone from his group had stopped by the mansion. He felt utterly surprised no one guarded the property or met him at the door.

"Hello?" he called, expecting to be caught inside the place ahead of the scheduled time.

No one answered.

A quick look around indicated four rooms on the lower level and sleeping quarters on the second floor. He ascended the stairs, finding each room with the intended occupant's name on the door in an etched copper nameplate.

Turner grunted to himself, uncertain of how to take assigned rooms, or the fact the mansion appeared abandoned. He found his room, slowly opening the door as though expecting to find a housekeeper desperately doing last-minute tidying.

As the door swung open, he stared inside, finding a king-size bed complete with satin sheets and what appeared to be a custom comforter. Several hardwood dressers with articulate engravings led Turner to believe they were antiques, sitting on either side of the bed. An end table with a Victorian-style lamp also rested beside the bed.

Much like a hotel suite, the room also contained a small desk with small amenities such as a calculator, laptop computer, desk lamp, and a printer/fax/copier combination. He suspected the mansion often served as an overnight residence for important people.

A sofa, television, and complete stereo system completed the room, leaving any guest little else to long for, short of food.

By no means a celebrity, Turner's profile was slightly more public than those of his investment colleagues. Almost ten years working as a model for a western wear distributer from the Nashville area left Turner wealthy enough to buy into the company when the time came for a 'fresh face' to model their clothing lines.

Shortly after a few gray hairs replaced their black counterparts, and his face showed the first signs of aging, the company wanted younger talent. The trend in western wear had gone from realistic, rugged, and handsome to sexy and cute. Turner had never considered himself a male model in the traditional sense anyhow. He wasn't the type an underwear manufacturer might contact to stand half-naked in their ads.

Based on discussions over the years with the company's owners, he knew the day would come, but the Ranchero company continually showed a profit, even after the line dancing craze faded just before the new millennium.

They tapped into the internet market immediately, rather than waiting like some now defunct companies. Their return policies remained liberal throughout the years, satisfying many customers across the country. Ranchero also carried many of the top brands in cowboy boots, vests, blazers, and hats, rather than marketing cheap imitations.

His financial status never allowed him to gain controlling interest of the company, but Turner had some influence over their decisions. He made millions through his shares, helping promote the company personally, while using his experience to assist in marketing and product selection.

In turn, his newfound funds provided him ample opportunity to make more money when he joined Red Sanders and Lone Star Investments. They were introduced through a mutual friend at a charity dinner, but their conversation eventually gave way to their careers and a discussion about their retirement plans.

After doing some research and discussing the idea of joining Lone Star with his lawyer, Turner decided to branch out his earnings, seeing no way of losing money because he had a vote in where the group spent it.

Giving the room one last look from wall to wall, he decided to search for his investment partners elsewhere when a noise came from the next room, or perhaps the closet.

Sounding like a young child, a voice called out, somewhat muffled by walls or the closet door. Turner couldn't decipher exactly what the voice said, but it sounded as though it might be calling for a mother or father.

Then it came again.

"Mommy?" he heard more clearly this time as he stepped toward the closet.

He opened the door slowly, looking inside the darkened walk-in closet. Unable to see, he flipped the light switch, illuminating the area to reveal another door within the closet at the far end.

"What the hell?" he muttered, wondering if a child might be trapped within his closet.

Or worse, intentionally placed there.

Having two children of his own, Turner knew his ability to think and act for himself might literally fall apart if anything happened to them. Like most parents, he dreaded the thought of them being abducted or accidentally killed. He watched them like a hawk when he was home, which made him wonder if someone had done harm to a child literally this close to him.

Edging toward the door, he placed his hand on the knob, refusing to turn it. He wondered if he should get the police, or find someone else, before looking inside. If indeed someone had abducted a child, they might know he found the hiding place and take the kid somewhere else.

He had to act now.

Turning the knob, Turner found the room ahead entirely dark, and small. He found no light switch beside the door, meaning he needed to step inside a pitch black room or find a flashlight first.

"Hello?" he asked cautiously, taking his first step forward.

Sticking his left arm forward, he felt ahead of him for any objects, or perhaps a human being.

Feeling and hearing nothing, he stepped inside a bit further. Keeping his foot against the door, Turner felt nothing except bare walls all around him. It felt as though he might be inside a one-person elevator car.

He began feeling upward, wondering if there might be something on the walls that led somewhere else. Very little light followed him inside, so his search was blind. His hand patted the wall until one of his fingers touched something sharp, like a thorn, that pricked his finger.

Fighting the urge to withdraw his hand, he continued to probe the object more carefully, keeping his foot propped against the door. Some part of him feared being trapped inside the dark room, especially since no one seemed to be inside.

He wondered if the voice came from another room, or perhaps a partition above or below him. His fingers began to feel around the thorny area, discovering a leather strap of some sort amongst several thorns, as though they were one intertwined unit.

About to explore the device further through the sense of touch, Turner never received the opportunity as a metal brace wrapped around his hand, pulling him into the wall. He hit with a thud, seeing the light and any opportunity to escape the small room dissipate within a second.

He felt several metal thorns dig into his wrist as the brace clamped around it, keeping him trapped against the wall. Turner panicked, imprisoned within a tiny dark room, as his heart pounded within his chest. He tugged at the shackle, which only served to injure his wrist more as skin tore against the thorns and blood drizzled down his arm.

Making matters worse, he felt the entire room begin to move, exactly like an elevator, terrorizing the former model even worse. He was ascending into a world of darkness, unaware of what awaited him at the next stop.

This was no time to be proud.

"Help!" he screamed, feeling rather certain no one heard his pleas for assistance during the darkest hour of his life. "Help!"

Following the schedule Jana provided ahead of time, the investment team members met at the mansion up the hill from the hotel grounds, bringing their individual vehicles with them. Some had stayed at the French Lick Springs Resort overnight, while others had just arrived.

Duncan brought his suitcase through the front door with him, leaving his motorcycle secured and covered in the trailer behind his truck. A lone servant waited outside to bring in belongings and take their coats, but Duncan preferred to keep his suitcase with him. Only a few group members required pampering, while most of them had worked for a living at some time in their lives.

Water dripped onto his hands as though it were raining, but one look down told him that snowflakes had settled onto his clothing, then melted when he stepped inside.

"Pretty thick out there," Red noted as he walked through the door. "We don't get much of this in Tennessee, do we?"

Duncan smirked.

"We're lucky to survive springtime tornados down there."

Looking upward, Duncan noticed how open the mansion looked, even from the front door. Like the hotel, it drew attention to itself the moment a person entered its threshold. He saw no access to a floor above the second level, considering the possibility another set of stairs remained hidden from view.

He glanced at his watch, wondering how much time remained to explore the place before the tour.

11:45 a.m.

Setting down his suitcase, Duncan wandered to his left. Two rooms took up vast amounts of space along the left side, but the first room grabbed his attention. Like something out of the movies, the room held everything a person might want for entertaining himself on any given evening at home.

A customized red carpet ran the length of the room with gold trim around its outskirts and a center that looked like something out of a classic cathedral. Golden leaves and tails ran in and out of one another as far as the eye could see along the trim.

The entire back wall consisted of book shelves twice as tall as any normal man, with a rolling ladder to access the upper levels. Not one inch of the custom stained oak shelving remained empty.

Several decorative lamps rested atop end tables, or by themselves with elaborate stands, but the chandelier centered in the room drew Duncan's attention upward. Thousands of crystals shimmered from over a dozen bulbs in the fixture's center.

Along the outside wall, a fireplace contained a large fire while a small stack of evenly cut logs waited their turn to keep the fire going. Comprised of old stone, the fireplace looked like something from colonial days gone by, but Duncan suspected its aesthetic appearance gave way to contemporary housing codes.

Furniture appeared strategically placed throughout the room, giving it enough space for a person to walk around comfortably, but enough seating to entertain a moderate gathering.

Opposite the fireplace, a mounted stereo system played the soft jazz music Duncan heard from speakers all around him. He looked around, seeing no speakers readily visible, guessing they were hidden behind the love seats and chairs. Much like a bank or restaurant might have, the mansion likely had speakers built into the ceiling, with virtually invisible holes allowing sound to filter downward.

"What do you think?" Jana asked, taking his side.

"It's impressive. I guess I don't put much thought into decorating my houses."

Technically a bachelor, Duncan had no reason to spend money on home decor. Owning two houses dipped into his funds enough that he needed to watch how he spent his inheritance and earnings. If his company won the right to open a casino and own the hotel, he planned to sell his place in Tennessee and personally oversee local operations.

Much like his great-grandfather had.

"I moved the dinner from the sixth floor suite to the dining room here," Jana informed him. "With the snow piling up, I didn't want us to get stuck over there without supplies or any communication."

"You think it's going to get that bad?"

"The weather reports say we may get a foot or two dumped on us overnight. We're a day or two away from a significant warming trend, so it could get bad."

Duncan had no previous engagements, but most of his colleagues had to work on Monday. He knew Keith and a few others had flights scheduled to depart Sunday evening for the return trip to Texas.

Ending the tour on a sour note was the last thing Duncan wanted. Southern Indiana seldom saw two inches of snow an entire winter, much less two feet in a day's time. He looked outside the window, seeing little more than a white blur.

"You okay?" Jana asked him, breaking his train of thought from the depressing path laid before him.

"Yeah. I guess I'm thinking too much about everything that could go wrong to focus on getting the group to buy the place. There's no way I can afford the grounds by myself, so I'm relying on them for help."

Jana smiled easily.

"There *are* other investment groups."

"Yeah, but there's no time left. By March Mr. Clouse is going to make a decision. Isn't he?"

"His decision could be not to accept any of the applicants. He's picky about who takes over the hotel."

Duncan looked to his watch again, seeing it was nearly time to begin the tour.

"Hopefully my fellow investors can overlook the problems and see what a worthwhile place the hotel can be."

Jana nodded as they returned to the foyer, finding the rest of the group awaiting instructions.

Quickly counting heads, Duncan realized someone wasn't present.

"You seen Glenn Turner?" he asked Red.

"No. I think he was driving up, but I haven't seen his car anywhere."

"Maybe he stopped at the hotel," someone suggested.

Duncan wondered if the man might have encountered some bad weather during his trip. He watched Red pull out a cell phone, then search his contact list before hitting a button. Nearly half a minute passed before he folded the phone shut.

"I got his voice mail," Red reported.

From what little bit he knew of Turner, the man didn't seem like one to leave his phone too far behind. Turner wasn't absolutely needed, because a majority vote within the group determined if they were pursuing the hotel officially.

Or not.

Growing concerned, Duncan knew the group couldn't afford to wait long for Turner. It made no sense that he would still be in transit if he wasn't answering his cell phone.

"How long do we wait for him?" Jana asked, her tone indicating that waiting might prove troublesome.

"It's your gig, but I say we don't," Duncan answered just above a whisper.

He looked at his fellow investors, who appeared ready to take the tour, noticing a strange, almost quizzical stare from Dave McCully.

*   *   *

McCully couldn't help but look at Duncan, realizing the man looked very much like the man who spoke at the end of his vision.

Though he tried being coy about his observation, Duncan caught him.

McCully quickly diverted his eyes, taking notice of the two women in the group.

Laura Compton was close to his own age, finding success through wealthy parents and a strong education in business. He knew of rumors that she had some sort of relationship with Keith, despite him being old enough to be her father.

Beside her stood Judith Parks, a lovely brunette who kept her personal life a closed book to the others. She had briefly dated Red Sanders, but their day and night personalities kept it from working. They both had money, so McCully imagined their brief relationship blossomed from their business ties. She dressed fashionably, always in the latest styles, despite Red seldom changing a thing about his attire or his outlook on life.

He seldom saw them speak to one another unless they had business to discuss.

Of anyone in the group, Judith was the least likely to be sold on the idea of buying the hotel. She seldom liked anyone else's ideas, which tended to dissuade them from voting for her projects. McCully had been personally burned on an idea to buy land just outside of Knoxville for development.

He found a perfect lot for condos or a small hotel near a new housing development. New businesses had flocked to the area, so he wanted to buy the land for resale, if nothing else. Judith shot down his idea, saying their profit would have been minimal at best. Red stuck by her decision, despite knowing better, and swayed the group's vote.

McCully checked on the land a few months later, discovering it was bought by a Tampa company that had already begun construction on a Holiday Inn Express. Though not one to hold a grudge, McCully had voted against several of their ideas that seemed far less stable than his own potential venture. He didn't always win, but his point was taken by nearly everyone in the group.

Jana called for everyone's attention, which they readily gave.

"Due to the weather, we're not going to wait for Mr. Turner to arrive," she announced. "I have a shuttle van outside if you would all be so kind as to make your way out there."

She led the way toward the front door, already beginning part of the tour by taking them through the motions.

"We'll begin by touring the sunken garden outside the hotel itself. From there, we will quickly observe some of the out buildings before making our way inside."

A moment later, everyone was seated comfortably inside the already heated van, which had its own driver from the rental service. McCully sat beside Oswalt, who had been engaged in conversation with Red Sanders while they waited inside the mansion.

"Nice of you to join me," McCully commented with a verbal jab.

"It's not every day I get to see Red," Oswalt said in his defense. "I'm stuck with you all the time."

Grinning to himself, McCully realized how often he saw his agent, whether it was conducting music business, or their investment meetings.

Soon enough the group members found themselves at the hotel's front gate, huddled in a group like penguins to avoid the falling snow. McCully noticed the climate didn't feel too bad, considering the temperature remained near the freezing point. The wind chilled him a bit, but he hadn't expected a mild blizzard while he packed for his trip.

"I'll try to make this brief," Jana virtually yelled through the elements so the group could hear.

She led them down the path, explaining some of the hotel's history to them, until they walked into the garden. After a quick look around the snow-covered flowers and shrubs, which had already met their seasonal demise around the holidays, she took them inside one of the two remaining springs.

"This is Hygeia," Jana noted, waving one arm slowly around the open area like a game show hostess.

McCully noticed sound resonated nicely inside the glazed brick structure. The acoustics might provide a nice staging area for a small band, he decided.

Roomy enough to accommodate a small party, the spring had a nice walkway on two of its sides. McCully noticed withered vines still wrapped around the support columns and trellises along both ends. He suspected they created a form of privacy for anyone visiting the spring during the summer because the leafy vines became a wall of their own.

"The spring's name originates from the Greek goddess of health, and is where we get our modern day word 'hygiene' from.

"The Jesuits capped the spring when they took over the hotel because it was prone to flooding. At one time, guests walked fifteen feet down for a drink of the mineral water."

Subtle stained glass in some of the windows gave McCully the impression the Jesuits had left their mark when they owned the hotel. The interior was completely white, appearing more so with the falling snow outside the abundance of windows that allowed natural light to flood the spring building.

By no means heated, the building only offered partial shelter from the elements. McCully exhaled through his mouth, seeing his breath in the air. A peek outside one of the smaller windows indicated the snow was already several inches deep on the ground.

Chancing a glimpse toward Duncan, he noticed the normally rugged biker looked concerned, yet attentive. He knew this project meant everything to the man, because he failed to contain his enthusiasm on more than one occasion after their meetings.

McCully couldn't shake the feeling the man looked very much like the last person he saw in his vision. It seemed impossible because the scene he witnessed was nearly a hundred-years-old. To him, things weren't adding up.

Never had his visions taken him so far back in time, and lately he required little or no physical contact to initiate them. Something about the grounds he stood upon heightened the abilities he often wished he'd never possessed.

Even the foreshadowing of coming to West Baden triggered something inside his mind.

Whatever Jana said went unheard as he lost himself in thought, staring at the snowflakes floating downward outside.

"Let's head inside the main building and get warm," he finally heard her say.

Like everyone around him, McCully found himself awestruck at the sight of the atrium a few minutes later. Six levels of hotel rooms were in complete view from one spot, some with balconies, all of them surrounded by intricate paint and Victorian artwork. Above it all they spotted the chandelier below a round metal drum.

The roof consisted of glass and metal panels, aligned beside one another around the dome. It looked somewhat like a flying saucer with large windows from below. The huge windows allowed light to freely illuminate the entire atrium.

Instead of acting as an eyesore, the metal framework that supported the dome from the ground up was lost in the hand-painted artwork just above the rooms. The metal arms spanned from large pillars to the center drum above the chandelier, directly beneath the metal panels of the same sandy color, allowing them to virtually go unnoticed.

"The atrium has seen everything from dinners, to car shows, to circuses," Jana stated. "As you can see, it has space enough for virtually anything you might wish to hold in the hotel. The Jesuits found it too large for their needs, so they converted the lobby into their chapel."

Jana led them across the atrium, showing them the old office, what was a smoking room in its day, the dining room, the kitchen, and the old barber shop along the first floor. They stopped at the emporium, which appeared closed.

"This is where regular tourists purchase gifts after their tours," Jana explained. "Occasionally the gift shop management hosts book signings for authors who write about the area. We'll stop by here after we get done upstairs, because I think you'll like the museum in the back."

Jana took them to the second floor, showing them the ballroom, now finished by Clouse's development team. She explained the metal beams used to solidify the upper floors created a problem with the ballroom because the floor was raised almost two feet.

"You can imagine how it looked having windows that reached down to your feet," she said. "But Mr. Clouse came up with a solution that left the windows outside intact for historical purposes, but also made them pleasing in here."

McCully noticed small crescent tables placed before the windows with open bases that matched the room's decor. They each had a glass top, allowing light to shine upward through them, or stream outside their bases. He knelt beside one, noticing the rustic red color of the metal bars holding up the table. Inside he spied some sort of light orb, not much different from a rotating disco ball atop a base.

"Functional *and* pretty," McCully uttered barely above a whisper.

"Isn't it?" Oswalt asked in a somewhat huffed tone, as though the tour bored him.

"What crawled up your ass and died?"

His agent shrugged.

"I came here for the food and the company, not the grand tour."

"Ever the consummate respect for history and lore, I see."

Oswalt sighed, returning to the rest of the group.

Jana led them to several other areas, including a balcony overlooking the lobby where she said women once wrote letters home while the men enjoyed the outdoors. Able to see the intricate artwork up close, McCully virtually felt the place come alive inside his mind, and through his veins.

He was a complete stranger from another state, yet he shared an unfamiliar kinship with the hotel.

They visited another balcony that overlooked the atrium. It gave visitors a sense of anonymity when they viewed the atrium, because anyone below couldn't see them unless they stepped forward to the railing.

Most of the remaining floors looked the same, with finished rooms that Clouse and his team had completed several years prior. They were fully furnished with beds, desks, lamps, and beautiful bathrooms, topped off with fantastic views of either the atrium or the grounds. The view depended upon whether a person had a room on the inside ring, or the outside.

When they reached the sixth floor after a ride on one of the two elevators, the group followed Jana into a small lobby that led to a suite. At long last the investors found themselves in familiar territory because the suite came equipped with a conference table, big screen television, kitchenette, and two bedrooms. Each of the bedrooms came equipped with a full bath, their walls covered from floor to ceiling in tiles with a marble finish.

McCully found himself impressed by the hotel's design, particularly since it was built over a century prior. He liked the idea of the hotel coming to life again, but he felt biased after seeing how it looked when it was open for business.

Hesitantly, he touched the conference table, wondering if it might set off a vision in front of his colleagues.

Nothing happened.

Since the table was evidently new from the renovation, it held no memories to trigger his ability.

"You gonna propose to it or what?" Keith Sanders asked as he took McCully's side.

He felt somewhat taken aback that Keith spoke to him outside of a business meeting, because he sometimes wondered if the man knew anything outside of ranching and investing.

Slowly chuckling to himself, McCully figured he probably looked a bit strange running his fingers along a tabletop.

"Maybe I was admiring the finish."

"Uh huh," Keith said with a skeptical raise of one eyebrow.

Both stood there awkwardly a moment, unsure of what to say next. Jana led the rest of the group through the suite, then out to the lobby for a bird's-eye view of the atrium.

"What do you think of it?" he dared ask the unofficial leader of their firm.

"I like the place, but I'm still not sold on the casino notion."

"Ever known a casino to lose money? Or go bankrupt?"

Now it was Keith's turn to laugh.

"I guess not. It'll just take some time for our lawyers to go through the Indiana laws before we commit all the way."

"It's a bit different, isn't it?"

"How so?"

"Usually we're the middleman, buying then selling. This project requires some hands on operation."

Keith nodded in agreement.

"This place sat vacant for almost twenty years with a selling price a fraction of the price *we're* looking at paying. I guess it would be a sink or swim venture, wouldn't it?"

"I think Dan has enough inspiration for all of us."

"The lad certainly does. At first I wondered why he had such a hard-on for this place, but I'm beginning to understand. I just wish it wasn't in the middle of nowhere."

McCully followed Keith toward the group, catching part of Jana's latest speech about the only confirmed death at the hotel while it was operating. It seemed a professional baseball manager took his own life while the team was at the hotel for spring training.

A few minutes later the group members found themselves downstairs, wandering around the gift shop. McCully saw gift shops all around the nation whenever he toured, so he immediately looked for anything unique to the area. He seldom bought anything, because his house was already full of memorabilia from his father, and from the recording industry. His life had little room for hobbies and collectibles.

Finding little of interest, McCully milled toward the museum. Merely an extension of the larger gift shop, the museum was separated in principle only by an arched doorway. When McCully passed through the doorway, he felt strange, as though the room held something for him, bursting to reveal its secret.

Only Judith Parks stood inside the room with him, studying some before and after composites placed on the walls. The photos depicted the hotel when weeds overtook the lawn and garden areas, the fallen wall portion, and the decay inside the atrium. Beside them, other photos displayed what the group had just seen.

A fully restored hotel.

Deciding to look at something other than the photos, McCully turned to his right, seeing old artifacts from the hotel's heyday, such as a dipping glass from the springs, and an old room key. He glided to his right, observing another glass case with different donations inside. Mostly old postcards and souvenirs such as plates and engraved spoons, the items took him back to the vision.

He had crouched for a better look at some of the items, but as he slowly stood, McCully's eyes fixed themselves on a photograph set atop the display case. Enlarged, the photograph displayed a dozen men seated upon a dark buggy named the 'Water Wagon' in bright paint along its side. Another man stood at the back of the wagon with his hands upon the wooden frame.

Impressive as the photo may have been on its own, giving visitors a glimpse of life around 1900, McCully focused on one man in particular. Wearing a dark suit and a tan cap, the man held a walking stick in his left hand, while his right thumbed a cigar.

"Dear God," McCully muttered as someone brushed his side.

As though in a dream, or some slow-motion movie sequence, he looked to his left, seeing Dan Duncan look at the photograph, then to him. If Duncan noticed the bewildered look scrawled across his face, it didn't register on his.

"That why you've been giving me funny stares all morning?" Duncan inquired, though not rudely.

McCully couldn't readily answer.

Of course the reason was the man in the photo, but he couldn't begin to conjure up a story to explain how he had virtually traveled back in time to see the man.

He looked from the man in the photo to Duncan once more, seeing only subtle differences between the two men. Duncan had a lighter-colored mustache, being blond instead of dark brown, and his face appeared a bit more weathered.

"Who is he?" McCully asked his investment partner, sensing Duncan knew the answer.

Duncan looked at him suspiciously a moment before answering.

"My grandfather."

9

"Did you ever meet him?" McCully asked as they both looked to the photograph.

"No. He died pretty young."

Judith passed them as she left the room.

"What do you know about my grandfather?" Duncan virtually demanded in a hushed tone.

"I've seen him before. These images are for sale on eBay all the time."

He hated telling a white lie, but had little choice.

Saying "I had a flashback to a time when your grandfather was a regular at this place" didn't sound very appropriate.

Or sane.

McCully had indeed searched online auctions for the hotel's memorabilia, which provided him the excuse. It seemed the old Water Wagon was somewhat of a photo backdrop, in addition to traveling around the grounds to provide mineral water. Many images were converted into postcards sold at the hotel, now stuffed in shoe boxes and old scrapbooks inside closets or garages.

Many were probably lost forever.

"What was his name?" McCully asked Duncan, though unsure why he pressed the issue, or even wanted to know.

"Andrew. He was actually my great-grandfather."

Duncan still appeared somewhat concerned that McCully had any kind of connection to his family, legitimate or not.

"I see the connection," McCully said, staring intently at the photograph.

He wanted to touch it, but not in front of anyone. If it was indeed an original, it would probably send him into a vision. Though his visions sometimes unfolded over minutes inside his mind, only a second or two passed in real life.

People had reported how his body stiffened or he appeared clinically insane for those few seconds, as though possessed. McCully had no desire to carry out any theatrics, intentional or not, before his fellow investors.

Only Oswalt had ever seen him in the strange condition, and he never pretended to understand in any capacity.

Oswalt was very much old-fashioned, explaining why George McCully chose him as his agent. He didn't believe in aliens, government conspiracies, or using the stock market, much less psychic powers.

"I realize we don't know one another much beyond our business," Duncan said, "but I get the impression you know something you're not telling me."

McCully ignored the statement, seeing no positives about telling the truth.

"Your grandfather dressed fairly plain, didn't he?"

"That wasn't plain back then," Duncan noted. "How often do you wear a carnation pinned on your sport coat these days?"

McCully nodded, getting the point.

Each of the men in the photograph had a flower pinned to their jacket. They wore vests, and while some of them wore ties, others had on shirts with turtlenecks. Their head dress was a potpourri of derby hats and cloth caps.

"Is he the reason you're so interested in this place?"

Duncan seemed to light up at the idea of talking about his interest in West Baden. He obviously knew bidding on the place was a hard sell to his colleagues.

"He helped bring the railroad here in 1887. It shaped the course of history as far as this area is concerned, and he made his fortune."

"When was this photo taken?"

"Probably sometime between 1899 and 1917, before they reno-vated the grounds," Duncan surmised. "A lot of these photos are taken near the old opera house and the early wooden springs."

"When did he die, if you don't mind my asking?"

"There was an accident in 1923. They found him one morning along the railroad tracks."

McCully simply nodded, not wishing to press the issue. The year sounded very much like the era during his vision.

"We're not so different," he said instead. "My family had success before I was born."

Duncan didn't appear sold, but he wasn't about to lose an ally in the battle to own the property.

"I've worked for a living," he said.

"You may not consider learning to play three instruments and touring the country on weekends and holidays work, but it isn't easy."

Duncan looked to the photo once more, letting a strange, almost remorseful grin cross his face.

"We should probably get back," he said uneasily.

"Yeah," McCully said under his breath as the grandson of a train baron left the room.

Looking to the photograph, McCully caught himself reaching for it as his fingers neared the frame. He hesitated, seeing no one look-ing his way. Wondering if anything would even happen, he let his fingertips draw near the wooden frame's finish.

Somehow doubting the picture could trigger an event, he let one finger graze the frame, instantly transplanting his mind and body to another time.

Outside once more, McCully took a quick look around, seeing wooden structures everywhere on what seemed to be otherwise familiar ground. Everything appeared lush and green around him, unlike the sepia images representing the only captured moments of the hotel's better days.

Nearby he spied the Water Wagon parked within the area he now knew as the sunken garden. Very little about the grounds appeared the same, aside from the general shape. None of the buildings had brick exteriors, the bicycle track loomed in the background, and the church stood atop the hill, overlooking the original hotel.

"Come on, Andy," a man said beside the wagon.

McCully noticed a group of men nearby, some appearing agitated as this man tried convincing Andrew Duncan of something.

"One picture isn't going to kill you," the man continued.

McCully seemed to recognize him as one of the men beside Duncan in his earlier vision. Apparently they shared some sort of friendship, or at least a partnership.

Shaking his head negatively, Duncan seemed to give in, stepping toward the wagon. A photographer lined them up on the wagon, putting Duncan near the center. He asked for a show of hands about how many of the men wanted copies.

McCully realized he was witnessing the creation of the modern day postcards he occasionally saw online. The photographer took orders, because he needed to shoot a photograph for each individual who wanted a personalized postcard made. To his surprise, Duncan raised his hand with several others.

Duncan's friend stood proudly behind him, wearing a light derby. Duncan himself looked away on most of the shots, appearing timid about looking directly at the camera. Perhaps the flash bothered him, but McCully sensed something deeper about his reluctance.

As the flash went off the third or fourth time, McCully's eyes diverted to the grounds, finding several people walking around while others milled near the springs. Compared to modern life, everything looked and felt tranquil. The highway was nothing more than a dirt path, people rode horses or took buggies for transportation, and nature looked unblemished everywhere around him.

Watching the people walk around the grounds felt something like viewing a slow-motion movie scene. In the distance, some of them looked like ants because the vast grounds appeared to have no end.

"You okay, Andy?" the friend asked once they were done, stepping off the wagon.

"I'm fine. Just a busy day ahead of me is all."

Duncan seemed like a local learning the walk and talk of the ritzy people who visited the grounds.

"Surely the wealthiest man in the valley doesn't have worries," his friend said playfully.

Giving an uneasy smile, Duncan led the way toward the hotel, noticing several people looking his way when his friend said the words. McCully observed this carefully, noting that Andrew Duncan was a private individual. For a railroad baron, he didn't fit the typical mold.

"I'm having lunch with the wealthiest man in the valley, Ben. Or high tea, or whatever the hell it is they call it. I can't get used to all these rituals."

"Then why do them?"

"It's expected," Duncan answered as though God Himself might strike him down if he failed to attend functions in the valley.

"You wanted money and power when you bought up railroad shares, Andy. You can't deny it. What you do with your life is your business, but you shouldn't be living to satisfy other people."

Shrugging uneasily, Duncan took a book of matches from inside his sport coat, lighting the cigar he had been toying with since the Water Wagon photo. He drew on it for several seconds before watching a smoke ring dissipate into the air when he exhaled.

"When you have lunch with Sinclair, just remember he wouldn't have found this hotel if you hadn't put the wheels in motion for the railroad that brought him."

Duncan didn't appear convinced.

"The hotel was up and running before he ever traveled this way. He just took advantage of a situation like I did."

"We're getting off the topic. We were talking about your goals now that you've accomplished riches and a title. If you were in England you might be knighted, you know."

Chuckling, Duncan appeared far more at ease around his friend than he had moments prior.

"So, we were talking about my goals, were we?"

"Good man, certainly you have ambitions to marry and spread your seed across the valley, don't you?"

Duncan appeared amused at the statement.

"Mr. Williams, I believe what you are suggesting would make me the father of many a bastard child."

"I suggest no such thing."

Puffing on his cigar to keep it from dying off, Duncan kept one eye fixed on his friend, waiting for an elaboration.

"It just so happens there is a beautiful young lady a few miles away who has asked yours truly about any single friends he might know."

Williams held out an open palm toward his friend, indicating Duncan needed to indicate interest, or manufacture an excellent excuse if he wasn't interested.

"I suppose we *could* go for a horseback ride this afternoon," he said after a few seconds. "There are always a few detours along the way, aren't there?"

"That's the spirit, Andy."

McCully felt a presence beside him that brought him back to his current snowy world.

He looked to his left, seeing Jana staring at him with a concerned, curious look.

"You okay?" she asked. "You've been staring at the photo for a few minutes now."

"I guess you could say I was somewhere else."

"Well, everyone else is getting into the van. I was going to lock up the emporium if you were ready to go."

Feeling as though he had been disturbed during a deep sleep, McCully wanted to see the vision through, suspecting it might lead him down a disturbing path. He typically disliked his abilities, but something about the hotel grounds intensified them, teasing him with bygone images.

As he followed Jana to the door, he wondered if they might be warning him about impending danger. Trying to shake the feeling from his mind, he walked toward the glass entrance doors, seeing snow piling up outside. The sunken garden and buildings beyond the van barely remained visible through the falling flakes.

While Tennessee felt some cold temperatures during the winter months, the state seldom saw any snow accumulation.

Something about the weather worried him, though he lacked any evidence why it might prove harmful. He opened the door for Jana, following her into the cold, wondering what events the evening held for his group.

10

When the group returned to the mansion Duncan noticed it was almost two in the afternoon. A few inches of snow now rested atop his truck and the trailer hauling his motorcycle. He groaned inwardly at the thought of lost enjoyment during his weekend homecoming.

Stepping from the van, he stood outside as everyone else went inside. Thoughts of the hotel ran through his mind, along with a burning desire to own or run the building.

His conversation with McCully plagued him, but he didn't suspect the man harbored any dark secrets. If anything, his interest in Andrew Duncan seemed genuine, though awkward in its timing.

Once everyone exited the van, it departed through the front gate, leaving the guests by themselves at the mansion.

Another tour was planned for the next morning in case the group had any concerns or questions about the hotel. Jana had taken them through the entire hotel, though somewhat quickly. Duncan felt bad that the garden and some of the outlying buildings were skimmed over during the walk because of the weather.

Though the highway was plowed, the road from the hotel to the mansion remained very much snow covered. If the front gate was capable of being closed, it might remain stuck if the snow froze it to the ground.

Duncan doubted any looters or thieves dared brave the elements to visit the seldom inhabited mansion. Turning around, he noticed everyone else had retreated to warmer shelter, so he decided to do the same. As he sauntered toward the front door, the images carved along the front of the building caught his attention.

He took a moment to study the carving nearest the door, finding its craftsmanship impeccable. In great detail, it showed an image of a young man tied down atop a stone tablet with an older man ready to plunge a dagger into his heart. Behind them, tangled in the brush stood a ram, bringing to mind an old biblical story about Abraham being tested by God. Prepared to sacrifice his son to honor the Lord's wishes, God then spoke to him and told him it was simply a test. Abraham then found a nearby ram to offer as a sacrifice instead.

Beneath the image, also carved into the mansion's stone foundation, Duncan found a set of numbers.

6:14.

Far removed from his church school days, Duncan believed most or all passages from the Bible had some sort of notation preceding their numbered paragraphs. He wondered if his guess about Abraham was accurate, deciding to check his room for a Bible later.

He stepped inside, wondering what the group was supposed to do for entertainment the rest of the evening. Most of his colleagues were already out of sight, likely unpacking inside their private rooms.

No one really gave him much indication about their impressions of the hotel. He caught several looks of astonishment when they entered the hotel's atrium, thinking perhaps they felt some of the nostalgia that ran through his veins.

"What happened to the servant?" he asked Jana as she passed him.

"He was just here for the morning," she explained. "I have the caterer here now. Was there something you needed?"

"No. Not at all."

Duncan put forth a cheerful look, though his insides felt like a dishrag being wrung out.

Picking up his suitcase, he started toward the stairway, hesitating on the second step as an uncomfortable feeling overtook his mind. He realized the probability of being snowed in for a day or two worried some of his partners, but something felt dangerous about his surroundings.

Glancing around, he saw no one wandering through the mansion, but several pleasant aromas rose from the kitchen. Letting his mind return to unpacking and relaxing, Duncan entertained notions of driving to the hotel later. His truck possessed off-road capabilities, so wintery weather typically did little to slow it down.

Supper was the only scheduled event left for the evening, then the guests were free to discuss the hotel or do as they pleased. Though the van driver had left, Jana remained behind, likely spending the evening with them. Radio reports indicated most of the highways were treacherous, with a dozen accidents already preoccupying police and county road crews.

Duncan trudged upstairs, his mind never venturing far from thoughts of the nearby hotel grounds until he noticed McCully emerge from his room.

Both men exchanged uncomfortable looks, then avoided one another as they passed in the second floor hallway.

Reading the placards along each door until he found his room, he turned the knob, stepping inside. Though he liked the room, he set down his suitcase, opting to return downstairs to get a feel for the opinions of his fellow investors.

He removed his heavy jacket, tossing it to the bed as his mind reflected on the day's events.

Glenn Turner had yet to show up or call. Red had tried phoning him several times, to no avail.

At first Duncan felt angry, thinking Turner shrugged off the tour, or simply chickened out. Now he worried the weather might have incapacitated Turner, or left him stranded somewhere. The man was professional enough to answer his phone, or at least return a call the moment he found himself free to do so.

Sighing outwardly, he sauntered down the stairs, prepared to see if there were any new developments.

11

In downtown French Lick, the sheriff of Orange County sat inside a local bar he had frequented for years, sipping a beer from his chilled mug.

The bar had gone through several name changes over the years, the latest coming when a retired couple bought the place and named it Berkie's. The atmosphere changed little, as did the clientele, but Sheriff Roland Brown made certain the riffraff stayed clear of the place.

With the prospect of a casino coming to town, his job was suddenly observed more heavily by the local media. The following year was an election year, and with one more term available to him, Brown wanted to make certain West Baden and French Lick remained free of problems.

Sitting across from his son at a table, he looked to the clock since none of the windows allowed a clear view of the snow falling outside.

"Almost four," he said in his son's general direction.

"In a hurry?" Arlan Brown asked.

"It's just this shitty weather. You know how things get when it snows just a few inches. People drive worse than usual around here."

Arlan took a swig from his beer bottle. This was his first of two days off.

Roland kept a tighter leash on his son than any of his other deputies. They seldom worked together, but away from work they were

71

virtually inseparable. Between fishing, horseback riding, and traveling to watch sporting events, few days passed when they didn't see or talk to one another.

"You got plans tonight?" Roland asked his son.

"Not really. I might stop by the video store on the way home."

His son had been dating the young woman who owned the local video store in West Baden. Until the casino was built, bringing all kinds of national chains to their little towns, she provided the only means of DVD and video rentals.

For the longest time his son hadn't dated after coming off a bad relationship. He was in his early thirties, thinking he was on the road to marriage when his world came crashing down.

Roland hadn't been the best role model, divorcing twice before he turned fifty. After retiring from a local police chief's position, he ran for county sheriff and won, to his own surprise. Luckily Arlan already had a job with the county force, sparing them from nepotism claims.

"What are you doing?" Arlan inquired.

The sheriff thought a moment before answering, staring at the nearly empty mug on the table. One beer was his limit on any given night, because his job required him to remain on-call all day and night.

"I'll probably take a few runs through town before heading home. The locals like seeing us out there doing our job."

Arlan flashed a crooked grin.

"Shaking hands and kissing babies *will* get you further."

Shoving his mug away from him, Roland groaned to himself. He believed the public liked seeing the sheriff in person, instead of viewing him as a photo in the paper after a big arrest or publicity function. He attended the largest church in the area simply to make himself known. Major crimes seldom occurred within the county, forcing Roland to draw attention to public relations. Because of limited crime, his force remained relatively small.

Nine officers served under him, which would likely increase after the casino issue was settled. Part of his structured redevelopment was to have his intern write grants for new officer positions to the government. Though the intern received no pay for such tedious work, he had the opportunity to create himself a position within the department if the federal government deemed the department worthy of funding.

Roland knew how to use incentives to his advantage.

His mind wandered to the fact that another group was touring the hotel, then staying overnight in the mansion. Thankfully things had gone smoothly with the first two tours.

Roland came into his position toward the end of the West Baden fiasco revolving around Paul Clouse. Very little about the hotel's history, or Martin Smith, made sense to him. Conflicting stories made it difficult to ascertain exactly what the hell happened on those grounds over a period of three years.

"You ever wonder how much things are going to change around here once the casino moves in?" he asked his son.

"Probably for the better. I keep hearing all about how New Albany and Corydon have better tax bases because of their casinos. I remember how rundown Corydon used to look when I was in school. They've changed that place for the better."

"Hopefully we can do the same here, son."

Arlan looked at him curiously.

"You okay? You seem on edge tonight."

"I don't know what it is. This snow, the hotel being looked at … something feels real strange."

Finishing his beer, Arlan set the bottle down hard enough that it thumped against the table.

"You grew up around here. I don't imagine you've seen much of this stuff over the years."

Roland forced a chuckle.

"No, I don't suppose I have."

He paused momentarily, placing both hands before him on the table.

"I can remember a time when that hotel was nothing more than overgrown weeds and crumbling walls. Now they're talking about making it a Five Star affair. We've never had anything like that before, and I'm afraid it's going to get fucked up like it did the last time they tried opening it."

"You worry too much," his son noted, stretching his arms as he stood. "I'm getting home so I can shovel my drive."

"I'll see you in the morning."

Arlan nodded, giving an informal salute before he headed for the door.

With his son gone, only Roland and two other patrons remained inside the bar. Tom Watkins, the man who owned the establishment, remained behind the bar as he cleaned glasses, then swept the floor.

Suspecting the man wanted to close up and get home, Roland decided to leave for the night when his cellular phone rang. Plucking it from his belt, he noticed the number coming from the West Baden Springs Hotel where a few of his state police buddies sometimes worked security.

"Hello?" he answered simply.

"Roland, this is Brent Guthrie. I'm working at the hotel tonight, and I have a little situation I want you to look at."

"Something bad?"

"I hate to drag you out in the weather, but it's something I really can't discuss on the phone."

Exhaling through his nose in thought, the sheriff wondered why in the world Guthrie wanted him specifically at the hotel. He also questioned why the retired state trooper phoned him directly when there were obviously county units on patrol.

"I'm just down the road," he finally answered. "Give me ten minutes."

"Okay. Be careful."

A click reached the sheriff's ears, but something about the way Guthrie ended the call worried him. The way he said 'be careful' sounded deeper than obvious concern over the weather. It occurred to him that Guthrie seldom spoke vaguely about any topic. They both knew cellular phone calls weren't traceable, short of high tech equipment.

Keeping his calm demeanor, Roland stood from the wooden chair. On his way out he gave Tom Watkins a quick wave, then decided to speak with the man as a precaution. Why he felt a need to let someone know his intentions eluded him, but something instinctively told him this was no ordinary night.

Perhaps the freak storm put him on edge, or the fact he was traveling to the hotel gave him goose bumps, but he needed to leave some kind of breadcrumb trail.

"If Arlan calls, I'm heading to the West Baden hotel," he told the establishment's owner. "I'll be heading home after I'm done there."

"Okay, Sheriff," Watkins said with an acknowledging nod.

"Take care, Tom."

Stepping outside, the sheriff encountered snow halfway to his knees. He looked up, pasted immediately in the face by giant white flakes. Walking toward the four-wheel-drive Ford Explorer he purchased almost immediately after taking office, he realized he now had justification for such a purchase.

Painted in the dull brown and tan colors of most all Indiana county police vehicles, it had a third color of snowy white atop the roof and hood. From the door, the Orange County seal shimmered against the exterior lights from the tavern. He opened the door, climbed in, and started the vehicle to let it warm up a few minutes.

When he stepped out of the Explorer, he fished a cigarette from his breast pocket, lighting it quickly before staring upward at the thousands of snowflakes dropping gracefully from the sky. Though most restaurants and bars still allowed smoking within their facilities, he chose to keep his habit from public view. Feeling as though he spent his career under a microscope, the sheriff attempted to be his own public relations specialist.

Elections brought out mudslinging, so he tried his best to maintain a flawless image and record while he held office.

A few minutes later his vehicle's heater produced adequate heat, so he took a final drag, flicked the cigarette away, then climbed inside. He flipped on the windshield wipers, ready to see what Guthrie needed at the dome.

Something told him he wasn't going to like what he found.

*   *   *

The drive to the hotel did little to knock the mounds of snow from Roland's vehicle. Unable to drive the speed limit because of the slick roads, it took longer than ten minutes to arrive.

Using the back entrance, which required a code to open the security gate, the sheriff typed in the code given to any police officers who patrolled the area. The gate slowly moved aside, revealing an unplowed road ahead.

"Shit," he muttered to himself, wishing the eventual change in ownership didn't create such piss poor conditions during the transition.

By no means a long driveway, Roland discovered it took several minutes to navigate because of snow drifts. Able to observe the grounds from the garden lighting, he saw nothing disturbed, and no vehicles other than Guthrie's sedan.

Considering at least one person remained on hotel security detail at any given time, county and local officers had no keys to the dome. The sheriff, on the other hand, had a master key for the hotel and several other significant buildings within his vehicle. Many local businesses allowed police and fire departments to keep copied keys on their vehicles to avoid broken windows or doors on emergency runs.

Stepping from his vehicle, Roland snatched the keys from behind his seat since Guthrie didn't step out the back door, or either of the main entrances, to meet him.

Instead of simply using the back door, the sheriff made his way along the veranda, which had only a dusting of snow the winds had deposited onto its concrete surface. The front steps, however, appeared engulfed by white mounds.

Like the rest of the grounds, they were left unattended during the brief snowstorm.

Roland preferred the days when volunteers participated on a daily basis. The hotel and grounds were always spotless back then, but since Clouse had decided to sell the place, their role diminished. No longer was the hotel a historic landmark needing to be saved. It now had a business face that indicated volunteers were being phased out once design teams stepped onto the grounds.

He reached the first set of glass doors, tugging lightly on one of them. Much to his surprise, it opened. The security personnel and volunteers typically kept it locked at all times after tours ended.

Hesitantly stepping inside, he pulled the next set of doors open. Once inside, he stood perfectly still a moment as his eyes adjusted to the low lighting inside the hotel. Even the atrium ahead seemed dim because snow covered the dome, and the dusk was readily approaching outside.

When he finally took a step, the noise echoed throughout the hotel, giving him the creeps. Roland immediately headed for the security office, prepared to demand some answers from Guthrie once he found him. Nothing seemed out of place *except* for the retired trooper's call.

The observation room where the security personnel monitored the hotel grounds was literally several feet down the hall. He walked the distance to the door, finding it slightly ajar, which seemed unusual. The troopers typically sat inside, keeping the door locked behind them, or locked whenever they walked their rounds.

While the hotel had no security cameras, the room itself provided a great vantage point because it allowed the troopers to observe the garden, the road leading to the front gate, and some of the back parking lot.

Pushing the door in slowly, he listened to it creak as he cautiously slid past the door itself. He focused on the far room where the troopers typically sat. The sheriff's trained eyes immediately spied a small crimson stream atop the floor, setting off alarms within his mind.

Instinctively, he reached for his firearm, but he had gone home to change before heading to the bar. Frequenting taverns in his official uniform made for bad public opinion during an election year.

As he moved closer to the room a black shoe came into view. Knowing Guthrie often wore casual dress attire, he swallowed hard, beginning to wonder if all the gruesome murder scenes he missed before taking office looked like this.

Guthrie was lying face-down on the floor, his eyes still open, with a pool of blood beneath his body. Roland felt horrified as he knelt beside the fresh corpse, seeing a stab wound in the man's back, but no knife. Looking to the man's clip-on holster, he also found no gun.

From habit alone, he touched the neck to feel for a pulse, finding none. No rise of the chest, or the back in this case, indicated Guthrie certainly wasn't breathing. Even if Roland attempted CPR, the lack of blood inside the retired trooper's body would make the effort futile.

He had just confirmed Guthrie was forced to call him, but by whom?

Before assessing the murder further, he looked around to ensure his own safety. Seeing no one, he wondered where the knife and the murderer had gone.

Carefully stepping around the body, he reached for the phone atop the desk. Plucking it from the receiver, he placed it near his ear, hearing no dial tone. Either the weather had somehow taken out the phone lines, or someone cut the hotel's phone line intentionally.

Roland suspected the latter.

"Shit."

He reached for his cellular phone, but a noise outside the main door drew his attention before he freed it from his belt.

Exercising extreme caution because he was unarmed, Roland walked toward the door, seeing nothing around him that appeared useful as a weapon. Why someone would kill Guthrie escaped him, but what concerned him more at the moment was why that person lured him to the hotel.

Nearing the door, he peered from side to side without framing himself directly inside the doorway. The last thing he wanted to do was make himself an easy target, so he looked across the room, seeing a second door within the same room. A bookshelf blocked it to prevent people from using it as an entrance to the security room.

He walked to it hurriedly, trying the knob without moving the shelving unit.

The knob refused to turn.

Deciding against smashing down the door and creating a ruckus, Roland moved toward the other door, giving a quick peek outside before stepping outside the door. He scooted to the area he knew was safe, giving a look the other way from the corner of his eye. Seeing he was safe, the sheriff breathed a sigh of relief, catching his breath a moment.

Able to see a little over twenty feet in either direction, the sheriff wondered if either of the bending hallways were safe to travel. The circular shape of the entire hotel made walking around the floors a mystery every time. Only the lights and doors seemed to remain in place, because the floor and ceiling were simply one continuous pattern if they were the only thing a walker looked at.

Picking a direction, Roland walked along the dim hallway. The only lighting came from small light bulbs shaped like candles in sets of three. They were spaced far enough apart that they lit the hallway, but didn't put out much overall light.

As he neared an entrance to the atrium, Roland pulled out his cell phone, using the contact function to call his department. Putting the phone up to his ear, he heard nothing but a strange airy silence.

One look at his phone indicated he had no signal. The severe weather likely blocked incoming and outgoing cell phone signals, as well as any satellite dish reception.

Alone and weaponless, Roland decided to go for help, rather than search for the killer himself. He crossed the atrium to the back exit where his Explorer was parked.

Pushing the white exit door open, he stood in shock a moment at the scene laid before him.

The hood of his vehicle looked like an open mouth, except its tongue had been ripped out. Strands of wires and spare parts were scattered randomly across the engine block. He didn't have to move from the doorway to know his Explorer wasn't starting anytime soon.

His mind raced for a solution to the dangerous dilemma he found himself trapped within. Walking seemed foolish because he wasn't dressed for long-term exposure to the cold, and he could envision a driver turning him into road kill after recklessly driving too fast in the snow and ice.

Besides, the closest business had to be almost a mile down the road. Many businesses closed early because of the storm, so finding one open might prove a craps shoot.

An idea suddenly struck him that the sixth floor suite had a phone, even if none of the other rooms did. Determined to exhaust every other possibility before walking, he turned around to find the nearest stairwell or elevator inside the hotel.

As he spun around a dark blur caught his eye before something heavy hit the side of his head, sending him spiraling down into an unconscious heap.

12

Throughout the afternoon the caterer provided snacks for the group until dinner was served in the late afternoon. Most of the guests, McCully included, spent the day milling around the mansion, thinking about the hotel.

Toward the end of their dinner, Laura stood up suddenly, stating she wasn't feeling very well. After barely eating, she excused herself from the table, informing Jana she planned to rest upstairs for an hour or two.

McCully had overheard part of the conversation, so he talked to Jana a moment after everyone had finished dinner. She walked with him into the living room, while most of the guests went upstairs or talked in the entertainment room.

"Was Laura okay?" he inquired.

"I think so. She said she had a headache and a little dizziness."

"So how does working for one of the richest men in the country suit you?"

Jana returned a cautious smile.

"I don't actually work for him. He's a client."

McCully shrugged.

"You know what I mean."

"I suppose I do. And to answer your question, it can be a little intimidating."

Both of them walked toward the fireplace, which radiated heat throughout the room while providing most of the light, since the overhead chandelier was dimmed.

"What about *you*?" Jana asked. "You must have stories from life on the road."

"You know, it looks the same everywhere we go. There isn't much to tell, because we're always crammed in some hotel room, or riding in the back of a tour bus. I don't get a whole lot of time for sightseeing."

"Still, it must be somewhat adventurous. I've only left Indiana a couple times my whole life."

"And I've only *been* to Indiana a few times. My father likes performing at the Little Nashville Opry."

"Maybe I'll come see you perform, since I have more time on my hands."

McCully turned to see her expression, finding her a bit glum.

"Been too busy living the American dream?" McCully asked as they stood before the roaring fire, sticking their hands out to absorb the heat.

Jana let a disgruntled sigh answer his question in part.

"I thought I was happily married, beginning the perfect family, but I guess we drifted apart without me knowing it."

"What happened?" McCully asked before realizing it sounded like he was prying. "If you don't mind my asking."

"I started hearing things at my old job about him. People raised questions, they asked me how life at home was going. That sort of thing. Then one day he served me with divorce papers at the worst possible time in my life."

McCully said nothing, simply trying to be a good listener. He could tell it pained Jana to speak about the divorce, yet it appeared therapeutic for her.

"He timed it perfectly so that he could get custody of our daughter, then he ran off to Georgia with his new fling. Now I only get to see Miranda once a month on weekends, and some holidays. I've been saving back for a good lawyer, so I can take him to court for full custody."

"How old is your daughter?"

"Four. She's been confused by all of this."

"I'd imagine so. Sounds like your ex wanted his cake and ate it, too."

Jana wiped her eye, though she hadn't cried. McCully felt bad for her, coming from a very close family himself. If his father had ever been unfaithful, he did an incredible job of covering his tracks.

"I'm sorry," Jana apologized. "I didn't mean to bring this down on you."

"It's okay. Really."

"No it's not. I'm supposed to be the professional salesperson and here I am babbling on about my personal woes."

McCully understood exactly what it was like having no one to talk to. It felt good to release pent up frustration every so often.

"It's not that I really minded him wanting out of the marriage," Jana said almost as a way of closing their conversation. "It's just the way he went about it, waiting until I was making less money at work so he could take me to the cleaners in court."

"Some people think the world revolves around them," McCully offered. "I still tend to think people who fight the good fight find true happiness in the end."

Jana looked at him, almost amused by the words.

"True words from a songwriter?"

"I like to think so."

Jana looked toward the foyer.

"I guess I'd better get back to some hostess duties before they have to come find me."

McCully nodded, thinking he had a few things to discuss with Oswalt when he found his agent. But first, he wanted a few minutes of quiet time.

He discovered some of the group members talking within their cliques when he passed the living room area. Not much for conversation about stocks, economic development, or war stories, he walked upstairs, finding a set of double doors along the mansion's rear.

He opened them, then stepped onto a second story deck providing a beautiful view of the woods behind the mansion.

Though cool outside, it felt nice to be in the elements a moment. He felt a need to clear his head, because the visions had left him worried about the overnight stay. Granted, nothing within them indicated danger, but his visions typically ended badly. They were appearing inside his mind for a reason.

"You okay, kid?" Oswalt asked, stepping onto the deck with him a moment later, packing his pipe with tobacco.

"I'm not sure. This whole trip seems warped."

Giving a suspicious smirk, his agent seemed to sense he wasn't getting the full story.

"I'm sure the fact that you're keeping your distance like the rest of us were lepers isn't helping much."

"Sorry about that. I just have a lot on my mind."

"You were a chatterbox until we got here, Dave. If you don't tell me what's the matter, I'll have to tell your daddy you were misbehaving under my care."

McCully chuckled. His father tended to have a mother hen nature concerning his band members, but it stopped short of having Oswalt report to him.

He hoped.

"Something about this whole trip is giving me the willies, Frank. Duncan thinks I'm nuts, but there was a photo of his grandfather in the museum, and I think I've seen the guy before."

McCully knew he was telling a half-truth to his agent, but he needed to say something about what he'd seen before he went crazy.

Oswalt lit his pipe before exhaling bluish-gray smoke as he stared at the snow, evidently digesting what McCully told him.

"You having one of those, uh, episodes again?"

"You might say that."

An uncomfortable silence fell between them for several seconds.

"We're in the middle of some highly unusual weather for this area, I've got what I can only imagine might be ghosts inside my mind, and this mansion doesn't do much to reassure me that we're in safe seclusion."

"You're paranoid, Dave. I think your schedule is getting to you."

"Maybe I am a little worried, but my schedule has nothing to do with it. I heard through the grapevine Martin Smith built this mansion before his death."

Oswalt puffed on his pipe, the name obviously not registering in his mind.

"Dr. Smith," McCully repeated again. "The guy they think was responsible for close to two dozen deaths around the hotel grounds."

"I thought he died in some accident outside the hotel."

"I don't think so."

Oswalt appeared openly skeptical.

"You think he's back from the dead to come after us?"

"No, but this mansion is extremely weird the way it's laid out. The stone carvings, the open second floor, the fact that we can't access the third level."

"You're being paranoid. That's all there is to it."

McCully nearly missed the last statement because his eyes fell to the ground below them, spying a set of footprints in otherwise undisturbed snow. He followed them to the mansion, needing to lean over the top of the railing to see that they ended to his right.

The kitchen area? he wondered.

Some sort of steel access door had created a snow angel wing of sorts across the ground when it opened. McCully gauged that it was recently used, having no idea where it led. If the caterer had used it to discard something, no evidence remained atop the snowy accumulation.

"You even listening to me?" Oswalt asked testily, catching his attention, though he had missed the past few statements his agent issued.

"Something about me being paranoid and a disgrace to my family?"

"Right on one count. You might be the other if you keep acting so odd."

McCully decided against pointing out the footsteps to Oswalt, suspecting his agent might get the others to lock him inside a closet.

"Let's talk about something else," he suggested instead.

"Good idea."

Oswalt sounded concerned, yet somewhat irritated. He hated hearing anything about the visions, probably because he knew they typically led to disaster somewhere for someone.

Visions about the hotel had to make him uneasy, much like they kept McCully on edge.

Knocking his pipe against the balcony railing, Oswalt let the tobacco fall to the ground below, obviously perturbed from their discussion. His shoulders openly shivered, indicating his indoor attire no longer protected him from the elements.

"You know, I think I'll join the others downstairs," he said suddenly. "I need to clear my mind."

"I'll catch up," McCully said, wanting some more time to himself.

Perhaps enough time to investigate the tracks below him.

He was about to head inside when Duncan appeared, blocking his egress from the balcony.

"What brings you up here?"

Duncan produced a humidor from inside his leather jacket, pulling a cigar from it, saying nothing. McCully suddenly felt uncomfortable around the man, as though they were both on the verge of spilling secrets, but neither wanted to speak first.

"I always enjoy an after-dinner cigar," Duncan confessed as he sliced one end evenly with a guillotine cigar cutter, sauntering past McCully on the balcony.

"Can't say I've ever taken up the habit."

"Not really a habit," Duncan corrected him. "These are all natural, so they don't have the addictive chemicals like cigarettes. Some people like wine, just like some of us like cigars. It's not a fix, but rather a satisfaction."

McCully wasn't sure what brought about the sermon, but as Duncan used a butane lighter to light the cigar in front of him, rather than traditionally, he felt compelled to ask.

"Why do you light it down there?"

"Butane gives it better flavor than a regular lighter. You don't taste any of the gas this way. And it makes for a more even burn."

McCully nodded, though still uneducated on the finer points of cigar etiquette. He had enough pointers for one night, so he decided to leave, or steer the conversation elsewhere.

The one thing he clearly understood was the bond, perhaps more than simple lineage, that Duncan shared with his great-grandfather. Their bond transcended time. Both enjoyed cigars and vast wealth, but their traits and appearance seemed remarkably similar to the casual observer lucky enough to know both of them in a limited way.

Andrew rode horses, while his grandson preferred the newer, steel version of riding adventure.

"You going to shave that rug of yours anytime soon?" Duncan inquired momentarily, making conversation since they both skirted the real issue between them.

McCully rubbed his new beard almost absently. He had grown it during the holidays, since his father's band didn't have another gig until February. George McCully believed in family time around the holidays, and despite pleas from his fans, took nearly a month off from touring every year around the holiday season.

"I kind of like it, but my father will say it's not very traditional bluegrass."

"You're lucky. I can't even grow a good one."

"It'll be gone by the time we hit the road again," McCully stated, always the dutiful son. "West Coast in February, the central states in March, and back home for spring. Not much ever changes with our schedule."

"Weekends only," Duncan commented thoughtfully. "Must be a bummer sometimes."

"It's not so bad. We practice during the week, but I have a lot of time to write songs and get things done."

"I don't see a wedding band on that strumming hand of yours."

McCully realized this was probably the deepest conversation he and Duncan had ever engaged in. Still, it seemed to be leading back to the topic he wanted to avoid.

"Seems to me you don't have one, either, Dan. Or was that a common-law marriage you ended last year?"

Duncan cleared his throat, indicating McCully had gone a bit far with his retaliation.

"I'd really appreciate it if you came clean with me about my grandfather," Duncan finally said after a few puffs on the cigar.

"I really don't know much," McCully replied. "You're not going to believe me, but I saw your great-grandfather in a dream of sorts. Except it was real."

Standing with his hands placed carefully atop the railing, Duncan stared at the nearby barren trees. His eyes wandered to the ground, evidently noticing the footprints in the snow by the way his eyes widened momentarily. Even so, he said nothing for a moment.

"Andrew died under strange circumstances," he finally said. "I thought maybe you knew something about his death that you weren't telling me."

"I only know what I've seen," McCully said. "Did he have a friend named Ben Williams?"

Duncan shrugged.

"I heard a lot of the stories about him when I was a kid. I've slept since then."

"I'll take that as a 'no'?"

It took a moment for Duncan to answer. He appeared discontent with their direction of their conversation.

"I'm not sure where you're going with this dream thing, but I wish you'd be straight with me about what you know."

"I don't know the whole story, and you're not telling me how your grandfather died."

McCully hesitated before making his next statement.

"I understand you're very much for buying the hotel, but something isn't right about those grounds. How much do you know about what happened there a few years ago?"

Duncan stood a moment, fingering his cigar before taking a thoughtful drag.

"Enough to know it's over and Mr. Clouse is moving on. You've got to understand this is my one shot to live out my life's dream. There are people in the valley counting on me to pull this off."

"I'm not against you. In fact, I might be the only one guaranteed to vote your way when the time comes. That's assuming nothing comes up that changes my mind."

"Such as?"

"Like finding out what happened here a few years ago isn't going to happen all over again. You live around here half the year. What happened?"

Duncan grunted to himself.

"I was in Tennessee when most of it unfolded. The locals say there was a coverup of sorts, but they aren't sure what happened."

"What kind of coverup?"

"They think Clouse paid off police, and possibly the newspaper, to keep things under wraps, because the cops were very tight-lipped about the findings on the hotel grounds."

"What do *you* think?"

"I'm a businessman. What I think is irrelevant to what the future holds. What *our* future holds if we buy the place."

McCully preferred Oswalt's cold shoulder to his present company. The idea of Duncan neglecting the hotel's sordid past worried him.

"It's getting cold out here," he said, trying to brush past Duncan to the warm interior inviting him back.

"Wait," Duncan said, clasping his hand.

McCully felt as though static electricity passed through his body, but in reality his mind traveled to a different time and place once again.

*   *   *

"You can't possibly pass up an opportunity like this," the man McCully now knew as Ben Williams told Andrew Duncan.

McCully recognized the area as the rear of the hotel, probably in the early 1920s, picking up where his first hotel vision left off. Apparently several years later than the vision where Williams and Duncan planned to ride horseback, things seemed more tense between them.

The third man appeared stoic, almost unmoving and uncaring. Oswalt was the most driven man McCully knew personally, but this man seemed set on one goal, his green eyes burning into Andrew Duncan.

"What you're proposing isn't right," Duncan argued. "On so many levels it's just not right."

"There's going to come a day when you and the millions you've amassed are going to retire and live it up," Williams stated. "But one day you're going to grow old and all the money in the world isn't going to change the fact that you're a mortal man. What I'm proposing isn't something we don't do anyway, in some shape or form."

"What you're proposing is *murder*, plain and simple," Duncan virtually spat back.

He nervously puffed on his cigar a moment more, refusing to look the third man in the eye. He barely glanced at the man, and never more than a split-second at a time. It appeared Williams was the one vote he needed to swing his way, because he wanted no part of whatever conspiracy had been forged without his full consent.

Though he respected Duncan's moral stand, McCully felt appalled such a conversation ever took place on the hotel grounds. He might have expected mob hits ordered by Al Capone or other notorious gangsters who stayed in the valley, but this was something completely out of the blue.

What on earth did these two men want done?

"Think of it as an insurance policy," Williams said, unwavering against his friend's argument.

"I can't believe we're even having this conversation, Ben. First of all, we're talking a lot of money, second of all, you don't know if these cubes do anything or not, and thirdly, you're talking about taking human lives to find out if they work."

"They work. I've seen it."

Drawing on his cigar, Duncan appeared unconvinced, and as visibly hostile to the idea as ever.

"Seen it, huh?"

Williams nodded, not revealing any details. The look on his friend's face soured completely, knowing Williams had crossed the line of no return in both their friendship and moral corruption.

"If they work, who would be willing to sell off such a device?"

Duncan was obviously covering every angle to distance himself from whatever proposition Williams and the mystery man brought to him.

"We've found a man whose father used the cubes before his murder. I told him we'd bury the things where no one would ever find them and he believed me. The fool doesn't see what a complete waste that would be."

"I think the man knows what happened to his father was a result of using those cubes. Whether they work or not, they have a power over people, Ben. Now you're falling prey to it."

"You're not looking at this the right way, Andy. This is an opportunity. A dream come true."

The look on Duncan's face indicated he had heard enough, and there was no changing his mind. He gave an unsettled look to his friend, then a downright hateful stare toward the other man.

"You can both go to hell," he said before storming off toward the main entrance. "And you probably will."

Both men looked after him a moment, then turned grim as they continued their conversation.

"I thought you said he'd back us on this," the mysterious man said.

"Give me another day or two. I can bring Andy around to our way of thinking."

"No," the other said sternly. "He's a liability. We can't afford the risk of him telling anyone else our plans."

Williams apparently understood exactly what the man meant. He appeared unhappy about the idea of killing his friend, but a realization crossed his face that indicated the plan came before all else.

"What do you have in mind?" he asked.

Another jolt took hold of McCully's body and mind, returning him to the present.

He felt unnerved a moment, looking at Duncan, but he reassured himself it was the great-grandson standing before him, and not the man who refused unethical advances.

"What the hell was that?" Duncan asked, a perplexed, worrisome look scrawled across his face.

"Your grandfather was murdered," McCully stated as no other words came to mind.

Taking a step back, Duncan dropped his cigar, which the snowy balcony instantly swallowed whole. He didn't bother to pick it up because his eyes locked on McCully without blinking.

"Murdered how?"

"I'm not sure the 'how' is as important as the 'why' in this case."

Duncan shook his head in disbelief.

"You're telling me you just saw in a split-second's time why my great-grandfather died?"

"It was only a second?" McCully questioned, wondering how his mind processed the visions so quickly.

"You jumped like your ass had just been bit, kid."

McCully decided not to pursue any more answers because he felt it was more important to focus on solving the mystery that revealed itself in pieces.

"Your grandfather was involved with some shady individuals," he stated. "They wanted his money to fund some kind of buy, but he refused to give his support. He knew they were going to murder someone, so he refused to help. After he left, they decided to kill him so he wouldn't foil their plans."

Duncan appeared skeptical, but in some small way, accepting. He walked around a moment, occasionally scratching his head. McCully knew people liked to test psychic powers, to see if the bearers were legitimate, and he sensed Duncan wanted proof of his abilities. The great-grandson seemed to sense McCully's ability, though unable to verbalize his accusation.

Unlike regular psychic powers, visions chose to appear when they wanted to. McCully couldn't simply touch objects and pick up mental images of the owner's life. He could only report the facts.

"It's been said Andrew's son thought he was killed to cover something up," Duncan finally revealed. "My family thought it was something more than an accident, but they could never prove anything."

"How did he die?"

"That's what seemed really odd, almost symbolic if you think about it. He was found with severe head injuries beside the Monon Route railroad tracks. The authorities said they thought he got drunk and walked into a moving locomotive. There were two problems with that. One, he seldom drank heavily, and two, he knew the railroad exceptionally well after helping bring it to the valley."

"Whatever he got involved in is still a danger today, or I wouldn't have seen it."

Duncan's face corkscrewed.

"Are you a psychic or something?"

"I have … abilities. And until now, I've been able to suppress them. Something about this place is bringing them back with a vengeance."

Duncan appeared openly perplexed. Not only was he digesting information from the vision, but his dreams of owning the hotel were teetering atop a dangerous slope.

"Unless you come up with some proof that we're in danger, I don't want to tell the others anything about this."

"Me neither. I'm not going to endanger your pet project unless I know what's wrong around here."

"How can you be sure something *is* wrong?"

"These visions don't come to me unless something bad is coming. I've never had a vision go back in time before, so there must be something important I need to know."

Duncan turned, opening the door with a purpose to return inside. He stopped in the threshold, facing McCully once again.

"If you find anything else out, I'd like a heads up."

"So you believe me?"

"I don't think you're completely crazy. Right now, that's the best I can give you."

He stepped inside, shutting the door behind him.

"I guess that'll have to do," McCully muttered to himself.

13

Jana watched as the caterer pulled out of the driveway, chancing the trip home through the snowstorm.

She felt somewhat depressed because she hadn't planned on staying overnight at the mansion. With no change of clothes, and no room to speak of, she would stay in the servants' quarters, or one of the empty rooms upstairs.

When she last listened to the radio, the news sounded bleak. Traffic jams lined the roads between West Baden and Bloomington because over a foot of snow had already fallen. Southern Indiana townships typically remain unprepared for anything more than a dusting of snow. Most small towns purchase only one snowplow, putting tax dollars toward more practical equipment.

Most everything else had gone according to plan. The tour went well, the dinner was excellent, and plenty of snacks and leftovers remained. One thing the guests didn't have to fear was starvation.

"You look bummed," Keith Sanders said as he approached her, putting forth an understanding grin.

"It could be worse," Jana thought aloud. "Better to stay here than ruin tomorrow for all of you."

Keith stared outside a moment, seeming to admire the white flakes drifting toward the ground.

"We don't see that down in Texas."

"I suspect you don't," Jana said, giggling conservatively.

She hated appearing the least bit unprofessional around the group. Judith Parks in particular seemed to eye her every move like a madam grooming a pageant candidate.

Accustomed to the pressure of being perfect around investment groups, Jana presented the hotel tour equally well to all three groups. Being around this set of investors felt good, especially because Keith and Red were such characters.

Every so often during the tour they made quirky remarks or played tricks on one another. Their brotherhood was evident, despite the fact they lived hundreds of miles apart.

"Can I ask you something?" Jana asked, noticing Keith hadn't once removed his hat all day long.

Even at dinner he kept it on after Red removed his.

"You've had that on all day," she said, nodding toward his Stetson. "Is that customary for ranchers?"

"Ah," Keith said thoughtfully. "A true cowboy doesn't take off his hat," he admitted, "but *my* reason for leaving it on is the diminishing hairline underneath it."

"Someone in your position shouldn't have to worry about his image," Jana said, trying to avoid saying something inappropriate.

"Maybe I just don't have enough other things to worry about."

Jana looked out the window, wondering how any of them would escape the confines of the mansion grounds if no one plowed or shoveled the driveway. She doubted the small county road beside the West Baden Springs Hotel would receive professional plowing anytime soon.

Keith spoke a moment later, breaking her concentration.

"You mentioned during dinner there was a DVD presentation about the hotel we could watch if we wanted to. Duncan's been pestering us to watch the dang thing, so I thought we could gather the troops and get it over with."

Jana glanced into the living room space, seeing several of the Star Investments members killing time.

"We'll have to get everyone into the entertainment room," Jana informed him. "I'll look upstairs if you want to rally everyone down here."

Most everyone had to be in one of two rooms downstairs, if they hadn't retreated to private quarters on the second floor.

"Sure," Keith said before walking into the mammoth living room.

Jana heard him yell something playfully at his brother while she ascended the stairs.

Within a few minutes she found McCully returning from the outside balcony, Duncan unpacking a few things, and Judith exiting her room after a change of clothes. Even in casual dress she appeared somewhat regal. Jana thought she conducted herself very well now that she had met the woman. Everything she had heard suggested Judith Parks was a battleaxe in the business world, but she said nothing unkind about the hotel or anyone around her.

Skipping Laura Compton's room because of her early departure from dinner, Jana walked downstairs. When she entered the entertainment room Jana did a quick headcount, finding everyone present except Laura.

"I decided not to knock on her door," Jana said.

Red looked to Keith, who returned a sour stare, as though they were airing dirty laundry.

"I'll go check on her and see if she's feeling better," Keith finally said, heading out of the room.

Oswalt leaned in toward Jana.

"Keith and Laura had something going a couple years back," he said just above a whisper.

Jana realized the rancher certainly did have a thing for younger women, wondering how innocent their first encounter had really been.

A few minutes later, Keith returned to the room, calling for Red to join him. Everyone sensed something odd had Keith worried.

The brothers walked upstairs together, then returned a few minutes later with worried expressions.

"She wasn't up there," Keith finally announced. "We gave every room a quick search and didn't find her."

Everyone suddenly appeared a bit more concerned.

Jana suspected Laura wasn't one to go exploring the mansion alone, probably having little need to see either kitchen area, or the dining room they used just over an hour ago.

Going outside seemed completely insane, while the idea of her exploring other guest rooms upstairs was unlikely. Somehow, without explanation, Laura had vanished from the mansion. Jana wondered if her early departure from dinner might have been an excuse for something else altogether.

"We saw footsteps out back," McCully said, thumbing toward Oswalt.

Everyone looked their way with mixed reactions.

"We didn't think anything of it," Oswalt spoke up. "There was one set of tracks that looked like they came from the woods toward the hotel."

"Let's take a look then," Keith ordered more than suggested.

Jana had an idea he was the group leader in more than one capacity.

Everyone moved toward the double French doors beside the entertainment room. Jana followed Keith outside, noticing the footsteps indeed pointed toward the hotel, namely a steel door with a pushbutton code box above the handle.

"What's the combination?" Keith asked her.

"I don't know."

"Where does it lead?"

"I'm not sure. Probably the basement, because there's no door in the upper kitchen area."

Keith's expression crossed between exasperation and dread as Jana suspected he somehow blamed her for Laura's disappearance.

While the group stood awkwardly at the doorway, Jana stole a glance their way, noticing more carvings along the mansion's foundation. Subconsciously she wondered if the six out front were equaled by six more along the back.

Everyone made room for Keith as he returned inside, his cowboy boots covered with snow. He quickly stomped the white powder off, then looked to Jana.

"Let's have a look downstairs," he stated. "I'll let you lead the way."

No one else moved from the lobby area, worrying Jana because Keith was acting erratically compared to his normal composure.

Jana led him through the kitchen, then into the cooking and storage area downstairs. They reached the bottom step rather quickly, allowing Keith to search around the walls for a doorway.

She hesitantly followed his lead, wondering where the steel door went, if not the basement. Agreeing with Oswalt's assessment that the footsteps aimed toward the building instead of the woods, she wondered if the group had two mysteries to solve.

"This is all concrete down here," Keith noted, staring at the walls.

A large storage shelf covered the back wall of a portion that jutted back from the main wall. Keith walked up to the shelf, examining it carefully. From what Jana could see behind the shelving unit, everything appeared concrete.

Just like every other inch of the walls.

"Damn it," he said through clenched teeth.

"We still haven't checked the rest of the mansion," Jana said calmly. "There are a lot of rooms, including closets, pantries, and bathrooms we can check."

"She's not a kid," Keith said a bit more harshly than he likely planned to. "She's not going to hide somewhere."

Unsure of what else to say, Jana turned to head upstairs. Keith lingered a moment, looking around to ensure he didn't miss any possible clue, then followed Jana.

When they reached the main floor, half the group was missing. Jana felt as though she was losing control of the situation, but after dinner the guests were on their own whether she stayed overnight or not.

Regardless of her liability, Jana wanted the guests to remain comfortable. What seemed like a flawless tour and layover, except for the snowstorm, seemed to be spiraling out of control.

"They went looking upstairs for Laura," Judith announced, calming Keith somewhat.

"We haven't checked out front," Jana suggested, never once imagining Laura had any reason to walk around outside.

Deciding to take initiative, mostly to keep Keith from suspecting her of wrongdoing, Jana took long strides toward the front door, unlocking three locks before pulling it open.

She gasped at the sight of a bearded man in camouflage, holding a hunting rifle, looking equally wide-eyed as though he were caught breaking the law.

14

Jana thought momentarily about slamming the door and locking it, but the man pulled his free arm back from where the doorbell was located. His look went from surprised to somewhat needful. Reading his chocolate-colored eyes, Jana sensed he was no threat, but rather in danger of succumbing to the elements if he remained outside.

"Are you okay?" she asked, noticing he was shaking visibly, barely able to keep hold of the rifle through his gloves.

He stammered as he spoke.

"I can't find my dog," he stated as his teeth chattered.

Jana knew it wasn't extremely cold outside, but he wasn't dressed for a prolonged stay outside, wearing only one layer of clothing beneath his camouflage bib overalls. Much of his clothing appeared soaked, as though he had taken several tumbles in the snow, perhaps into some puddles.

"Who's this?" Keith questioned, approaching her from behind.

"I'm not sure. I think he's lost."

Giving what Jana termed a low growl, Keith stood there momentarily as though debating whether to continue searching for Laura or interrogate the lost hunter standing on their doorstep.

"Come in," Jana said, taking the man's hand to lead him inside.

Keith snatched the rifle away from the hunter as though he might be a terrorist luring everyone into a false sense of security before striking.

A fleeting glance was all the hunter gave his rifle, apparently thrilled to be indoors. He didn't show much emotion because he appeared to be in some form of mild shock.

Leading him toward a chair in the living room area, Jana helped him remove his jacket before sitting him down. His teeth continued to chatter, despite being in warmer quarters.

Duncan and Red entered the room, standing behind Jana like watchdogs.

"He's completely drenched," Jana said as she began removing his overalls. "We need to get him a change of clothes."

"I think the bedrooms have spare clothes in the closets," Red stated. "I'll see what I can find."

He looked to Duncan before walking away, indicating he shouldn't leave Jana alone with the stranger.

"What's your name, buddy?" Duncan asked, kneeling beside the stranger.

"Craig," the hunter answered with slow deliberation, as though he needed a moment to think about it. "Craig Jennings."

Duncan helped Jana pull down the overalls, revealing soaked blue jeans and a tattered flannel shirt. They were cold to the touch.

"Craig, I'm suspecting you weren't making snow angels out there, so how about you tell us what happened?"

"I decided I wanted to go rabbit hunting in the snow," he said slowly, though a bit more evenly with his drenched clothes being removed. "We just don't get snow down here very often, and they *are* in season."

He made the last statement defensively, as though someone might question his legal right to hunt.

"My dog went running into the woods and I couldn't find him. Before I knew it, I got lost because my tracks kept disappearing. Then I came across this place."

"Do you know where you are?" Jana asked.

"The mansion. No one's ever here, but I saw the cars outside, so I thought I'd try the buzzer."

Without Jennings noticing, Duncan made a strange face at Jana, as though he didn't believe the story, or thought it seemed suspicious.

"Do you work around here?" Jana asked him, deciding she wanted more information.

"I'm a shop teacher at the high school," he readily answered.

She didn't notice a wedding band on his left hand, so she decided to probe a bit further.

"Married?"

"Yeah," he answered, his head drooping a bit from embarrassment. "The whole reason I left the house was because me and the wife had a fight. I took the dog and went out to cool off."

He chuckled only a second or two.

"No pun intended."

Jana felt reasonably convinced the man spoke the truth, but Duncan proved to be a harder sell.

"We'll be right back, buddy," he said to Jennings before subtly leading Jana out of the room.

"What's the matter?" she asked once they were a distance away.

"Laura comes up missing and this guy shows up? It's gotta be more than coincidence."

"Have you seen what it's like out there?" she countered. "I'm surprised we haven't had stranded motorists asking for our help."

Duncan remained unwavering.

"It might be about time we call the police," he said.

"You're jumping to conclusions. Laura might still turn up, and this poor guy may simply be lost in the woods like he says."

"It's not likely she's going to turn up," McCully said as he approached them. "We've been everywhere in this place and there's no sign of her."

"What about outside?" Duncan asked, glancing toward Jennings, who shivered slightly as he sat in the cozy chair a room away.

McCully looked skeptical.

"Why the hell would she go outside?"

"I don't know," Duncan said, "but Keith is going to fly off the handle if we don't find her soon."

"Guilty conscience?" McCully asked with a sharp tone.

The exact meaning of the words eluded Jana, but she deeply suspected Laura and Keith had a relationship that somehow ended badly.

"Just get someone to go with you and check outside so he doesn't freak out," Duncan insisted.

McCully nodded before leaving to continue the search.

"We're treating this as though Laura was a defenseless creature left in the woods," Jana told Duncan. "You're all very quick to assume she hasn't wandered off somewhere on her own."

"Call me paranoid, but I'm beginning to wonder why Glenn Turner never showed up. All day we haven't been able to reach him, and now Laura disappears. I know there's a blizzard outside, but I'm starting to think Dave was right. Whatever bad karma the hotel has might be rubbing off on this place."

"We don't know that for certain, Mr. Duncan."

He shook his head negatively. Secretly, Jana couldn't help but share his concerns. Absolutely nothing had gone wrong with the first two visiting groups, but it seemed like nothing could go right for these people.

"Someone doesn't want this place to be bought," Duncan said. "It's just like before. Someone is going to do whatever it takes to scare people away from the hotel, even if it means taking innocent lives."

Jana felt as though her whole world was collapsing around her. Within ten minutes the investment group's male members were reverting back to some primitive state of mind, prepared to suspect everyone around them with little or no proof of wrongdoing.

Even Duncan, whose dream since childhood was to own the hotel, seemed susceptible to the curse.

The lights flickered twice within an instant, bringing them back to the reality that there was indeed a snowstorm outside, and one of their companions was missing. Jana began to realize a walk outside was pure madness, drawing near the closest window to see the flakes falling faster, and more abundantly, than before.

"Does this place have a generator?" Keith asked, returning to her side.

"Yes," Jana answered from memory alone. "I believe it's outside."

A thought suddenly came to her.

"I think there are some cottages out back as well."

"Why didn't you mention that sooner?"

"My boss mentioned it in passing one time. They're down near the tree line, so you wouldn't see them unless you went looking for them."

Now dressed for the outdoors, as much as one could expect, Keith stood beside McCully, who had donned a coat to brave the cold weather. The pair reminded Jana of witch hunters, ready to go outside and cleanse the mansion of whatever evil was abducting its membership.

McCully looked less than thrilled about venturing outside, but the way his eyes kept shifting toward Keith indicated his faith in the man's leadership might be faltering.

Jana doubted some homicidal maniac was waiting to pick them off one by one, but she shared some of their concern over Laura's disappearance. All of the trouble at the hotel during Clouse's employment there, and his ownership later, supposedly concluded two years prior.

"Let's go," Keith told McCully, who followed him outside to brave the elements.

A moment later, Red returned from his upstairs search, carrying a small pile of clothes with him.

"I found some shirts and pants that look to be in his size," he said. "And a blanket to help warm him up."

Jana followed him into the room where Jennings warmed his bones, beginning to remove more of his wet clothing by himself. Duncan tagged along because there was nothing else for him to do. Since their new guest had started to move, perhaps he could talk and reveal more of his story to them.

If he didn't, she feared the group might torture him until they heard something they wanted to hear, even if it wasn't true.

*   *   *

"It's freezing out here," McCully commented as he followed Keith down the length of the mansion's facade.

The reply came in the form of another grunt from Keith, likely suggesting he thought his colleague was spoiled. He often talked about the tough times in his life, and how he'd worked since his teenage years, breaking horses and mending fences to make ends meet.

To him, everyone else had life so much easier because they never worked nearly as hard for anything.

Every several yards McCully noticed a stone carving along the wall. They looked impressive, but he had little time to study them because keeping up with Keith's brisk pace required his full attention.

Snow came up to his knees, letting him know how Jennings got so wet during his trek. If not for the good lighting inside the mansion gleaming through the windows, their journey would be pitch black. The pair quickly made it to the far corner, peeking around to discover the cottages were little more than silhouettes half a football field's length away from them.

McCully wished he had found a flashlight somewhere within the mansion before stepping outside, but his day was comprised of one misfortune after another.

By no means a tracker or even a weekend camper, McCully had enough sense to realize there was no evidence of footprints outside the mansion's front door, except for the hunter's.

Jennings' footprints came directly from the road, without any sign of outgoing tracks.

When they reached the back corner of the grand building, he saw no tracks leading toward the cottages. Despite the snowfall, some evidence of tracks would have survived during the short time between Laura's disappearance and the present.

"No one's been there," he told Keith, who simply looked back at him with a look of disdain.

What's his problem? McCully wondered to himself. It seemed as though he had some duty to find Laura at any cost.

Perhaps Keith figured the others would hold him responsible, or think *he* personally had something to do with her disappearance. McCully recalled him being around his brother most of the time, and close to several others, so Keith was undoubtedly innocent of any wrongdoing.

"Stay there in case anything happens," Keith ordered.

McCully sighed audibly, but Keith never heard him because he was already halfway across the lawn toward the cottages. Staying at the corner, McCully split his attention between Keith and the engraving near the end of the mansion.

He hadn't really seen any of the carved messages along the back wall yet, but this one appeared far different than any of the six along the front. An unusual piece of artwork, the carving displayed a man smearing the blood of a human and a sacrificial lamb, both of which lay to either side of him. A pool of blood drained from each corpse as the man swiped them both with his hands, creating a mixture.

"Weird," McCully commented, seeing a number below the sculpted piece.

9:7.

He looked up again, finding Keith peering through the cottage windows like a child at a candy store, with both hands against the glass.

"Find anything?" he called.

Keith shook his head negatively.

"The rooms look empty. I need a flashlight."

"Good luck with that," McCully muttered to himself.

As though Keith understood what he said, McCully received a long, hard stare. It took a moment, but he then realized his colleague wanted him to find a flashlight inside the mansion. So far he hadn't seen any, but Jana probably knew where most things were located.

"I'll see what I can find," he said before turning toward the front.

Somewhat thankful to see the warm indoors, if only for a moment, he trudged through the snow until he reached the front door. As he turned the doorknob he realized how cold his feet were from standing in snow for several minutes.

Jana stood outside the living room area as Red and Duncan helped Jennings change clothes, as though making certain they didn't mishandle him.

"Are there any flashlights around here?" he asked without hesitation.

"The kitchen," she answered, leading him that way.

"Is the hunter talking?" McCully asked as they crossed the foyer.

"He says he was hunting rabbits with his dog and got lost in the snow. He lives a few miles away, outside of town."

McCully realized little else aside from fields and a few swampy areas surrounded the mansion as far as the eye could see, which made the story plausible. The man's timing, however, seemed absolutely terrible considering the events after dinner.

"Have we called the police, or let him phone his relatives?"

"We called 911, but they told us it might be hours before they can send someone out. Their cars can barely get through the snow, and they've been swamped with wrecks and people stuck in snowdrifts."

"So we're on our own," McCully muttered, beginning to believe Laura's only hope of being found was a larger search party.

Jana led him into the kitchen, finding several rechargeable flashlights alongside cupboards. She opened a few of the cupboard doors, showing him they had candles in case the power failed completely.

He picked out one of the flashlights with an orange exterior and large square ends like fire departments often use. He suspected it put out sufficient light for any situation, deciding to wait until he stepped outside before he tried it out.

"I'd better go check on his highness before he comes looking for me."

Jana's expression showed she agreed, but a guilty wave came over her, wiping it from her face immediately.

As McCully turned to leave, Jana called after him.

"Good luck."

He turned just long enough to give a reassuring grin, then opened the front door to find Keith before the older man did something to get himself into trouble.

When he returned to the rear corner, McCully switched on the light, seeing no one in sight. Two trails of tracks seemed to lead everywhere around the cottages, then along the back of the mansion. His heart skipped a beat, immediately fearing the worst, but McCully calmed himself enough to begin looking.

For some reason the present situation reminded him a little bit of playing hide and seek with his cousins during childhood. He always remembered following their tracks through mud or snow, finding them quicker than they ever found him.

"Keith?" he called out.

No answer returned.

He yelled a bit louder several times over, receiving no reply.

Taking a quick look around the cottages and the nearby generator, McCully found no sign of Keith. He then followed the tracks behind the mansion, realizing halfway along the building's rear side they veered into the woods.

"Damn it," he said under his breath, quickly following them.

The tracks appeared to be made by one person, so if Keith was in any way abducted, he was slung over someone's shoulder. Since there was no sign of his Stetson anywhere, McCully felt somewhat relieved, knowing it would have toppled to the ground during a struggle.

"Keith?" he called out once more, praying for some kind of response.

A few seconds later, it came.

"Get over here, kid," he heard the man's soft drawl call through the woods.

Glancing to his left, he found the cattle rancher centered in a small clearing, staring at the mansion from a distance.

"What the hell are you doing?" McCully asked pointedly, since he feared the worst when he couldn't find the man.

"Look how tall that place is," Keith noted. "We only get to go up two floors."

"So?"

"So there's at least one more floor up there."

"You trying to say this place has secret passageways and tunnels?"

"It has *something*. It's just stone and plasterboard, kid. We can bust through it if we have to."

McCully felt his feet begin to tingle again from the cold.

"Let's make our way inside, unless you've got something else you want to search for out here."

Keith's head dejectedly bowed toward the ground, his thoughts likely consumed with finding Laura and shame for not having done so yet.

"Let's check these cabins real quick, then we can get warm."

15

"Can I call my wife?" Jennings asked Red once he was changed into warmer clothing.

"Sure," Red answered, trying to think of where the closest phone might be.

For some reason the living room and entertainment room didn't have phones, but the dining area and kitchen both did.

Thankfully the hunter had recovered enough to undress himself and put new clothes on without assistance. Red and Duncan simply watched over him to make sure he remained in good health, and didn't mean harm to the guests.

When they removed his camouflage cap, they realized why Jennings needed headgear in the cold climate. His dark brown hair had receded to little more than a fringe, despite his relatively young age. Red guessed the man to be close to ten years younger than himself.

Once he warmed up, the hunter spoke a little more often, giving Red hope that he was exactly who he said he was. Jennings appeared thankful for the hospitality, cautiously flashing a smile every so often.

"Come with me," Red instructed Jennings, who seemed somewhat stiff as he rose from the chair.

His new clothes weren't a perfect fit, but he seemed much more comfortable, and warm, inside them.

Duncan and Jana remained behind as Red took Jennings to the phone inside the dining room. They observed the new guest carefully, but remained in the foyer.

"Everyone's acting a little tense around here," Jennings noted. "Any particular reason why?"

"Let's just say you picked a bad time to arrive. Things have kind of fallen apart around here in the last hour."

Jennings gave him a quizzical look, but didn't press the issue.

Red handed him the receiver, watching as the hunter dialed a number, hating to deny the man privacy, but feeling little other choice.

Jennings seemed to sense mild trepidation, even hostility toward his arrival, but said very little about the subject. No one had taken the time to thoroughly explain Laura's disappearance to him, hoping perhaps he might say something out of place to reveal his true nature.

If he was hiding something.

"The line's dead," the hunter announced after a few seconds, when he finally placed the receiver to his ear.

Red hung up the phone, picked it up, then placed it to his own ear.

Dead silence.

"Shit," he grumbled.

Plucking the cellular phone from his side, he saw absolutely no signal bars visible, indicating the precipitation, and the clouds that brought it, blocked his phone's signal.

Inhaling deeply through his nose, Red tried to think of any reasonable means of communication, but none came to mind. Either local phone lines were down, or someone had cut the line leading into the mansion.

Neither prospect sounded good, but he dreaded the latter, wondering if someone had diabolical plans for the groups.

His mind wandered further, wondering if that particular someone might be part of his group.

"What's the matter?" Jennings asked while Red continued to stare at his cell phone.

"I guess we're cut off from the real world, my friend."

Red realized if someone had intentionally cut the phone line, which was still only a possibility, the hunter had to be innocent.

Unless he had a partner.

After all, he was already inside when the group dialed 911 for help.

Driving himself crazy over conspiracy theories wasn't productive, so Red shook his head, trying to free his mind of all negative thoughts. The possibility remained that a series of strange coincidences, beginning with Laura's disappearance, put the group on edge.

Red debated his next move when his brother walked through the door with McCully.

"Find anything?" he asked Keith.

"Not yet. The cottages were empty, but the generator looks good if we have any power problems."

Though not fantastic news, Red felt comforted that his brother returned so quickly with assurances that not every comfort inside the mansion was jeopardized. Without power, the group would be hard-pressed to stay warm, particularly over a two or three day span.

Keith shot Jennings a hard stare without provocation, so Red drew close to his brother.

"Take it easy," he said in a hushed voice. "I don't think he had anything to do with Laura disappearing."

"He better not have," Keith growled, "or he'll be getting the pointy end of my boot up his ass."

Red patted his brother on the shoulder gently.

"Take it easy, big brother. We'll find her."

"But in what condition?" Keith questioned, his blue eyes a bit misty from either concern over his former girlfriend, or the harsh weather.

Red knew better than anyone else in the group what Keith and Laura shared. His older brother had a reputation for dating younger women after his divorce almost ten years prior. The divorce stemmed from his wife wanting half of his money and a new life, but she made the mistake of waiting until their three children were legally adults, receiving far less in the settlement than she wanted.

Not until the divorce was final did Keith officially lay the groundwork for Lone Star Investments. He met Laura several years later, dating her a few years after that. Their relationship lasted just over a year, but it ended well, leaving their friendship and partnership through the firm intact.

So far as Red knew, the two never took their relationship to a sexual level again, though they remained close.

Now engaged to be married, Keith had dated the young lady for nearly two years, earning him a reputation as sugar daddy among some of his peers. Red knew they shared the same interests, originally set up on a blind date by a common friend. Keith didn't worry much about what other people thought, so Red turned the other cheek when he heard derogatory remarks about his brother's social life.

"What do we do now?" he asked of Keith.

"We search this place from head to tail until we figure out how to get to the third floor."

"Third floor?"

"You didn't notice how tall this place is?" Keith questioned.

"I guess I didn't think much about it."

Keith stood a moment, stealing a glance at Jennings, who had engaged McCully in conversation. Just when Red figured he was lost in thought, he spoke again.

"There aren't any doors or stairways leading up there, so I'm wondering if we can find an access hatchway to the attic, or whatever's up there."

"Shouldn't be hard to find."

"If we don't find anything, I want to tear through the ceiling until we find our way up there."

Red couldn't help chuckling, despite the irritated expression his brother gave him.

"In case you didn't notice, we don't exactly have heavy tools around here."

"I'll use a screwdriver and pry away the ceiling tile if I have to."

Realizing his brother was serious, Red decided to suggest more logical alternatives.

"We'll help you look for a way up there. Maybe there's some tools and ladders in the garage."

Located on the other side of the mansion from the cottages and generator, the spacious garage had yet to be accessed by anyone from the group. Red had just remembered its existence himself.

"I can't believe I forgot all about checking back there," Keith said, ready to begin his search anew.

He started toward the door until Red caught him by the shoulder, lightly pulling him back.

"You're not going out there alone."

Keith's eyes immediately went toward McCully, but Red intervened, knowing the songwriter wasn't anxious to step outside again.

"I'll go with you."

Red thought a fresh pair of eyes might be useful if anyone was going outside again.

"Why don't you let me take someone else with me? You can start your search in here and save some time."

Keith looked hesitant about turning over control of the exterior search.

"You trust me, don't you?" Red prodded.

Continuing to balk, Keith's chest rose and fell as he took several deep, thoughtful breaths.

"Okay. But don't leave one stone unturned, little brother."

"I promise."

*   *   *

When searching for a companion to search the garage with, Red found himself limited on choices.

Oswalt was grumpy, not wishing to venture outside, Jennings was out of the question, McCully had just returned from the chilly weather, Jana and Judith couldn't help very well with moving heavy objects, and Duncan seemed preoccupied with his thoughts.

Red couldn't imagine Judith doing any kind of intensive labor to help him. By no means a lifetime prima donna, she had stated on more than one occasion her working days were well behind her because her money afforded her workers for her every need. He had little to say to her after their brief relationship, and faking any sort of friendship made it worse. What drew them together was their opposite nature.

Later, it served to drive them apart.

After weighing his options, he selected Duncan by default.

"You want me to go out to the garage with you?" were the first words Duncan uttered after Red explained the situation to him.

"It'll just take a minute," Red replied without trying to sound desperate. "We go out there, check for Laura, and come right back in. Keith is happy, every square inch of the grounds is checked, and we can sit back and wait for the police."

Duncan didn't appear impressed by the plan, but quickly resolved to get their task out of the way.

"I have to get my jacket and gloves," he said. "I'll be right back."

Red watched Duncan trudge upstairs to fetch his gear from his quarters. He couldn't understand how a simple overnight stay now bordered on complete disaster.

A few minutes later, Duncan returned with his motorcycle jacket and thick gloves. He even put on a cloth skullcap to keep his head warm. Anxious to get the task over with, he opened the front door for Red, who gladly led the way toward the garage.

With the snow falling indiscriminately, the driveway and yard appeared the same. Both had over a foot of white precipitation covering them, so Red simply walked behind the main building, looking for the garage near the woods.

Luckily he had snagged the flashlight from McCully before venturing outside, but it did little to penetrate the swirling mist of snow still coming down.

"Is that it?" Duncan asked, squinting to see through the white flakes.

"I think so," Red answered, discovering the outline of what appeared to be a large building a short distance from the mansion.

Set back from the main building, the garage was found down a small hill, which obscured it from view unless someone walked toward it.

"You can keep your shitty weather," Red commented as they drew near the building.

"This is new to me," Duncan replied. "It takes us years to accumulate this many inches of snow."

When the two finally reached the side door that accessed the garage, they looked to the door with a padlock in addition to a deadbolt and conventional lock, then exchanged weary glances.

"Figures," Red stated sourly. "I don't suppose you saw any remotes for the overhead doors around?"

"Can't say I did."

Red looked around for any other way into the garage, finding several windows too far off the ground, the sealed overhead doors, and nothing else.

Since Duncan was wearing his heavy biker boots, Red decided to ask him the obvious question.

"Can you kick that door in?"

The reply came in the form of a strange expression and raised eyebrows.

"Please tell me you're kidding."

"I wish I were. If you can't, we're going to have to find some kind of battering ram."

Quickly sighing, Duncan turned his back to the door, kicking forcefully backward like a mule three times before the door began awkwardly falling inward along the hinged side. Strangely, the three locks continued to hold the secured side until Duncan gave the door one more swift kick, groaning painfully as he did so.

"You okay?" Red asked.

"Yeah," Duncan answered slowly. "My knees just aren't what they used to be."

He held his right knee gingerly a moment before taking a few hesitant steps.

"I'll be fine," he finally said.

Red stepped inside first, feeling for a light switch until he remembered to turn on the flashlight in his other hand.

After switching on the light, he found a panel nearby, bringing the entire garage's interior into plain view. One switch brought every fluorescent light overhead to life, while the second switch Red flipped turned on four powerful bulb lights that slowly gained strength over several seconds, much like gymnasium lighting.

Impressively large as the garage might have been, it held no vehicles, displaying everything openly to its two visitors. A smooth concrete floor awaited new vehicles, while the white aluminum walls looked brand new, with no discoloration, and no visible wear.

Able to hold four vehicles behind its overhead doors, the building contained additional square footage on a second level, only partially visible to the two men because stairs in the opposite corner invited them up to a wooden loft. They could see along the closest edge of the loft, but the rest was lost in the vast square footage.

"Take a look at that," Duncan said.

Red followed the man's stare to a smudged footprint near one of the overhead doors. What looked like a greasy outline from a distance horrified Red as he drew closer, kneeling down to examine it.

"Blood," he said, swiping a wet trace of the substance with two fingers. "And it's fresh."

Considering it wasn't dried or frozen, it had to be quite fresh.

"But there weren't any footprints outside," Duncan pointed out.

"No, but the way this snow is falling, it doesn't take long for tracks to get buried."

"But why just one print?"

Red shrugged, then looked toward the loft area.

Duncan appeared very uncertain about checking the upstairs.

"I promised Keith I'd check every square inch of the place," Red told his colleague.

"I'm right behind you," Duncan reluctantly replied.

The entire climb up the stairs was well-lit, removing any apprehension Red might have otherwise felt. Because they were constructed of wood they creaked, but neither man showed any outward fear as they neared the top.

Red felt certain he was going to find some bloody corpse atop the stairs, or a severed limb. Instead of finding the stuff of nightmares, he only noticed two small crates the size of footlockers in the far corner.

"You know, maybe I'm getting too caught up in this area's past," he confessed to Duncan. "I keep expecting all of these bad things, and none of them have turned up."

"I know what you mean."

While he popped the top off one crate, Duncan worked on the other. A few seconds later, both were open, revealing their contents.

"Now I kinda feel bad for kicking in the door," Duncan stated as he lifted several photographs and postcards out of the crate.

Red's box contained more of the same. Dozens of photographs, postcards, and souvenirs lined the crates from top to bottom, most of which appeared to capture the West Baden Springs Hotel during its heyday.

While Red contemplated his next move, Duncan continued to paw through the items until he stopped at one particular scrapbook, staring at a particular newspaper clipping inside it.

"What's wrong?" Red questioned.

"This is the newspaper article about my great-grandfather's death," he answered. "I haven't seen one like it for years."

"Did he die *here*?" Red felt compelled to ask.

"In the valley, near the railroad tracks," Duncan answered almost blankly before his eyes showed signs of life. "Can you help me carry one of these inside? I'd like to have a look through both boxes."

Not in the mood to argue, Red nodded affirmatively. He decided it wasn't much work carrying a little crate inside the mansion, though he questioned Duncan's thought process, considering they had more pressing issues to confront.

He continued to hold out hope that Laura's disappearance was her own doing, but as he descended the stairs, he knew Keith wasn't going to be pleased about their lack of findings.

Somehow, he suspected his older brother had occupied his time with a new search and rescue tactic.

16

"I'm starting to think he's gone insane," McCully confessed to Jana as he watched Keith go from room to room, checking every ceiling, wall, and door he encountered.

No visible proof that a third floor even existed presented itself, but Keith seemed certain there was some kind of anomaly in the mansion that accessed such a place. McCully had seen movies with secret rooms and false bookcases that granted access to other areas of the house, but they typically had farfetched monsters and schemes he didn't see here.

"I'm starting to think Laura found a place to hide out for awhile," Jana replied. "She hasn't even been gone that long."

Strangely enough, Judith and Oswalt kept the hunter company while McCully and Jana monitored Keith. Had Keith approached him with a sound, more sane plan, McCully might have been inclined to offer help, but Keith wanted to check the entire second floor himself. The way things stood, McCully felt certain Oswalt and Judith had outsmarted him by rushing downstairs.

"I was never told of a third floor," Jana informed him, "and my job was to sell the place with the hotel if possible."

"You say 'was' like your career is over."

"I dare say it's not looking very promising at the moment."

"This isn't your fault," McCully said in his best assuring tone. "You weren't our babysitter."

Both of them paused to observe Keith leaving one room, entering the next in line just as quickly.

"I can't help but wonder what happened to Mr. Turner," Jana wondered aloud.

"He probably stopped off somewhere to get a motel with some bimbo."

McCully realized he had probably revealed too much about a fellow business partner.

"Strike that from the record," he added.

Jana laughed just a bit at the remark, despite the dire circumstances surrounding them.

"Glenn tends to get distracted easily," McCully said in place of his initial comment. "He probably meant to come up here and had something come up at the last minute."

"But why wouldn't he answer his phone?"

"He probably thinks we're pissed at him and doesn't want to hear about it."

Hearing a noise downstairs, McCully walked to the railing to find Red and Duncan returning from their outdoor expedition. Duncan's eyes immediately locked on him, but his look appeared almost excitable, far different from the skeptical terms they last parted on.

"Got a minute?" he called from below.

"Sure," McCully answered, seeing each man carrying a small crate.

He turned to Jana.

"Can you keep an eye on Keith in case he goes completely batty?"

"I could call the men in white coats, but they'd probably take longer than the police."

Now McCully chuckled.

"That's probably true."

McCully headed downstairs, wondering what brought about Duncan's change of attitude toward him.

"Please tell me you found something good out there," he commented when he reached the bottom step.

"Just heavy as a stack of Bibles," Red mumbled as he set down his crate, looking to the second floor. "Is my brother on a mission?"

"Quite," McCully answered.

Red gave little more than a sigh before ascending the stairs to take McCully's place at Jana's side.

"What's going on?" McCully asked Duncan once they were fairly isolated from the others.

"This," Duncan answered, virtually thrusting a scrapbook toward McCully, which he reluctantly accepted.

As McCully began flipping through the pages, he noticed Duncan studying him, as though expecting him to stiffen any moment when a new vision hit him.

"Can I ask what you're expecting from this?" McCully finally asked as he turned to the fifth page.

"There's an article in there about my grandfather's death. I thought it might complete the mystery for you."

McCully intentionally gave him a discouraging stare.

"For *me*, huh?" He paused. "It doesn't work like that. Just because I touch something doesn't mean I'm guaranteed to have a vision about it."

"But you said the grounds were bringing out the best of your, uh, abilities," Duncan said with unwavering optimism.

"I can't believe you're asking me to do this while everyone else is still looking for Laura," he said quietly enough that no one within earshot could hear.

Duncan appeared unaffected by the words.

"You said yourself we were possibly in danger. Maybe if you figure out what happened to my great-grandfather, you'll know what's wrong with this place."

"I feel used," McCully said evenly as he turned to the article.

"Well, don't. I'll be the first to admit I want to know what happened to my grandfather, but I'd also like to see this meeting have a happy ending."

Giving a tired sigh, McCully placed his palm on top of the article.

Nothing happened.

His eyes met Duncan's, seeing all hope drain from the man's face.

"Like I said, it doesn't usually work like that."

"Then try this," Duncan said, thrusting his hand forward, clasping McCully's right hand.

Before McCully could even think to pull his appendage away, he was transported to another time and place, much different than the warm confines of the mansion.

He saw Ben Williams standing with two men in the dark of night beside a train depot. Though he had no proof, McCully suspected it was the route that brought thousands to West Baden over the span of five decades.

At the moment, no train was stationed at the depot, leaving empty tracks and what appeared to be an empty building where tickets were bought. A clock inside revealed it was well past the witching hour, so the depot was abandoned of all life, aside from Williams and the two men.

In the chilly night he saw the breath of all three men in the air when they exhaled. While Williams stood in the open, beside the station, the other two men remained beside the wall, concealed from anyone walking toward the depot from the staging area.

Williams' companions looked like well-dressed bouncers from a nightclub, but he noticed a scar across the larger man's chin. These men were hardened, probably the type who worked for money without a care for the poor sap they injured. Their fists looked hardened with what McCully thought might be blood streaks, but a closer examination revealed detailed scars.

A light, misty fog lingered near the ground, but the eerie silence caught McCully's attention more than anything. The occasional cricket chirped, but the sounds of traffic and city life were something unknown to the valley in those days. Even the train yard appeared devoid of activity in the early morning hours.

Something felt very wrong, because they seemed to be waiting for something to happen.

Or someone to show up.

Suddenly wishing he weren't there to witness what he suspected was Andrew Duncan's demise, he wanted to turn around and run.

Unfortunately, he was a captive within his own visions, forced to witness whatever event he was meant to see.

A moment later, Duncan approached his longtime friend with an unhappy look. Despite the late hour, Duncan was dressed as nicely as ever, sporting a full suit and shined shoes. A fedora hat covered his head, but beneath the brim his eyes appeared troubled and sleepless.

McCully wondered why the man even bothered to show up, suspecting Williams used some ploy to lure him there.

"You have some nerve threatening my family," Duncan said with controlled rage, his right hand already curled into a fist. "My wife almost saw that little memo you sent to my house this morning."

"I'm just glad you got the message," Williams said somewhat coldly. "This is the last time we'll be seeing one another."

"It had better be. You got what you wanted, so there's no need for you to play me like a fiddle any more."

At this point the two men stepped forward, openly concerning Duncan as his eyes shifted between them and Williams. To McCully, they looked like mafia types from the big city, hired for one single purpose.

Duncan looked as though he wanted to run, but the thought was fleeting. Whatever fate Williams planned for him ended here, or it would spill over to his family. He seemed resolved in accepting whatever evil plan his former friend had in store for him, but he wasn't about to lie down like a dog waiting to be shot.

When Williams turned his back, as though unable to bear the impending sight of his friend being tortured, Duncan jabbed the first large thug in the jaw, flooring him against the wooden platform.

He ducked a punch from the second man, swiftly launching his own fist into the man's chin, phasing him temporarily. McCully was impressed the doomed man put up such a fight. By this time he had to be in his late forties at best, but his riches hadn't softened him.

The advantage was temporary, however, because both men regrouped before attacking a second time. While one held Duncan from behind, the other launched fists across his face, and into his stomach, quickly subduing him. His fedora hat fell to the ground with several speckles of blood covering its otherwise brown felt.

"Here," Williams said, thrusting some sort of alcoholic bottle into one of the thug's hands. "Take him down the tracks and finish it."

Cramming Duncan's hat onto his head, the two men began dragging him down the tracks, occasionally having to strike him because he resisted their efforts.

Williams looked around, seeing no witnesses, then walked the stretch of the platform to return to wherever he was staying. McCully, on the other hand, followed the action down the tracks. Compelled to see the end result, he found the men nearly a hundred yards down the track, forcing Duncan to drink heavily from the bottle. They tipped the bottle upward, forcing him to drink down whatever he could until he needed to breathe.

Whenever he put up resistence, they struck him with fists or feet until he cooperated. McCully hardly called it cooperation, because the man continued to spit up what little bit of the alcohol he could.

By this time his nose was obviously broken. Blood leaked from several opened gashes along his face and forehead. McCully couldn't believe a friendship was torn apart over money so easily. Whatever Williams purchased was apparently worth killing his good friend over, to keep it secret for all time.

McCully shuddered, turning away momentarily as the thrashing continued.

When he finally dared look again, he heard Duncan moaning in agony, barely conscious, as the two large thugs each held one of his arms. Basically the only thing keeping him from collapsing entirely, the men paused momentarily to assess the damage. One finally displayed the bottle to the other, indicating some unsaid signal between them.

The second man placed Duncan on his knees and elbows, barely keeping him off the ground as the man with the bottle swung it downward across the helpless man's head.

Duncan collapsed in a heap with a final moan as the shattered bottle landed beside him.

"He's still breathing," one of the men said after momentarily observing their prey.

"Grab a rock. The boss said to finish it."

"He also said to make it look like an accident," the other argued.

"It will. Just grab the goddamn rock, will ya?"

McCully watched the man wander just a few feet away, picking up a stone slightly larger than his fist, holding it with a solid grip. He desperately wanted to interfere, but he was no time traveler. In fact, he was a specter, unable to touch anything, and completely undetectable to everyone around him because he didn't exist when such events transpired.

His heart went out to Duncan, because the man obviously had a family at this point in life. Why he chose this path, rather than contacting police, or hiring his own help, was beyond McCully's comprehension. Perhaps he clung to hope that Williams might change, or had no idea what evil things his friend was capable of doing.

Barely able to watch, McCully witnessed the man with the rock clubbing Duncan in the back of the skull twice. While the first blow seemed like a warmup swing, the second cracked Duncan's skull, drawing both blood and tissue. McCully wasn't sure there weren't some bone fragments mixed in the fleshy gash.

He felt sick, wanting to vomit, but ghosts and holographs did no such thing, so he simply continued letting the events lead him.

Both men waited a moment to see if their victim had expired, which he apparently had, because they each took one end of Duncan's body, moving it near the tracks.

"Let's go celebrate," one said as though they had just won a company softball game, rather than murdered a human being. "I've got another bottle where that came from."

How heartless, McCully thought, taking a step toward the body, wishing he knew more about Andrew Duncan and the man's life. Somehow seeing random highlights didn't feel satisfactory to him, particularly since most of them related to his demise.

He still had no idea why Williams needed him dead. It had something to do with the purchase Williams made, but the story about cubes made little sense. McCully wished he knew more about the man's evil motivations, but his time viewing the past had come to an end.

17

"Dear Jesus," McCully muttered when his eyes found the contemporary Duncan standing in front of him.

"What happened?" Duncan asked with concern.

Taking a moment to collect himself, McCully pushed both Duncan and the scrapbook away from him to ensure no other gruesome scenes overtook his conscious mind.

Duncan stayed a few steps away. The look on his face indicated he understood his investment partner had seen something few human beings ever witnessed.

"Was he murdered?" he finally asked.

"Yes."

An uncomfortable silence surrounded both men momentarily as everyone else was preoccupied elsewhere in the mansion.

"What does it have to do with us?" Duncan questioned once enough time passed.

"Nothing," McCully answered. "At least not that I saw."

"Can you talk about it?"

Nervously rubbing his jawbone, McCully had no idea where to begin such a woeful tale.

"Your great-grandfather's best friend had him killed by two thugs," he said a moment later. "It was staged to look like a railroad accident, but they beat him up, forced him to down a bottle of whiskey, then knocked him over the head with a large rock."

There, that's it, McCully thought, hoping Duncan didn't press with more questions.

"But why?"

"He refused to help his friend buy some objects because it meant killing people, and his friend couldn't afford the risk of your grandfather telling anyone about it."

"What the hell was it?"

"Some sort of cubes."

"Cubes?" Duncan asked skeptically.

"That's what I thought, but there's something more to it that I never got to see."

Duncan stood silently a moment, pondering something, but Keith came down the stairs before their discussion concluded. His face bore a disgusted look, which McCully couldn't decipher. Keith was either irritated because they weren't helping in the search for Laura, or because he hadn't found her.

"This is bullshit," Keith stammered angrily. "We're stuck here, we can't call for help, and two of our members are missing."

"Two?" McCully asked.

"Well, Glenn never made it. How do we know something didn't happen to him?"

"We don't," Duncan answered. "But that doesn't mean someone has it in for us. Two other groups walked away from this place without any issues, so we're just having some bad luck."

"Bad luck?" Keith fired back. "The *Titanic* sinking was bad luck. People disappearing for no reason has nothing to do with luck, or karma, or any of that shit."

McCully continued questioning whether Laura's disappearance might be her own doing. They had no evidence of an abduction, and so far as he knew, no one could enter the mansion unless they used the front door.

"Laura isn't in this building," he dared say, contradicting Keith's opinion. "Maybe we should get everyone together so we can figure this out."

Keith considered the idea momentarily, looking up to the second floor as though not convinced he was wrong about a third floor.

"We need to contact someone right away," he finally said. "I don't care what it's doing outside."

"That means one or more of us trying to get somewhere else, because none of the phones work in this building," McCully stated. "Can you get everyone to meet down here?"

Keith looked around, noticing most everyone nearby as McCully already had. He stared a bit longer at Jennings, but returned his attention to McCully a moment later.

"I can get everyone down here, but what do you have in mind?"

"The hotel isn't that far from here. If I can't find a vehicle able to cut through the snow, I can probably walk there. I can take someone with me and leave the bulk of you here, so no one else gets lost or hurt."

"What if *you* get lost or hurt?" Keith countered.

"You aren't the only one who grew up in a tough environment, Keith. I can take care of myself, and like I said, I'll have someone with me."

Duncan looked toward him, but McCully didn't feel the man was very excited about the notion of hiking to the hotel.

"Take Red with you," Keith said, leading McCully to wonder if Keith wanted him monitored by someone he trusted implicitly.

"Fine," McCully agreed. "Let's get everyone in the living room and explain what's going on."

*   *   *

Five minutes later, everyone took a seat or looked out a window into the darkness as McCully stood by Red, who had been informed of their impending journey.

One look outside informed McCully he had signed up for a perilous trek, even by modern standards, because he didn't pack for a hike through miles of snowdrifts. At least visibility seemed incredibly good for nighttime. Across the grounds and vehicles parked out front, pure white snow blanketed everything, helping illuminate the area as though experiencing a long dusk.

Not once had a plow, or any vehicle, passed by the mansion that anyone reported seeing. Of course the building was set back from the road, but McCully felt certain any of them would notice headlights, or hear the sound of a vehicle powerful enough to tame the drifting snow.

Looking around, he noticed Oswalt, Duncan, Jennings, Jana, Keith, and Judith all present. No one appeared thrilled about being summoned together, as though they held out hope for Laura to walk through the door any moment. McCully couldn't imagine what kind of explanation she would offer for being gone so long, so he didn't share their optimism.

"Dave and Red are going to the hotel to see if they can phone for help," Keith began rather bluntly, never one to mince words. "None of our cell phones are working in this storm, and all land lines to the mansion are dead."

"Wouldn't it be safer to stick together?" Judith asked.

Unlike everyone else in the group, she never lacked courage to question Keith's leadership and decisions when necessary.

"We *will* stick together," Keith insisted. "Red and Dave will be gone just long enough to phone for help, then they'll be back."

Jennings stepped forward, turning heads.

"I can help them get to the hotel quicker if they have to walk."

"We were hoping to drive there," McCully said. "Dan has a four-wheel-drive truck."

A skeptical look crossed the hunter's face. As someone who lived in the area, and experienced the storm's vicious nature first-hand, he would know whether or not a truck could navigate the roads.

"If those plows haven't come through, you're going to get stuck."

"And what exactly are you proposing?" Keith asked the hunter sharply.

"I know the area pretty well. We could cut across a few fields and be there in no time."

Keith gave a chuckle, but it was laced with ill intentions.

"This coming from a guy who got lost after taking a walk out of his own yard?"

"I didn't get lost," Jennings said, losing patience with the cattle rancher. "I wouldn't have inconvenienced your dysfunctional meeting if I hadn't almost froze to death."

"You watch your tone, mister," Keith said, taking a step forward before Oswalt intercepted him. "One of our people is missing, and I'm not convinced you're not responsible."

Jennings shook his head with a frustrated look. For some reason he couldn't explain, McCully tended to believe the hunter was entirely innocent. If he had anything to do with Laura's disappearance, Jennings had no reason to return to the mansion.

Unless, of course, he got stuck down the road while attempting his escape.

"Can I have a second?" he asked, directing his question toward Keith.

Both men left the room before McCully offered a modified proposal toward the investment group's leader.

"I want him with us," he stated.

"Why? He's nothing but trouble."

"Maybe. Maybe not. You aren't going to have the resources to monitor him and see if Laura comes back. And *if* he had anything to do with her disappearance, this is my one chance to see if he slips up and lets us know something. Red and I can handle ourselves."

Keith seemed convinced, but concerned.

"There's something you're not telling me, kid."

"If anyone took Laura anywhere, they didn't get far. This is hypothetical of course, but if he, or anyone, drove away with her, there's a good chance their vehicle is stuck along the side of the road."

"But if you take him, you're not going to use the road, are you?"

"I need a look at the roads first. Maybe Dan's truck can make it if the drifts aren't too bad. I'll just tell him I want him along as backup."

An uneasy moment passed between them. Keith made no secret of the fact he had trust issues with the hunter. Now McCully was asking him to send the man with his brother to an isolated location.

"What if you can't even get inside the hotel?" he questioned.

"We'll find a way inside. There's supposed to be security there around the clock."

"Okay," Keith said with as much resolve as he could muster. "But watch your back."

He motioned for his brother to join them. A few minutes later, Red understood what Keith expected, then the three returned to the room, finding curious stares directed their way.

"Your clothes dry?" Red asked Jennings, keeping his brother from speaking with the man.

Jennings nodded, gathering them from one of the nearby fireplaces. He left the room to change, likely glad he was leaving the turmoil of the mansion behind.

"Dan, can we borrow your truck?" McCully asked Duncan officially.

"I'll have to take the trailer off the ball hitch," came the answer with an affirmative nod.

McCully threw a coat on, following Duncan outside. A moment later the two began undoing the restraint that kept the trailer attached to the truck's hitch.

"I hope you guys are careful," Duncan commented.

"I'll try not to wreck it."

"I wasn't talking about the truck. It's insured."

McCully caught his drift.

"Just make sure you lock up behind us. We don't want anyone getting into the mansion who shouldn't be there."

"That shouldn't be a problem. Keith will probably shoot anyone who doesn't know the secret knock."

"Please tell me he doesn't have a gun."

Duncan smirked.

"Well, he took the hunter's rifle."

"Great."

Carefully removing the trailer's connection from his truck, Duncan shoved it back. He handed McCully the keys to his truck rather slowly, as though expecting to shock the country songwriter into another vision.

Taking the keys, McCully half expected the same result, but it never happened. He pocketed the keys, allowing Duncan to lead him toward the front door.

Stopping just short of the threshold, Duncan turned to him.

"Did you really mean everything you said about my grandfather dying over some cubes?"

"They were something special, maybe valuable. And I'm not sure they were worth dollars so much as holding a different importance to Andrew's buddy."

"I can't honestly say I understand what you're telling me."

"It doesn't make much sense to me either, but maybe this little trip to the hotel will help me figure things out."

Duncan nodded, opening the door for them to step inside.

Keith greeted them immediately, with Jennings remaining a few steps behind the figurative leader. The hunter had changed to his warmer gear once more, appearing anxious to leave the premises.

Technically, the hunter had the option of leaving at any given time, so McCully wondered why he continued to stay with the group. Perhaps a sense of obligation, returning the favor for their help, kept him around. The way Keith had badgered the man with his rants and raves, they were lucky Jennings hadn't abandoned him the second his clothes dried.

"Good luck," Keith said, giving his younger brother a quick embrace.

McCully saw him whisper something to Red, but couldn't decipher the words. Jennings didn't appear very comfortable around Keith, so McCully wondered if the two men had heated words while he helped Duncan outside.

Having someone around whom the group couldn't trust made McCully uneasy, but he wondered if his mistrust was simply an extension of Keith's worries. He opened the door for Red and Jennings, deciding to focus on the task ahead of them, rather than his faith in the two men accompanying him.

As he stepped outside, snowflakes immediately smacked him in the face as though to say they weren't letting up anytime soon. He pulled the truck's keys from his pocket, giving one last look back toward the window where Duncan and the others looked out toward the departing group.

A strange feeling came over him, as though he might be doing the wrong thing by leaving for help. He wondered if the others were somehow vulnerable since they were less in number, but shrugged the feeling out of his mind.

The three men spent a few minutes dusting snow off the truck's hood and windshield by hand so they could see.

One look toward the road revealed a treacherous course ahead because snow had drifted, creating pockets between six inches and two feet deep in random fashion.

"Ready for this?" he asked Red as they opened opposite doors.

"As I'll ever be."

McCully assumed the driver's seat, Red rode shotgun, and Jennings squeezed into the back through the truck's third door.

The hunter remained silent, which didn't alarm McCully. After all, the man was near Red, the brother of his one outspoken adversary since his arrival to the mansion.

After placing the key inside the ignition, McCully brought the truck to life with a roar from the engine. He hoped the truck's power on the road matched its bark, throwing the shifter into drive.

18

"I said this was a bad idea," were the first words Jennings muttered when McCully encountered their first large snowdrift halfway down the hill.

Unfortunately the snow accumulation was only half the problem. McCully quickly discovered brakes provided very little stopping power on the icy sheets beneath a deceptively fluffy covering.

Despite Duncan's truck having anti-lock brakes, McCully carefully tapped the brake pedal as the truck swerved violently like a hooked trout, fighting for its existence. Strangely, his surroundings remained highly visible, and for a fleeting moment he contemplated which tree might provide a less dangerous crash if no other way of stopping presented itself.

From memory he recalled that the hill didn't even out the least little bit until it reached the highway, meaning he had seconds to bring the truck under control or risk being smashed like a bug against a snowplow or building.

"What's wrong?" Red asked from the passenger's seat.

"It's sheer ice under us," McCully answered quickly, still tapping the brakes as the truck began to respond.

Apparently the road wasn't completely ice, because the truck skidded to a stop within twenty feet, allowing McCully to observe his surroundings as he caught his breath.

"This is going to be problematic," he noted aloud. "Even if we make it down the hill in one piece, we may never make it uphill to the mansion."

He turned to Jennings.

"Which way is it to the hotel from here on foot, and how far are we talking?"

Jennings pointed out the direction, taking a moment to decide the distance.

"It's almost a straight line there," he finally answered. "Maybe a mile or so if we cut through the woods and a couple fields."

Red looked dissatisfied when McCully turned his way.

"If we make it to the bottom of the hill, we can pull up to the hotel," he said with confidence. "That way we don't have to walk through all of this shit both ways."

Realistically, they didn't need to make it all the way to the bottom, McCully deduced. The side entrance to the hotel had an electronic gate where he could park the truck, leaving them only a few hundred yards to walk. Of course that particular location would leave them almost all of the hill to climb with the truck before reaching the mansion as well.

"If I start this thing and don't get control of it within a few seconds, we're basically going to be riding a roller coaster with no safety features," he informed Red.

"I'm willing to take that chance."

Jennings shook his head negatively, openly against the idea of driving any further. Considering he was dressed for the elements, a hike probably didn't sound quite so hazardous to him.

"Screw it," McCully said, easing off the brake, wondering if he was going to maintain control of the truck, or send it spiraling toward a dangerous collision course.

His answer seemed the latter momentarily as the truck refused to brake when he touched the pedal again, but after a few seconds the tires touched paved road once more, allowing McCully to steer toward the side. Though the shoulder of the road was barely a foot in width before extending to a large ditch, it provided a hard dirt surface for the right tire to grip.

Answering his silent prayer, the truck stayed a straight course because very little snow accumulated on the shoulder. Near the edge, the drifts leveled out as the snow toppled into the ditch.

"I hate to think what'll happen if we come across another vehicle," he said, talking to calm himself more than make conversation.

"I'd say our chances are slim," Red answered grimly.

It took several minutes, but McCully navigated the truck down the slope until their salvation came into view. Through the falling snow he spied the side gate that led into the hotel grounds. Considering it was on the opposite side of the road, he needed to steer the truck perfectly into the small drive beside the gate while maintaining an ideal speed.

"Heads up," Jennings said, taking notice of the gate coming quicker than any of them wanted it to.

Once more McCully carefully tapped the brakes, finding more success as he brought the truck gently over to the opposite shoulder. The gravel beneath the snow kept the truck under control while he steered it into the short driveway until it came within inches of the gate.

"I don't suppose you know the combination to get in," Red inquired.

"There's no need. It's a short walk to the hotel."

"And a long hike back to the mansion," Jennings said.

All three men exited the truck rather quickly, finding the wind circling and howling around them. McCully and Red bundled up the best they could, pulling their jackets up to their cheeks while Jennings stood calmly near the truck's front end.

"Let's go," Red stated, taking charge much like his brother often did.

McCully walked around the gate's side, quickly returning to the red brick path, now covered in layers of snow, because he had no idea how the grounds were laid out. He knew a stream ran through part of the sunken garden, but he didn't know if other watery areas existed around the satellite buildings. Falling into a sinkhole was about the last thing he wanted to do after seeing the hunter's fate earlier.

Trudging through the snow proved more difficult than McCully envisioned, particularly without good boots on his feet. Snow immediately found its way into the exposed areas of his clothing, instantly melting into frigid sprinkles of displeasure. The thick socks he had found at the mansion did little except hold the miserable reminders of winter against his skin longer.

The three men drew near the cemetery where several dozen Jesuit priests were buried. A concrete walkway jaggedly led the way to the tombstones placed further up the hill. Surrounded by shrubs that acted as a railing of sorts, the steps were now entirely covered in snow, while the grave markers barely peeked above the accumulation.

Without realizing it, McCully stopped momentarily. He stared at the graveyard as the vision of a disturbed grave during the fall flashed through his mind in an instant. Unblinking, his eyes remained fixed on the wintery scene as another vision raced across his mind.

This one seemed far more disturbing because it also looked like the fall season based on the foliage coloration. A number of specters dressed like robed priests stared back at him from various positions behind tombstones. Some of them appeared injured, almost like zombies, because of head wounds or blood smeared across their faces. Several had agape mouths, but they all maintained blank stares, as though waiting in some sort of purgatory for the appropriate action to free them.

One in particular seemed to stare directly at him. His flesh appeared burned in some areas, very much charred in others. Fleshy tissue hung from his face along the cheeks and forehead, but his eyes caught McCully's attention the most.

Unlike the others, this man didn't appear very much like a priest at all, mainly because his stare felt as heated as his burned flesh looked. Tattered clothes hung from his body, also damaged from fire, which led McCully to suspect he died a horrible, fiery death.

To McCully, the priest's stare felt scolding, like his life as a specter had been disrupted by the man's visions. He suddenly realized the hotel's past contained other mysteries his powers had yet to reveal.

Like snapshots, the visions were gone, leaving McCully in the cold with fewer answers than questions. He quickly took up walking again before his two companions noticed his awkward stare.

Most of the buildings, and even the sunken garden itself, seemed indiscernible under sheets of white. Only the hotel was mammoth enough to resist being covered in any sense. The yellow lamp posts combined with the bright ground illuminated the large building. Very few lights were visible inside the structure, even as they drew near, because only a few lights were necessary to run the building.

Only light enough to run tours and guide security through the building seemed necessary, but several lights on the upper floors caught McCully's attention. He witnessed one bulb go out, then another turn on just a few rooms down, along the third floor.

"Did you guys see that?" he asked, wondering if ghosts were indeed toying with him.

Both turned around to look at him, then stared upward where his eyes remained locked.

"No," Red answered. "What was it?"

"A light just switched off up there."

"So the security guard is probably doing rounds. No big deal."

McCully thought differently, but said nothing as he followed Red's lead toward the front door. Two sets of double glass doors prevented their entry as Red tried every single door without success.

"I'll try the back," McCully suggested, starting to walk that way.

He stepped over a few large piles of snow, then made his way toward the rear entrance, seeing what looked like an unmarked police car, and beside it, a Ford Explorer with police decals. The second vehicle worried McCully a bit, because several wires dangled along the side from beneath the hood. Either someone had serious engine trouble, or the vehicle was sabotaged in a major way.

Trying to subdue the worries that crept through his mind, McCully reached the white door in the back, finding it opened without hesitation. He slipped inside, making his way around the first floor hallway toward the lobby doors. After passing the restrooms and the gift shop, he unlocked the first set of double glass doors by turning a lock at their base, then stepped into a short lobby. Undoing the lock to the outside glass doors, he let Red and Jennings inside.

Both men visibly shrugged off the cold as they stared into the darkened atrium, then the hallway to either side.

"The security office was to the right, wasn't it?" Red asked, the exterior doors to his back.

Every sound they made echoed throughout the vacant building, including speech.

"This way," McCully said, leading the way toward the office Jana pointed out during their tour.

Mere paces down the curved hallway, he found the security office door slightly ajar with a single light source barely visible from around a doorway partly obscured by a hanging cloth.

Not quite finished, the office had bare floors and walls desperately in need of paint or wallpaper. McCully found a light switch to one side, flipped it, and found a single, dim overhead light came to life.

The room the three men stood within was devoid of furniture and accessories, as though a front for something else. Beyond the room, divided by the cloth, the security room awaited the visitors. McCully now saw the single light source was a television playing some sort of movie from a DVD player beside it.

Since the hotel had no cable or satellite dish connections, he suspected watching movies was how the state troopers entertained themselves when not on rounds. Brushing the curtain aside, he also questioned why the hotel had absolutely no cameras or monitors.

A quick examination of the room revealed no clues about Brent Guthrie's whereabouts. McCully found no personal belongings, except for a paperback novel set atop the table, and a lunch box. The single rolling desk chair sat in the far corner, which seemed odd.

"He must be walking upstairs like I said," Red stated in a partially reassured voice.

"I'm not so sure about that," McCully answered, kneeling down to swipe up a shimmering liquid with his two forefingers.

"What is it?" Jennings asked.

"Blood. And there's a lot of it."

Someone had done a sloppy job of cleaning up a fairly large pool of blood. Despite the obvious smears and smudges along the floor's concrete surface, enough remained that McCully doubted it found its way to the floor by accident.

Red searched the desk, finding a phone on the opposite side of the television. He scooped up the receiver, placed it to his ear, and displayed a discouraged frown almost immediately.

"Dead."

"What a wasted trip," McCully muttered, turning to see Jennings shifting uneasily as his eyes panned the small room.

Looking up to Red, McCully waited a moment until his stare was returned.

"What now?" he asked once he had the man's attention.

"There has to be another phone in this place, or some way to get help."

"Either the phones are dead throughout the town, or someone cut the lines at the mansion and this place."

Silence filled the room momentarily.

"I don't like this," Jennings complained just above a whisper.

"And we didn't ask you to stumble into our lives," Red responded in an unfriendly tone, not much different than his brother's.

"I'll gladly hike back to my house if you prefer."

"You're not leaving my sight until I know you aren't responsible for Laura's disappearance."

Now Red sounded *exactly* like his brother. Just when McCully thought the number of sane people in his group outnumbered the psychological breakdowns, Red made him rethink his situation.

"Maybe we should have a look around the place before we take off," McCully suggested. "I'll take Craig with me and we can explore the first three floors. You can get the top three, and we'll meet back here."

Red didn't seem fond of the idea, perhaps because it wasn't his own, but he slowly nodded in agreement.

"Be careful," the older man warned, though McCully wasn't sure if he meant to be cautious around the darkened hotel floors, or Jennings.

*   *   *

Jana had the feeling everything had spiraled out of her control.

Keith had more or less ordered her, and everyone else, to remain downstairs while he continued his search for Laura. She understood how dogs felt when their owners left them chained up while they left to do errands.

"This is bullshit," Duncan stated to no one in particular. "He tells us to stick together while he runs off to find his ex. That's a bit hypocritical."

"More than a bit," Judith said, not hiding her irritation.

She was the only one seated within the room.

"I'm a bit confused," Jana admitted. "He's acting like she's the love of his life the way he's gone looking for her."

"You've got to understand Keith," Oswalt said. "He has a one-track mind once he decides on something."

What she truly couldn't grasp was why he wanted to continue the search by himself when he apparently thought some form of danger existed toward the group. His logic made sense, because the mansion appeared far more vast from the outside than the two finished levels.

"You're the authority on this area," Oswalt noted. "What happened here a few years ago?"

"That's a good question," she replied. "The newspapers and authorities kept everything very much under wraps to protect the hotel and Paul Clouse. There's no denying there *were* murders at the hotel. Of that, I can assure you."

Duncan appeared openly unhappy about her statement.

"We all thought it was behind us," Jana said for his benefit. "I believe Mr. Clouse understands there are families out there who will never get over what happened, which is part of the reason he decided to sell."

"Sounds like the place is cursed," Oswalt stated.

"I don't know about that," Jana said in the hotel's defense. "The legend of a Jesuit priest named Ernest has passed down through the decades, but what happened a few years ago was the result of one man."

"Who?"

"Martin Smith, the hotel's previous owner. Again, much of it was covered up, but it seems he was the puppeteer behind most, or all, of the murders."

Everyone digested her words a moment.

"What about this place?" Oswalt inquired. "What's the story behind it?"

"Smith built this after his acquisition of the hotel so he had someplace to stay nearby. There's a mansion between French Lick and here, but it was turned into a museum, so he had to compromise."

Silence filled the room as everyone looked away from Jana. She felt as though she had said something terrible and didn't realize it.

"What's wrong?"

A few more seconds passed, then Duncan spoke.

"You just said Smith caused several murders just a few years ago, and he owned this place."

"I made no secret about that information earlier today."

"True, but you didn't connect all the dots, either. Is it possible the man brought harm to Glenn and Laura?"

"He's dead," Jana said assuredly.

Then a memory struck her like a knife through the heart.

The image of a disturbed grave during the fall entered her mind, as well as a newspaper article from several years prior. A catalyst, or at least the first chapter, of the tragic events while Clouse worked at the hotel began with an illegally exhumed body.

She shook off the idea that someone returned from the grave to commit murder, but wondered if someone might be using the past to carry out a new agenda.

Only one person came to mind who might know the two properties well enough to devise such an evil plan, but Paul Clouse had no motive.

Unless he had slowly gone insane.

"You know, I'm going to buck the system and step outside a moment," Oswalt said, plucking his pipe and tobacco pouch from inside his sport coat.

"You probably shouldn't go alone," Duncan teased, though he showed no inclination to join the talent agent.

Jana wanted to look outside, mainly to see if there was any hope of assistance coming their way anytime soon.

"I'll keep you safe," she kidded, grabbing her coat from a nearby chair.

"Well, there you go," Oswalt said to Duncan.

Judith stood from her chair, openly unhappy.

"I don't care what Mr. Sanders thinks we are, but I'm not sitting around like a grounded child. I'll be in my room if any of you need me."

Everyone simply exchanged stunned glances as she left the room, too stupefied to say a word.

Oswalt simply grunted to himself, walking toward the front door. Jana followed him, but looked back to see Judith ascending the stairs without an ounce of fear, considering she directly disobeyed Keith's orders.

"Shouldn't one of us go after her?" Jana asked as she stepped into the winter wonderland beyond the front door.

"Won't do any good," Oswalt answered, lighting his pipe. "She's too stubborn to listen to *any* of us, much less Keith."

"I'm sorry things have gone so wrong," she apologized, though entirely unsure why she said the words at that particular moment.

"It's not your fault. There's probably a logical explanation to all of this. Glenn probably got stuck somewhere between Tennessee and here, and Laura might have wandered off."

Jana looked out to their vehicles, now looking more like snow forts than machines. She felt unprofessional, perhaps even stupid, for not making better preparations. Everything she planned turned out perfectly until two feet of snow landed in the valley. Very few professional snow removers lived in the West Baden area, but she could have found one, had any of the phones worked.

Now they were stranded without police assistance, and no chance of reaching main roads, even if the roads were plowed by morning, because the driveway was littered with white powder.

"It figures the weekend we come up here, the whole place falls apart," Oswalt said with a light chuckle. "We hardly ever see snow around Nashville."

"Southern Indiana isn't much different. If we get an inch or two, it's usually enough to cancel school and every public meeting in the area."

Jana turned around, seeing one of the stone carvings near her with the strange number beneath it. A few exterior Victorian-style lamps illuminated the front yard, allowing her to see most of the mansion's lower front wall.

She sauntered toward the second engraved image without much thought. The snow easily reached her knees, but she didn't care. A plethora of blankets and a hearty fire awaited her inside. Without much to do, she could wait inside until help arrived, or McCully and the others returned from the hotel.

Ignoring the image a moment, she looked to the number scrawled beneath it.

11:2.

"Hey, that's my birthday," Oswalt stated offhandedly, startling her a bit as his approach had gone unheard.

"Birthday?" she asked before she even realized it.

The numbers all seemed the same. One number, a colon, then another number.

Jana instinctively thought they were biblically tied, never considering the notion of them standing for something else.

Of course biblical numbers by themselves were worthless without a testament name to accompany them.

She wanted to walk to the end of the mansion to examine the rest of the numbers, but Oswalt stared inside one of the windows, then looked to her uneasily.

"There's no one in there."

"Where did Duncan go?"

"I don't know, but we'd better find out."

Oswalt knocked out his pipe against one of the pillars near the front door, then opened the door for Jana. She stepped inside first, looking around to find no one nearby. An eerie silence overtook the mansion, and as she moved forward, the sound of her own steps was the only noise entering her ears.

"Dan?" Oswalt called out.

Jana suspected Judith had retired for the evening, or simply didn't want company. No one knew where Keith had gone, or what his agenda might be. She only knew it didn't include room for anyone else.

A moment later, Duncan appeared at the balcony atop the stairs with a worrisome look.

"I heard a scream, but when I got up here to check, Judith was gone."

Oswalt shot Jana the briefest of skeptical looks, as though suddenly not trusting Duncan, then bolted up the stairway for a firsthand look.

Quickly following, Jana began fearing the plan to split the group might be the worst possible idea. Now two groups remained isolated, and ripe for the pickings, if someone had evil intentions in mind.

19

"This isn't how I planned on spending my night," McCully confessed as he and Jennings walked along the second floor.

"Me neither."

The pair had quickly checked the third floor, finding nothing out of place. Every room was unlocked, allowing them a brief search inside, but nothing turned up. A descent of the nearest stairwell brought them to the second floor where they immediately began opening doors to opposite rooms across the hallway.

McCully didn't dare fully trust Jennings, but to state his mistrust meant alienating the hunter. He tried to tell himself he was falling into Keith's cynical trap, but the fact that the hunter showed up right after their problems began did seem suspicious.

For the moment he continued to check the rooms on the inner hallway that faced the grand atrium. He consciously scanned the floor for any further bloodstains or other evidence, but found nothing along the dark carpeting.

Saying nothing, he ducked inside several more rooms, meeting Jennings in the hallway as they exited their rooms simultaneously.

"Nothing," the hunter said.

"Same here."

A thought occurred to McCully that they hadn't checked the vehicles parked beside the building before walking inside. At the time, they had no reason to think the security guard would be missing, much less wounded or dead.

Dead.

Missing.

He pondered the two thoughts for a moment, then looked to Jennings, wondering exactly what the hunter had done before reaching the mansion.

"What's that look for?" Jennings inquired somewhat defensively.

McCully realized he had left his emotions on his sleeve. Anything he said now would sound like backpedaling, so he decided not to make excuses.

"Nothing. I just wish we could find the security guard and get out of here."

He began doubting their chances of locating the guard alive. It felt as though their entire trip, even the weather, had been custom ordered by someone with an agenda.

They checked several more rooms until McCully stared out a window toward the atrium. Lit only by the atrium's overhead windows and a few dim bulbs scattered along the various floors, he found himself able to see much of the building's interior. Movement along the first floor caught his attention, but someone crossed one of the four atrium thresholds before he noticed any details.

Unless Red opened no doors whatsoever, then dashed downstairs, there was absolutely no way he cast the shadow McCully saw near the entrance. He continued to stare downward until a hand touched his lower back, startling him enough that he jumped an inch off the ground.

"Christ," he muttered, regaining his composure after the unusual outburst, considering he worked on several gospel albums with his father.

Jennings had a worried look, glancing from McCully to the first floor through the window. He appeared on edge, almost as though he sensed something evil stalked them through the hotel's hallways.

"What's wrong?" he asked.

"Someone was walking through the downstairs."

Jennings stood there a moment, just gawking at him as though wrestling with his thoughts.

"We're almost done on this floor. You wanna head down there?"

"We probably should," McCully decided aloud.

His trust in the hunter reached a new high after seeing an unidentified stranger along the first floor. He doubted the security guard had any reason to be sneaking around, and based on the bloody streaks in the office, he doubted the man was in any condition to walk.

Leading Jennings to the next set of stairs, he put his hand on the guide rail, wondering how many times Andrew Duncan had descended the same set of stairs before his untimely death. In a sense, the hotel shared his fate. Though rich with history, hosting thousands of guests during its first century, the building virtually died the day of the stock market crash.

Yes, it functioned in some capacity during the following decades, but lost its title and purpose as a hotel. The grandest, most expensive resort of its day no longer catered to the rich and famous, hosted professional baseball teams, or bubbled mineral water in its garden.

Like most things in the world, it changed and adapted through its ownership, lucky to have survived so many threats over the years.

McCully admired the building, both architecturally and historically, wishing for some way to avoid the deadly collision course it seemed he and his group were destined to find.

"You visited this place much?" he asked Jennings just above a whisper as they followed the turns of the staircase.

"As a kid, I used to sneak in here for looks at the atrium. It wasn't much to look at back then, but it was still awesome. It was overgrown outside, and the atrium was in disrepair, but you could still see the craftsmanship through the mold and faded paint."

"I'll bet."

McCully recalled viewing some photos of the hotel during its gravest era. How the building remained standing before the historical preservation groups stepped in was beyond his comprehension.

He reached the bottom step, looking around cautiously before walking onto the floor. They were now in the main lobby, an area with tiled floor, which muffled little or no sound when walked upon.

When empty, much of the hotel echoed and reverberated any speech or footsteps. He didn't like the idea of separating from Jennings, but decided quickly their search would produce better results if they split up.

"Check that way and I'll meet you in the middle," he said softly enough to the hunter that it didn't sound like an order.

Jennings nodded, walking in the opposite direction.

Able to hear his own steps, McCully thankfully exited the lobby quickly, knowing only a handful of small rooms stood between him and Jennings around the circular hallway.

After taking a look through an open lounge, McCully walked until he came across a storage room on his right, which had been carpeted during renovation, but left bare otherwise. He slowly opened the door, peeked inside, then closed the door, wondering if the person he saw wished to remain inconspicuous.

As he closed the door, the answer came to his left.

Holding a revolver pointed directly at McCully's face, a younger man wearing a thick duster gave him a dead-serious look with unblinking blue eyes. His right hand brushed back the duster, as though in an old western, to reveal a silver star along his torso that revealed he was a deputy for the county police.

"This isn't how it looks," McCully quickly stated.

"You have about thirty seconds to explain exactly how it *does* look, or I put a bullet between your eyes."

20

In absolute frustration, Keith tore through the basement inside the mansion, tossing pots and pans as he searched for some way to reach the third level he felt positive existed.

Oblivious to his colleagues' whereabouts during his search, he suspected they would do as they were told. He led the group in virtually every way, and they typically obeyed him. Red certainly listened to him, providing him some assistance by leaving the mansion with McCully and the troublesome hunter.

He patted his hands along every wall, looking for some secret passage, or perhaps some shaft that led upward. The dumbwaiter had definite ends in the basement kitchen and the first floor.

Finding Laura became his number one priority the second he discovered she went missing.

No harm came to anyone in his group while he was in charge, and a quick survey of the grounds outside revealed it highly unlikely she had strolled out either doorway. Turner not showing up for the tour could be dismissed several ways, but Laura was not one to simply disappear.

By no means needy or starved for attention, she had intelligence and an enduring will to get her by. Keith enjoyed the brief time they dated, but both realized business came first, and their relationship hurt the firm.

To him, leadership meant more than just guiding his people. He needed to take care of them as well, which meant discovering why Laura had disappeared.

Technically, taking care of his remaining people was important as well, but his standing order should have kept them safe, if they listened. They were responsible adults, capable of reason. Knowing there might be danger from outside forces, or Keith himself if they disobeyed, they would stay put.

He ran his hand along the inside wall, finding nothing unusual. Metal work tables stood in the room's center, and along several walls, creating a protective blanket around the room that Keith decided might harbor the mansion's darker secrets.

Quickly checking several cabinets along a different wall, he found more utensils, but no secrets. He removed his leather sport coat and black Stetson, which was far less common for him to do, but sweat continued to pour down his face and forehead. Setting the two items atop the center counter, he began his search anew.

Wiping his forehead with his shirt's long sleeve, Keith looked around the room, spying a shelving unit sitting in front of what he considered an unusual section of the wall. About four square feet of indentation broke up what was otherwise a solid wall the length of the room. Though an industrial woven metal shelf currently sat there, he suspected the area served a dual purpose.

A small table sat directly in front of the shelving unit, which made it appear even more odd, as though someone had deliberately cluttered the area to keep anyone from snooping.

Keith easily moved the table aside, examining the twisted metal fibers that comprised the unit as he ran his hands along their polished grooves. He noticed only a few large cans of food occupied the shelves, so he shoved them aside, reaching to the back end of the unit to touch the wall.

His fingertips and palm pressed to the wall like a child might absently touch the glass display of a candy store. What he felt, however, came nowhere close to what he expected.

Aside from being raised around horses, Keith learned quite a bit about construction from his father. His hands found the surface of the wall to be some kind of wallpaper that had yet to finish drying. Several air pockets refused to dissipate, meaning someone hurriedly put the wallpaper up very recently.

His knuckles tapped against the surface, allowing him to discover the paper covered a thin particle board. Yanking the shelving toward him, Keith tossed it behind him, having no concern about who heard the noise, or found the damage. He suspected the fledgling wall was placed there to hide something, so he looked for the quickest means with which to tear it down.

He never expected to find tools within a restaurant-style kitchen, but one of the drawers contained several screwdrivers, wrenches, and a hammer. Grabbing the hammer from the drawer, Keith began smashing into the thin covering, revealing something that widened his blue eyes momentarily.

Shimmering elevator doors gave him the assurance he needed, informing him that his hunch was accurate. Without taking a moment to assess the situation, he pressed the button with the up arrow, immediately regretting the decision.

"Damn," he muttered, wondering if he might have tipped off someone lying in wait upstairs.

Strength in numbers sounded much more reasonable, but the elevator was already coming down. Frantically looking around, he spied a knife rack nearby, snatching a sharpened blade from the wooden rack in case he needed to defend himself.

The option of retreat remained, but he doubted anyone upstairs might provide him much support in any kind of skirmish.

He also doubted anyone was riding the elevator down.

Except for the button, the elevator displayed no other features. There was no floor indicator, because the device only linked two distinct areas. Considering no evidence of an elevator existed on the second floor, Keith knew he had guessed correctly.

Some form of a third floor awaited him.

A ding alerted him that the doors were about to draw open, but as they did so, a darkly-clad figure immediately burst forth, catching him by surprise before he could raise the knife to defend himself.

Armed with a knife himself, the figure simply raised the blade upward, catching the underside of Keith's left arm with the sharpened end, creating a red slit. Groaning in pain, Keith punched the man in the side of the head, refusing to be a victim. He stunned the man momentarily, but as he went to use the blade, his wrist was struck.

His knife dropped uselessly to the ground, so Keith wrapped his hands around the assailant's neck as the two bounded from wall to wall, struggling and grappling. It took most of his effort to keep the attacker's knife from plunging into his chest, assuming that's where it was aimed.

Keith maneuvered the arm away from his body, pointing the blade toward the attacker as he kneed the man in the groin, doubling him over.

He immediately had the choice of fleeing, or taking the elevator upstairs. A glance revealed that the mobile box continued to wait for him, doors ajar, as though inviting him to see the secret it helped hide.

Lingering a moment too long, Keith allowed the dark figure to grasp his leg, but a swift kick from his boot to the head gave him time enough to stumble toward the open elevator.

As though desperate to keep some dark secret, the assailant grabbed Keith by the ankle, nearly pulling off his boot. Keith punched him in the head, near the temple, before he was tackled to the ground by the recovering figure.

Another skirmish ensued, but this time Keith threw several hard punches against the side of the man's head. The hood had some rubberized mask beneath it, absorbing some of his fury. He felt a powerful hand wrap itself around his throat, immediately cutting off the oxygen to his lungs.

Keith found a discarded frying pan nearby, using his fingers like feelers to find the handle before grasping it. When his knuckles finally locked around the wooden handle, he prepared to swing it, but found a knife swiftly swinging toward his chest. He went to block the blow, deflecting the blade enough that it lodged in his shoulder, dropping the frying utensil in the process.

As he yelled in pain, his left arm instinctively moved toward the wound to assess the damage or remove the knife. It bled, but the blade prevented the blood from gushing. Rolling over, he crawled and clawed his way toward the elevator, trying to distance himself from the dark figure.

Within a few seconds he neared the elevator, propped on his elbows to keep the knife's butt from touching the ground and sinking the blade further into his flesh. A strong hand grasped his foot as Keith drew near his discarded knife, with thoughts of certain escape crossing his mind.

His hand clasped the weapon's handle as he dared look behind him, his eyes adjusting too late to the dark shape now looming above him.

The delay cost him dearly as the frying pan, now wielded by the assailant, struck him upside the head, sending his consciousness spinning into a black void.

Leaving him at the mercy of a vicious stranger.

21

"Exactly who are you, and why did you break into the hotel?" the deputy asked McCully, who felt positive for the first time in his life he was about to die.

"My name is Dave McCully, and I didn't break in here. I'm with the investment group who toured the place earlier today."

"I didn't hear of any special tours."

A perplexed look crossed the deputy's face, indicating he really knew nothing about the group, making McCully's battle very much uphill.

"We got here and the security guard was missing," McCully explained. "We found blood near his post, so we went looking around."

The deputy didn't seem to buy his story, his hold on the gun unflinching.

McCully tried to think of some presentable proof, but nothing immediately came to mind. He wasn't issued a receipt or ticket, he had no letter from Jana Privett, and every form of communication appeared lost or broken.

His only hope was to explain his way out of this frightening situation.

"We're a group of perspective buyers for the property. We took a tour of the place this afternoon, and most of the group is up the hill at the old mansion."

"Who's here with you?"

"A few of us came down here to see if the phones were working. Our cell phones couldn't penetrate the storm."

Lowering the weapon just slightly, the man seemed to find some credibility in McCully's story.

"You didn't exactly answer my question," he stated just the same.

"I'm here with another member of my group," McCully told a partial truth, hoping if Jennings showed up he might know the deputy.

Or bail him out of trouble, even if he didn't.

Now the deputy pulled back on the revolver's hammer, aiming it straight at McCully's forehead. Appearing dead serious, he left the bluegrass singer wondering exactly why he was at the hotel in such ferocious weather, and why he acted so cross.

"I suspect you have better things to do than check on the hotel in this weather," he said, trying to get some answers. "And you're not in uniform, so this must be a personal matter."

"I'll ask the questions, mister, starting with the what you know about the vehicles parked out back."

"Absolutely nothing. They were here when we got here. The truck we brought down from the mansion is parked near the employee gate."

Taking a moment to digest the information, the deputy refused to lower his weapon. Their conversation came to a screeching halt when footsteps echoed down the hallway. The county officer motioned for McCully to quietly move to a nearby wall where they were out of sight from whomever approached the area.

If he were held at gunpoint by a kidnapper or known felon, McCully might have dared attack the man at a convenient moment, but this was an officer of the law. To this point, he had every reason to believe the man had only good intentions for stopping at the hotel, so he complied.

When Red stepped into view, it surprised McCully, but surprised the older man even more. Upon seeing the deputy's firearm, Red immediately held his hands halfway up in a defensive posture.

"I very much want to hear your version of things," the deputy said, waving the gun for Red to move beside McCully, which he did.

"My side?" Red questioned, giving McCully a questioning glance.

"Tell me what the fuck you're doing here."

The man flashed his badge toward Red, authenticating himself once more.

"Well, we were stuck at the mansion and one of our people went missing, so we thought we'd see if the phones down here worked," Red replied far more calmly than McCully had.

Everyone stood silently a moment.

"Can I ask what you're doing here in this weather, officer?" Red dared inquire. "We called 911 over an hour ago and they said the police were too busy at traffic wrecks to come help us."

Looking between McCully and Red, the deputy seemed to question why both of them had asked the same question. He appeared suspicious of them, as though they were the reason he felt compelled to brave the weather and check on the hotel.

"Someone important to me is missing," the deputy answered gruffly. "I tracked his movements to this location."

McCully recalled seeing the damaged county police vehicle outside.

"We saw the Ford outside," he said. "That wasn't yours, was it?"

"No. I got here the only way I could. Horseback."

McCully looked outside, though the dim lighting only provided a limited view of the grounds. Everything looked a hazy yellow from the limited bulb lighting and heavy snow.

"He's inside the old pavilion," the man answered, guessing his thoughts correctly.

"We might be able to help you find him or her," Red suggested in a neutral tone, still acting the calmest of the group.

"I don't think so. In fact, I have to decide what I'm going to do with you two while I search for him."

McCully looked from the corner of his eye toward Red, who didn't appear thrilled about their predicament. They had little time to waste, and a group of people at the mansion to rendezvous with before conditions grew any worse.

"You don't have to *do* anything," Red stated. "We're who we say we are, and we're here to get help. If you're really a deputy, we could use some assistance finding our missing person."

Now the man gave an uneasy chuckle.

"*If* I'm a deputy? I'm holding a gun, and I think that's about all the authority I need at the moment."

A thud surprised both McCully and Red as the deputy lurched forward, then collapsed to the ground, falling forward to reveal Jennings holding the culprit.

In his hands he clasped a short spade shovel.

"I found it in the basement after I saw you were in trouble," he informed McCully.

"You know who he is?" Red asked.

"He's the sheriff's son."

McCully and Red exchanged confused looks.

"And you still slugged him?"

"He gave me a speeding ticket last year I didn't deserve."

All three suppressed laughs, looking down at the unconscious deputy.

"What do we do with him now?" McCully asked once their chuckles subsided.

"We get that gun away from him and do what we came here to do," Red answered. "I couldn't find a phone on the sixth floor, but that doesn't mean we've struck out completely."

Unsure that he felt equally confident, McCully kicked the gun away from the deputy's limp hand, hoping things at the mansion were going smoother.

*   *   *

"I can't believe this," Oswalt commented, standing at the doorway of Judith's room.

Jana looked from him to Duncan, beginning to wonder who within the group could be trusted. Considering they hadn't heard one word from the three men who left for the hotel, it wasn't beyond the realm of possibility one of them incapacitated the other two and returned.

She tried to shake the feeling someone in the group came to Indiana with ill intent, because there seemed no other way anyone might enter the mansion.

Unless they had hidden away the entire time.

"I searched the whole room," Duncan said immediately, as though noticing their suspicions. "No sign of any foul play. She's just gone."

Everything inside the room appeared orderly to Jana. She checked the closet, under the bed, and inside the bathroom to confirm Duncan's report.

Oswalt shook his head, wearing a frustrated look. He left the doorway, calling back as he went down the stairway.

"I'm going to find Keith. You two can search the other rooms."

It sounded more like an order than a suggestion.

"Patsy," Duncan commented. "I think he's more devoted to Keith than he is his own clients."

Jana said nothing, contemplating their situation in her mind instead. A sinking feeling overtook her rational thoughts because Judith simply disappeared, just like Laura.

This wasn't a practical joke, she had decided. Obviously, leaving the mansion wasn't a realistic option. No help could be reached, and even if they talked to a dispatcher or police officer, the chances of them coming to the mansion remained slim. The only thing Jana thought might make the situation worse was a power outage.

Or being left completely alone.

She put aside any mistrust of Duncan, sensing he might be the one genuine person in the entire group. His love for the hotel, and its history, eliminated him as a suspect because he had no ulterior motive for harming his group members.

"Want to check the rest of these rooms real quick?" he asked her.

"You haven't already?"

"I called her name, but I didn't poke around a whole lot," he confessed.

Jana nodded easily, almost in defeat before they even began searching.

"Let's go check."

A little over ten minutes later the pair finished checking the upstairs with negative results. Oswalt had yet to return, so they walked down the main stairwell, utilizing the bird's-eye view to observe the area below.

Nothing stood out, so they made their way downstairs, finding the place extremely desolate without the sounds or sights of other people.

"Where the hell could he be?" Duncan questioned.

"Hopefully with Judith and Keith."

"Something tells me we're not that lucky."

As they reached the bottom stair, Duncan looked around the area with a concerned expression.

"Can you check those two rooms real quick?" he asked, nodding toward the living and entertainment rooms.

Alone? Jana thought, unsure of how the disappearances were occurring, but positive about one thing.

Everyone who came up missing had left the company of others.

"Okay," she answered anyway, deciding not to enter either room.

A quick glance inside each one would suffice.

And it did.

Jana saw nothing unusual in either room, beginning to wonder if aliens were transporting her guests into their flying saucers, completely undetected.

To her, Keith's third floor theory seemed unfounded, if not unsound, but unless the entire group was playing some sort of practical joke on her, she had no other realistic explanation.

She walked toward the middle of the room, expecting to find Duncan nearby. When Jana reached the stairway, she peered cautiously around, hoping to see someone familiar standing there.

"Dan?" she called, stepping toward the kitchen area on the other side of the stairs.

"I'm here," he said, suddenly emerging from the doorway, startling her.

He looked more concerned than ever.

"I didn't see anyone downstairs, but I found Keith's hat and coat. He was down there at some point."

Jana felt true panic for the first time, struggling to keep her composure. She knew Duncan was genuinely worried about his colleagues, but he said very little, keeping his thoughts to himself.

She wanted to check downstairs for herself, simply to eliminate him as a suspect from her mind more than anything else. Daring to request such a search provided no other positive aspects for her, so she said nothing.

Perhaps an opportunity to search downstairs might present itself later, so Jana decided to stay by Duncan's side, hoping any fears she harbored were unfounded.

"What are we going to do?" she asked him, wondering if any new ideas had come to the man who knew the area better than anyone in his group.

"We're screwed until the others get back," he answered. "They took my truck, which is the only good vehicle in this weather we have. If they get stuck down there, we may be on our own the rest of the night."

Jana didn't recall weather reports mentioning anything about a quick warmup after the initial snowfall hit. Sleeping at the mansion overnight might prove just the beginning of their stay if road conditions didn't improve.

"We should have left when we had the chance," Jana said with a sigh.

A loud series of knocks at the front door startled them both as their feet left the ground. After a moment of regaining their composure, Duncan and Jana looked to one another, then directed their attention toward the front door.

Jana wondered what other surprises awaited them, hoping one or all of the men who went to the hotel might be returning. She started toward the door to answer it, but Duncan caught her arm.

"Shouldn't we have a weapon or something?" he asked.

"Like what? A spatula from the kitchen?"

"That hunter's gun is somewhere around here."

Jana decided opening the door was a safe option if they ascertained the identity of the person on the other side.

"We don't have time for this," she stated more boldly than she intended. "Let's find out who's out there."

22

McCully waited by himself for the deputy to awaken within the security office. He should have felt comforted by the fact that the man, now identified as Arlan Brown, was bound to a chair.

But he didn't.

Before leaving to explore more of the hotel, Red and Jennings had pulled the deputy's license from his wallet. They now knew exactly who the man was, confirming the hunter's initial identification, but McCully wanted to know his motivation for holding them at gunpoint.

Jennings apparently had extensive knowledge in knots, because he tied the deputy to the chair quicker, and with better quality, than McCully recalled ever seeing any object bound. Almost twenty minutes had passed since Jennings struck the man, leaving Brown slumped in a chair with his chin buried in his chest.

McCully half expected to see him drooling on himself in his limp state, but it didn't happen. He wanted to converse with the man, if only to know what brought him to the hotel. Expecting assistance from Brown seemed farfetched, but beggars can't be choosers, he decided.

Despite the major storm gripping the valley, two group member disappearances seemed highly unlikely without some outside meddling. He considered Turner a missing person, since the man never called or showed up. Until the security guard came up missing, he felt most every odd occurrence could be explained.

Something felt wrong about separating the group at the hotel, as though they might be following an intended harmful path. McCully couldn't place the feeling, but his heightened awareness usually provided him better intuition.

To put his suspicions aside, more so than anything else, McCully reached over to touch the man's arm. His fingertips grazed the man's shirt sleeve, which typically provided a vision if one was to be found.

But nothing happened.

He would have breathed a sigh of relief if not for the man stiffening to a full upright position immediately. His eyes appeared wide with confusion, and possibly some anger, but they came to rest on McCully after surveying his surroundings.

"The last thing you want to do is keep me tied up," he said momentarily, after regaining his composure.

"Seems during our last encounter you had a gun pointed at my face," McCully answered, refusing to back down.

"Assaulting me is a criminal offense."

"Assaulting *anyone* is a criminal offense. And I believe battery is putting your hands on someone, isn't it?"

Brown didn't appear the least bit amused.

"Maybe if you had been more forthcoming, instead of accusing my friends and I of breaking and entering, we wouldn't be in this position," McCully offered.

"And you weren't breaking and entering?" Brown said, openly amused at such a statement.

"I suppose technically we were, but we were looking for help. One of our party is missing from the mansion up the hill. Care to tell me who you were looking for?"

"It would be a lot easier if you untied me."

McCully flashed a suspicious smile, but didn't budge from his position.

"I'd like to hear your story first."

Brown sighed, relegating himself to his current situation.

"My father came over here after a phone call, and I haven't seen or heard from him since."

"And you came out in this shitty weather to find him?"

"My dad was supposed to contact me, and never did. I couldn't get him by home phone, cell phone, or radio, so I knew something was wrong. He's always out working during storms and major events."

"Working?" McCully asked, trying to pry additional information from Brown to make their conversation a bit smoother.

"He's the sheriff."

McCully got what he wanted. Though he already knew that piece of information, he wanted Brown to say it. He could now take a different direction with his questions without implicating Jennings as the person who struck Brown in the head with the shovel.

"So that's his Ford out back?"

"Yes. And the sooner you get me out of here, the sooner I can get looking for him."

McCully recalled the engine compartment of the sheriff's vehicle openly displaying its damage.

"We've been through the whole place and found nothing," he revealed. "The security guard was missing, and we found a pool of blood near his desk."

"I know," Brown said impatiently. "That's why I figured you and your buddies took him out. I'm still not convinced otherwise."

"If I were murderous enough to kill a retired state trooper, do you really think I would have simply tied you up?"

Brown shrugged what little he could.

At the same time, McCully began wondering how interconnected the strange occurrences around them might tie into one another. The only logical explanation seemed to be an elaborate scheme to slowly break up the investment group, while taking out the sheriff to ensure the plan reached its conclusion.

Shaking his head, McCully felt certain his mind was wandering too far, because the weather could easily be the cause of Turner's disappearance, the sheriff's mishap, and possibly Laura wandering off and getting lost in the snow. It didn't feel right, but McCully had no explanation why someone might bring harm to anyone in the group.

"So you're really staying at the old mansion?" Brown asked, suddenly showing modest interest in McCully's story.

"Yes. I think we've covered this ground already. And, no, I haven't seen your father. In fact, you're the first stranger I've seen since we saw the security guy this afternoon."

McCully thought a moment.

"Well, I guess the catering crew was hired by our tour guide."

"Tour guide?"

"The woman who showed us the grounds this afternoon. We're the third group to come through here. Surely you've heard something about it."

Brown nodded.

"Sure. But I didn't hear much, because apparently the first two groups didn't cause much of a stir."

"Funny," McCully commented. "This place must be some bread and butter for you locals."

Now the deputy shot him an irritated stare.

"Is that how you think of us? As piss ant local hicks?"

"Not at all. Maybe I don't have the local connection to this place that my colleague Duncan does, but I understand the history of the place."

McCully dropped Duncan's name, hoping for a positive connection from the deputy, but it didn't come.

"You're wasting time I could be spending by searching for my father," he said instead.

McCully realized the man was right. He traveled to the hotel with Red and Jennings to find help, or Laura, so their situation had an eerie similarity.

"I'll get you out of here, but first I have to see what my two colleagues have found."

He hoped more than anything they hadn't found any corpses, but the grim reality that the storm brought more than just piles of snow settled in his mind.

"I'll be waiting," Brown said in a displeased tone.

McCully stepped into the hallway, instinctively looking both ways. He worked one summer in a factory, where he learned to always look both ways. Failure to do so got several workers struck by forklifts and machines carrying hot liquid metal. McCully listened during orientation to the horror stories, making certain he paid attention at all times.

After that summer, the habit stuck, no matter where he went.

Working in the factory was his father's idea, to teach him what real work was like, and it was that summer McCully decided he wanted to follow in George McCully's footsteps. Not that he minded hard work, but the entertainment business provided many more luxuries and fringe benefits.

He didn't dare call out for Jennings or Red, so he stepped as quietly as possible down the hallway, listening for their voices or footsteps.

No sound entered his eardrums, but he wondered if they might take the elevator instead of the stairs. Noise only carried so far throughout the hotel, despite the echoing effect when it was vacant.

McCully expected to hear conversation or doors closing at the very least. He reached a window in one of the first floor lounge rooms, staring outside momentarily.

Snow finally began tapering off, but the damage appeared to be done. Strong winds continued to create new drifts, and any lights normally seen beyond the end of the hotel's long driveway were hidden or nonexistent. For all he knew, West Baden might be a ghost town, partly or completely deprived of power.

The Victorian-style lanterns along the main drive remained lit, but the bulbs looked like hazy globes painted on canvas in the wintry night. At least the hotel had power, which meant the mansion probably continued to provide warmth for the people left behind.

McCully whirled around upon hearing conversation in the distance.

He walked briskly to the door, stepping into the hallway. Stopping just long enough to detect the area where Red and Jennings were walking, he heard a slight echo, guessing they might be crossing the grand atrium.

It took little time to reach the nearest of the four open entrances to the atrium. He found the two men near the center of the large open area, talking quietly as they walked. McCully felt better that the two were speaking at last, but noticed something in Red's right hand that looked like a sheet of paper.

Instead of calling to them, in case someone watched their activities from above, McCully stepped into the atrium, the echoes of his movements immediately alerting his colleagues to his presence.

"What are you doing out here?" Red asked once he intercepted them.

"I decided to check on you two. You were gone quite awhile."

"How's our deputy?" Jennings inquired, looking sheepishly guilty after whacking the man with a shovel.

"Grumpy. He's still tied up, but I found out a few things once I got him talking."

"Such as?" Red inquired, leading the way toward the security office.

McCully and Jennings quickly followed, not wishing to be left in the unnerving darkness of the atrium.

"His father is indeed the sheriff, and he came here looking for the man."

"So?"

"So, his father is missing, the security guy is missing, and Laura is missing. This place is a stone's throw from the mansion, so don't you think something weird is going on?"

Red stopped mid-stride to ponder the evidence presented to him. His upper body shivered as a cold draft passed through the group, and he said nothing for a moment.

"That police vehicle outside looked trashed," he finally stated. "We found this on the dashboard inside."

Red handed him a sheet of paper with some scribbled writing on it.

He read the note to himself.

Trouble at the old Smith mansion.
Two missing.

"'Two' missing?" McCully questioned. "What the hell?"

"That's what we were wondering," Jennings said.

McCully deduced the original message might have been inaccurate, the writer got the information wrong, or he and his two colleagues were a step behind someone's fiendish plan.

"We need to talk to our deputy," he said. "Maybe he has a clue about what's going on."

All three quickly made their way to the security room, but when they arrived it was vacant. The ropes formerly binding the deputy lay uselessly on the floor.

"Shit," McCully said under his breath.

Red had the man's gun, but there was no telling if the deputy planned to enlist help, track them down, or escape with his new-found freedom to search for his father.

"Well this isn't good," Jennings said, swallowing hard.

23

A pounding came to the front door several more times before Jana unlocked it, yanking it open to find Oswalt standing in the cold, his hands held in front of his chest as though he were in prayer.

They were a faded pink color, indicating the pose was meant to simply keep them warm.

"About time," he said gruffly as he stepped inside, immediately shivering.

"What happened to you?" Duncan questioned, thinking much like Jana that Oswalt had no reason to step outside without proper clothing.

"I thought I saw a streak of light outside, so I ran out there hoping to flag someone down."

"And?" Jana inquired.

"It was a snowplow, but they were too far gone to see me."

"Did you find Keith?"

"No. I found his stuff in the basement, but no sign of him."

Oswalt's voice trembled when he spoke, because the cold had numbed his body. Jana hadn't thought it was exceptionally cold outside, but she noticed the man wore nothing more than thin socks and some kind of sport sandals on his feet. Some of the guests had dressed down after dinner.

Everyone stood silently a moment. Oswalt continued to shiver, so Jana grabbed one of the blankets Jennings had used from a nearby chair.

"Thanks," he said, wrapping himself inside it like a cocooned worm.

He waited a few seconds to regain his composure before speaking again.

"We have other problems."

Duncan looked at him as though wondering how their situation could really get any worse.

"Every tire was slashed on every single vehicle."

Jana glanced at Duncan, who appeared to instantaneously be caught between rage and utter desperation. He darted to the window, looking outside for confirmation of Oswalt's news, but shook his head.

"I can't see anything out there," he reported, apparently having no desire to step outside by himself.

"Trust me," Oswalt said. "We aren't getting out of here tonight."

Duncan looked hard to Oswalt momentarily, then his expression changed when he looked to Jana. She read it plainly, fighting not to give away Duncan's secret message.

I'm not sure I trust him anymore.

The thought of Oswalt slashing every tire seemed preposterous to her, despite the length of time he was away from them. She knew something wasn't right about their stay at the mansion, but trusting absolutely no one seemed counterproductive.

She saw no motive in Oswalt harming Keith, or stranding them at the hotel, but she wasn't going to simply sit around and wait to disappear next.

"We have to do something to get out of here, or get help," she said.

"Like what?" Duncan asked. "You're the local person. If there was something we could do, wouldn't you have thought of it already?"

His argument was sound, but Jana had no friends or contacts as far south as West Baden. At this point, braving the elements to walk to the nearest police station or open business sounded better than waiting inside the mysterious building.

Jana decided if they couldn't leave the grounds, perhaps their time might be better spent solving the mystery at hand. Anything sounded better than waiting for McCully and the others to return, or searching the mansion for Laura and Keith.

She wanted them back safely, but they were simply nowhere to be found, and risking three more lives to find them sounded illogical.

"We have to find out what happened to Keith," she finally said, deciding it was time to check downstairs for herself.

Oswalt and Duncan had likely done hurried searches for their group's leader. Keith certainly hadn't vanished into thin air, and no signs of anyone exiting the building presented themselves.

Both men appeared reluctant to conduct another search, as though they might be next on someone's hit list.

"Fine," Jana said more sternly than she felt. "I'll go check by myself."

She knew, or at least hoped, they wouldn't *really* let her stray from them. Duncan stepped forward first, giving her an internal sigh of relief.

"I'll go. I didn't get to look around very much the first time, so maybe we'll find some clues."

Oswalt continued to shiver, pulling the blanket tighter around himself.

"You'll forgive me if I don't join you? I promise I won't go anywhere."

Jana nodded, then stepped toward the kitchen area with Duncan in tow. They quickly passed through the kitchen area, noticing the pleasant lingering odors of their evening meal remained. Jana opened the door to the downstairs, turned on the light, and took the lead.

"I think he's hiding something from us," Duncan commented on the way down.

"Something tells me if he was behind any of this, he would have been much smarter about it."

"What do you mean?"

"If Oswalt wanted the tires slashed, he could have done it hours ago. And why would he turn around and tell us about it?"

Duncan had no reply.

They reached the bottom step, but Jana turned to speak with Duncan, rather than immediately begin their search.

"Maybe he wanted half of the group gone so he could toy with us," Duncan said before she could offer a suggestion.

"I doubt it. Someone who knows this area and this mansion very well is behind the strange goings on."

Duncan reluctantly nodded in agreement.

Turning around, Jana wondered where to begin their search for Keith, because he certainly hadn't left them any clues.

*   *   *

"How do we know he's not still lurking around here?" Jennings questioned as the three men refused to leave the sanctity of the security office.

"And how do we know he isn't responsible for any of this?" Red questioned McCully, who still felt positive the deputy was truthful during their conversation, albeit while he was in captivity.

Jennings shook his head, disagreeing.

"He's kind of a jerk, but I don't think he's the homicidal type. If he was looking for his dad, he probably took off to the bar down the road. That's where the two of them hang out all the time."

"I doubt it," McCully muttered barely above a whisper.

Red clearly looked disturbed by the turn of events. He exhaled audibly through his nostrils before speaking.

"There's nothing in this place that's going to get us any help any sooner, and if he goes and finds his dad first, our situation might get worse."

"Are you suggesting we find him and toss him in the brig?" Jennings asked.

"No. I'm suggesting we find him and work this out before it gets messy. We don't have time to waste with all the weird stuff going on around here."

McCully had an idea where to find the deputy before the storm engulfed him.

"I'll check outside and see if there's any tracks."

Red nodded his approval, and said something that sounded like orders to Jennings as McCully wasted little time exiting through the building's front entrance. He supposed building security was hardly a worry when no one could feasibly step onto the grounds without adapted travel methods.

Despite the snow tapering off, he found himself unable to see past the brick driveway, now layered in pure white. McCully stepped forward, making his way toward the sunken garden through the impeding snow.

Feeling somewhat disadvantaged tracking an officer of the law, he wondered if Brown had really planned to retreat, or if the deputy planned on enacting some revenge. Standing completely still on the stairs, McCully looked cautiously around before continuing his descent. He then looked upward, studying the windows that loomed over six stories above.

No shadows broke any of the light patterns, and no lights switched on or off. Returning his attention to the garden, he stepped forward, finding a dark figure moving along the garden beside the closest spring.

Too large to be a person, McCully figured he had just found Bigfoot, or the deputy was on horseback.

"Shit," he muttered, wondering what Brown had in mind.

While the snow drifts reached his knees and beyond, McCully noticed the horse having little trouble navigating the garden as Brown directed him toward the side gate. A terrible thought crossed his mind as he contemplated the deputy taking the time to disable Duncan's truck.

If he even had the means to do so.

Most saddles can carry multiple objects, including shotguns, food, bedding, and possibly even a knife of some sort.

Another glance toward the garden revealed the shape nearing the gate. A mad dash through the snow might allow McCully to catch Brown in the act of slashing tires, if that was indeed his desire, but not in time to prevent the act entirely.

He quickly returned inside to inform Jennings and Red of their new problem. Even if Brown didn't slash their tires, he would certainly reach the mansion before any of them could. At this point, McCully had no idea what the man's frame of mind might be.

Yanking open one door, then the next, he reached the inside, hearing no sign of his two colleagues. Since they were the only people in the hotel, so far as he knew, he decided to call out this time.

"Red! Jennings!"

No answer.

"Red? Craig?"

A few seconds passed before a response came.

"Over here," Jennings called, entering the atrium from the other side.

Both men walked halfway across, meeting in the center beneath the overhead chandelier.

"Where's Red?"

"He said he wanted to check on something in the basement," Jennings answered.

"Our deputy is mobile, and he just took his horse out the side gate."

Jennings stood a moment, trying to reason what McCully's point was exactly. A strange look crossed his face when the answer came to him.

"He's heading for the mansion?"

"I sort of let him know there was a group of us staying up there."

"Yeah, but why would he care?"

"Maybe he thinks we did something with his dad."

Jennings soured a bit, openly trying to guess the deputy's typical movements.

"His dad and him are close. There's a chance he might have gone off the deep end if he thinks we did something to him."

McCully realized he had no time to waste.

"I'm heading for the mansion. He might have slashed the tires on the truck, but if he didn't, I'll be back for you."

"You can't just leave-"

"I don't have a choice. Hell, I'm not even sure the truck will make that hill. In the meantime, you two can look for a way to contact the police, or maybe some blueprints from the mansion."

"That's a longshot," Jennings scoffed. "But I *can* take the shortcut back to the mansion if Red and I need to get back there."

McCully turned to leave, then turned around in mid-stride.

"And maybe our cell phones will start working with this storm front deteriorating."

Jennings nodded, allowing McCully to continue on his way, wondering exactly what had transpired at the mansion in his absence.

24

Oswalt felt warmer within a few minutes of being inside, but his extremities still tingled with numbness as they gradually regained their circulation. He flexed them in and out, trying to get them warm but they simply responded with shooting pain, as though he were trying to push a ping-pong ball through a straw.

His veins were no bigger than straws, meaning they could only withstand so much regained blood flow at once.

Standing from the chair, he decided to walk around, hoping he might feel better. At the very least, he wanted to think about something other than the frigid weather.

A noise caught his attention from across the main entrance that sounded like a door latching.

Or locking.

He quickly dismissed it as Duncan and Jana conducting their search. Oswalt sensed they didn't fully trust him, but no definitive sign of Keith showed up during his personal search, and he had legitimately run outside to flag down some help. He suspected the plows were owned by the county, meaning the drivers likely had radio contact with a home base, or perhaps the police.

Feeling certain he had left the door unlocked when he stepped out, Oswalt dismissed his memory as fleeting because of the excitement. He wasn't ready to call himself absentminded just yet, because Keith was still missing, and either foul play was involved, or he and Laura had set them up for an well-planned prank.

But Turner had never shown up, either. The more he thought about it, the more Oswalt began to suspect someone had plans for his group.

And he suddenly didn't like being alone in the mammoth structure by himself.

Walking as far as the stairs, Oswalt stopped, peering toward the kitchen area, not daring to go any further. Jana and Duncan were together, so he dismissed the noise as them aggressively searching every inch of the basement. He immediately doubted his analysis, wondering if the mansion would actually allow noise of any kind to transcend its floors or walls.

He doubted it.

A different sound caught his attention, but this one came from above. More like a moan or cry, it sounded feminine, drawing him toward the staircase. Before he consciously realized it, his hand glided along the finished wooden railing as he dared take a step or two upward.

For some reason, his mind began contemplating how a devious mind might lure him upstairs under false pretenses. If not for people disappearing without reason, Oswalt would ordinarily rush upstairs to render help to whomever needed it. The investment group was a fairly close bunch, despite enjoying successes early in their lives.

He took a few steps upward, hearing a different sort of moan from above, more painful and drawn out.

"No way," he muttered, refusing to take another step forward.

Sensing something almost prodding him from behind, he slowly turned his head, then his upper torso, to look at the stairwell's base.

Standing there, as if on cue, a darkly cloaked figure held a knife in one hand, rubbing his thumb and forefinger along the blade's sides ominously. Oswalt fought the instinct to simply run upstairs, thinking he might have a chance to overpower the man, knowing this was no joke.

It took mere seconds for his mind to realize this man had likely murdered Jana and Duncan downstairs, which explained the closing door he heard. He knew just enough about the problems surrounding the hotel a few years prior to understand the dangerous situation he now found himself entangled within.

Deciding to save face while saving his own life, Oswalt slowly ascended the stairs, walking backwards to keep the figure in his view. For a moment the man stood there, looking upward through a dark mask that revealed no features. It wasn't until he charged upward that Oswalt felt enough urgency to do the same.

If nothing else, he at least wanted even ground on which to defend himself.

He reached the top step first, but the assailant tripped him by clasping his foot. Oswalt stumbled, then rolled several times over along the carpeted floor. His attacker definitely seemed younger and stronger, but Oswalt punched him defensively when he drew closer with the knife.

Looking desperately around for any kind of household item he might use to defend himself, the music agent saw nothing except a vase in one of the corners. He felt somewhat unmanly searching for a weapon, but the attacker did have a knife.

Oswalt reached the vase while the figure was stunned, striking him over the head with it, shattering the possibly rare antique into thousands of shards. The attack failed to do more than momentarily stun the man, leaving Oswalt at a loss for what to do. He had no phone, no one around, and very few places to hide.

Deciding his room might be as safe as any, he darted for it, slamming the door in the attacker's face before locking it. He knew the door provided a temporary safe haven at best, because its flimsy frame could easily be knocked down by an average man.

Knowing this, Oswalt rummaged through his belongings, hoping he brought something useful. He owned several firearms, but left them in Tennessee because they were unnecessary on what he considered a hospitable business trip.

He found nothing useful, but not one sound barged through the door from the other side. Leaving his baggage momentarily, Oswalt stood erect, listening for any sounds. Frozen to the spot, he didn't dare move forward in case the door burst toward him.

The last thing he wanted was a swinging door incapacitating him.

A few minutes passed, feeling more like an hour, as he remained perfectly still, breathing slowly and quietly enough that he barely heard his own exhales.

Oswalt had nearly decided to test the door when a moan originated from the closet within his room. His attention immediately focused on the closed door, wondering what awaited him on the other side.

He snagged a plastic letter opener from the desktop, thinking it was better than no defense whatsoever. Clutching it in his left hand, he slowly reached for the closet door with his right.

"Laura?" he asked cautiously toward the door.

No answer returned.

His hand had nearly reached the knob when the door to his room smashed open with wooden splinters hurling toward him, revealing his assailant once more. This time the man charged him immediately, blocking his attempt to use the letter opener, creating a bloody slit along Oswalt's arm as the knife traveled along his forearm in a flash. Though not deep, the injury proved painful, forcing a cry from the agent.

Without hesitation, the figure slugged him across the face, stunning him enough that the room began spinning. Oswalt could still see well enough to know the man was opening the closet door. Before he was able to put up any resistance, he felt himself being shoved into the room, the door slamming behind him.

Now locked in complete darkness, he tried to regain his senses, but the floor began moving upward, like an elevator. He felt his weight shift until he slammed into a wall, realizing too late the combination of being punched and losing some blood had taken a toll on his ability to function normally.

A sensation of complete helplessness overtook him as the ride turned bumpy, giving him an idea of what miners felt like when they rode rickety winch-driven elevators from the underground to the surface.

Except they had flashlights.

Seconds later, the ride abruptly stopped with a thud that sounded like metal against metal, leaving him to wonder exactly what his fate might be.

*   *   *

McCully didn't particularly like the idea of leaving Jennings and Red behind, but his primary concern steadfastly remained with the people at the mansion.

He trudged through the snow as quickly as his inappropriate winter gear and the elements allowed, finding the journey to the edge of the property difficult. His body tired quickly after repeatedly lifting his knees high enough to cross the snowdrifts, and McCully prayed Brown had passed the truck without disabling it.

Reasonably certain he locked it, McCully figured the only thing Brown might realistically do without breaking a window would be slashing the tires.

A few minutes later he neared the truck, finding his fears unwarranted.

Everything about the truck appeared fine, so he unlocked it, climbed inside, and found the cab equally cold to the outside. As he started the vehicle, he wondered if it possessed the ability to climb the hill. Duncan had done nothing to weight down the back for snowy conditions, because he obviously never expected to be driving in snow.

In his haste, McCully made the mistake of living for the moment, failing to weight down the back as well. He knew the truck could make the trip down the hill, but completely forgot about the notion of a return trip.

"Too late now," he muttered, putting the truck in reverse.

Much to his surprise, a snowplow had passed through, shoving the snow to one side of the road while dropping sand atop the slick surface.

He suddenly felt better about returning to the mansion in one piece as he aligned the truck with the plowed path. It immediately informed him a clear trail wasn't a perfect one as the tires struggled to grip the angled surface, spinning as the truck began traveling sideways toward the hotel's security gate.

"Fuck," he said in a raspy whisper to himself, struggling with the steering wheel and brake pedal to keep from wrecking his colleague's vehicle.

When the tires reached solid snow, they finally gripped, allowing him to begin his ascent toward the hotel, slow as it was destined to be.

He doubted the truck could catch Brown and his horse for two reasons. One, a horse could navigate the easiest path on or off the road. Two, the truck was already several minutes behind, and unable to reach what McCully considered a decent speed.

Looking at the dashboard to ensure the truck was in four-wheel-high, McCully listened to the vehicle struggling to maintain its uphill course. His mind raced to decide an appropriate action when he arrived at the mansion. With so many unknown factors, he knew the first thing he wanted to do was survey the property to see if Brown indeed beat him there.

It took several more minutes of navigating slick roads in virtually complete darkness. Even with snowfall tapering off, the headlights barely penetrated the strange foggy mist that seemed to come from changing air temperatures. McCully knew he would be giving away his destination to Brown if the deputy had chosen a path beside the road.

Cat and mouse games didn't suit him, but he wasn't about to let Brown torment anyone at the mansion in the search for his father.

Another concern passing through his mind was whether or not the deputy might be armed. McCully had no defense against a shotgun, and without warning, his colleagues at the hotel would have no time to find any of the weapons left at the mansion.

"Maybe I'm just blowing this out of proportion," he told himself when the mansion's iron gates finally came into view.

He stopped at the edge of the driveway, immediately noticing something wrong with the vehicles parked near the mansion. It took a moment before he registered that they sat a bit lower than usual, some extremely close to the ground.

Every tire on every vehicle had been slashed. Though he initially figured the deputy had gone insane and disabled the vehicles, he dismissed the notion just as quickly. If Brown had beaten him to the property, there wasn't time enough to do so much damage.

Which meant someone else meant to keep the group members exactly where they were.

McCully parked the truck at an awkward angle, quickly jumping out to discover the whereabouts and conditions of everyone left behind. He suddenly regretted leaving Red and Jennings behind, because both were obviously innocent of any wrongdoing.

Despite the cool breeze swirling inside his eardrums, McCully heard a snort that sounded distinctively like that of a horse. Unable to immediately determine the direction, he ducked behind the truck, hoping Brown hadn't spotted him. He suspected the deputy was just reaching the property, but whether or not Brown would recognize the truck had yet to be determined.

He heard another snort, then heavy footsteps, meaning the horse drew closer, rather than simply standing in one spot.

McCully waited and listened for the moment when he could jump the deputy, not wanting to complicate whatever problems might be happening inside. Feeling his muscles tense, he waited for the moment when the deputy crossed his path, ready to strike like a cobra.

25

"I can't believe he left us here for dead."

Red virtually spat the words after Jennings explained their current situation to him.

"I didn't exactly say he abandoned us," Jennings corrected him. "The deputy took off, so he went after him to protect the others at the mansion. He didn't feel there was time to find both of us before he left."

Taking a moment to think things over, and pace the tiled floor of the lobby, Red didn't like being left behind, especially since there was nothing left to accomplish at the hotel.

"We can get back there through the fields," Jennings offered.

"How long would it take?"

"Maybe fifteen minutes."

Red contemplated the urgency of the situation, trying to think of any stone left unturned before they left the grounds.

"We really didn't turn over those two cars out back, did we?" he thought aloud.

Jennings nodded. They had found the strange note and abandoned their search of the vehicles rather quickly.

"What are you hoping to find?" Jennings inquired.

"Maybe a cell phone with better tower coverage, or another gun. I want to find something useful before we go hiking."

He walked toward the back door with the hunter close behind, thinking something was deeply wrong with their situation. Someone had devised a plan long before his group ever arrived, which targeted them and anyone who made contact with them. Divide and conquer came to mind, but he hoped to turn the tables by making haste in returning to the mansion.

Red shoved the back door open, immediately spotting the two disabled vehicles nearby. Jennings pulled out a flashlight they had found in the security office, turning it on before shining its beam into the sheriff's vehicle.

"What if the deputy killed his father and made up a story about it?" Jennings asked.

"You know him better than we do," Red answered. "What do you think?"

The hunter shrugged.

"Stranger things have happened."

Red examined the back of the Ford, finding several locked strong boxes he assumed contained guns and other police items the common public shouldn't have access to. The locks were embedded within the cases, meaning he needed the keys to open either one.

"Seen any keys for this thing?" he asked Jennings.

"Sure haven't."

Jennings immediately checked the overhead visor, and under the seat, just in case. He then checked the drink holder in the middle just to be certain.

"Nothing."

Red rummaged through the remaining items in the back, discovering the truck had already been ransacked by someone else, based on the loose papers and debris scattered everywhere. He wished time permitted to force the containers open, but getting back to the mansion was his number one priority.

"Anything in the car?" he asked Jennings as the hunter accessed the interior of the car with his flashlight beam.

"No keys in there, and it's locked," he replied.

"Par for the course," Red muttered disgustedly.

Jennings walked around the car to try every door of the four-door sedan, finding them all locked. Because the car had been parked beside the building, the snow drifts around it were considerably lower, since the hotel blocked much of the wind and snow.

Jennings dropped to his knees, shining the flashlight underneath and around the vehicle.

"We don't have time for this," Red stated, assuming the man was looking for discarded keys.

His words apparently went unheard as Jennings fished through the snow, bobbing his beam in front of him as he went. While he continued to search, Red opened his cell phone, seeing no signal bars in the top left corner. He dialed 911, but a scolding series of beeps reached his ear, indicating his call was going nowhere.

Jennings made a strange gleeful sound, smiling cautiously as he returned into view, jingling a set of car keys in one hand.

"Where were those?"

"In a little snowbank a few feet from the car. I saw a hole, so I dug around a little bit."

Jennings removed a glove to gain a better grip on the keys, then unlocked the driver's side door. Red watched as he poked around inside, finding nothing useful.

"What about the glove compartment?" Red asked, wondering if all cops kept spare firearms nearby in case of emergency.

Even if they didn't all carry spare guns, he was glad the retired state trooper did, because Jennings came up with a small revolver.

"Keep it," Red stated, already armed with the deputy's confiscated handgun.

Jennings pocketed the gun, finding a red button inside the glove compartment. He pushed it, allowing a ca-chunk noise to enter their ears when the trunk popped open.

Both men briskly walked to the back of the car, where the trunk lid sat just above its seam, waiting to be lifted fully open.

Red wasn't sure why he felt hesitant about opening it until he saw a few speckles of blood beneath one of the taillights. He groaned inwardly, lifting the trunk to find what he least wanted, but half expected to find.

"Shit," Jennings muttered nervously, initially turning away from the sight.

Despite killing and gutting deer, he seemed squeamish about seeing a deceased human being.

Placed awkwardly on his side, with appendages lying in various directions, the retired state trooper he remembered seeing during their tour had a large bloody wound in his back. His eyes remained open, his mouth partly agape, as though forever frozen in the moment where he was surprised from behind by an attacker.

Jennings recovered, reaching inside the trunk, which prompted Red to grasp his hand.

"You probably don't want to touch the body," he advised.

"I was just going to see if his gun was still there."

"How many do you think we need?"

Jennings shrugged defensively.

Preserving the body seemed trivial compared to the other concerns weighing on Red's mind. He now had confirmation the retired trooper was murdered, meaning Laura's disappearance, and Turner never showing up, were probably planned events.

"We have to get back there," he said without even realizing it.

In response, Jennings gave him a gravely concerned look.

"What's wrong?"

"You're talking about walking into the lion's den," he replied. "What if it's a trap, and every one of you ends up springing it?"

Red considered the man was trying to back out of assisting him, but realized the hunter had no vested interest in their dilemma, and probably had a family awaiting his return. And, if he was right, both of them walking into a trap left no one to seek help if their situation became otherwise hopeless.

"Despite what happened earlier, I don't want to see anything happen to any of you," Jennings said. "We have local authorities in West Baden, and maybe I can find someone at the police station if I walk there."

"How far is it?"

"Farther than the mansion, but I can make it."

Red looked to the wooded area behind him, then to the road leading toward the side gate where McCully had gone to retrieve the truck. God only knew what had become of McCully and the deputy, since someone had likely done harm to the sheriff. If it *was* his son, then every single one of them was in danger.

"How do I get back?"

"I'd suggest you take the road in case your buddy's truck had problems."

Red had new respect for the hunter, because the man seemed wise and levelheaded, even in the face of danger.

Extending his hand, Red waited until Jennings reluctantly shook it like a dead fish. Neither wanted to admit it, but they knew this might be the last time they saw one another, at least under decent circumstances.

"If I get help, I'll be up there lickety-split," Jennings promised.

"Hopefully there won't be a need for the police, other than this poor fellow in the trunk, but I'm not holding my breath."

"Just be careful."

Jennings looked to the gate on the far end of the driveway.

"I can at least walk with you that far."

Red nodded, feeling as though they were two friends destined to part ways for the summer, not knowing if they would meet again. Their dire surroundings quickly brought his mind back to the reality that he might not survive to see Jennings again if he wasn't careful.

Walking to the mansion was half the battle, but getting inside safely might prove far more difficult. In the back of his mind he hoped everyone would be at the front door awaiting his safe return, but a pang in his stomach suggested to expect otherwise.

A few minutes later the two men reached the edge of the brick drive, looking at one another momentarily without words.

"Good luck," Jennings said, offering his hand this time.

"Thanks," Red replied as they shook. "I know you have nothing in this, so I appreciate your help that much more. And I'm sorry we doubted you in the beginning."

Jennings let a smirk slip.

"Well, it's understandable."

A moment of silence passed between them, neither knowing the appropriate words to say before parting.

"I'll see you in a little bit," Jennings finally said. "I know the way there."

"Glad *you* do," Red replied, implying he wasn't so certain about his own sense of direction. "Take care of yourself."

Jennings gave a nod, and the two men walked in opposite directions, each hoping to complete a small objective that might ultimately save lives. Red had no idea why anyone wanted to harm his group, much less murder a retired state trooper, but he intended to find out why. His right hand patted the gun tucked inside his coat as he trudged up the snowy hill.

Taking notice of the plowed road, Red tested the ground, finding it reasonably tolerant of human footprints. The sand kept him from slipping, but the surface felt like sheer ice in some areas. Red chose to maintain his present course, rather than wear himself out by stepping over and around snow mounds beside the road.

He quickly realized the trek would take far longer than a few minutes, but he pressed onward, hoping to find his brother alive and well. He wanted answers, beginning to understand why some locals claimed the hotel was cursed. If only he would have paid more attention to the hotel's history, he might have gained an understanding of the plot unfolding around him.

Realizing it was too late to change the past, he trudged forward, determined to reach the mansion before anyone else came up missing, or got hurt.

26

McCully waited patiently, unable to see anything from his vantage point. If he dared peek over the top of the truck, Brown would spot him. He tried peering under the truck, but snow mounds everywhere prevented him from seeing anything except the color white.

While his position felt uncomfortable, he deemed it necessary. Cold from the snow began soaking his pants, but he remained still, listening for the deputy's movements. Another snort from the horse reached his ears, as well as the clop from its hooves as it stepped onto the concrete driveway.

McCully had been in one fistfight in his life, and it was broken up by a teacher. By nature he was a pacifist, not because of his religion or family beliefs, but mostly because of his public image. After releasing a solo album, and being part of a group effort with his family, he refused to do anything that might embarrass them.

His stand on violence caused him to rethink his strategy. If the deputy was a reasonable man, telling him the truth at the hotel, then he might work with McCully, saving them both painful swelling and bruises.

What seemed a noble thought cost him the advantage in what he termed the worst scenario possible. Before dismounting, Brown surveyed the area, spotting McCully after his horse passed the truck. His eyes widened as he reached for something on the opposite side, forcing McCully into action as he sprang to his feet, grabbing the deputy by his free left foot, flipping him completely over the horse.

Brown landed hard, never grabbing whatever object he reached for, with a bewildered look that McCully had beaten him to the mansion. McCully refused to waste one second against a seasoned peace officer, scurrying around the horse to confront the grounded deputy. He slipped along the ice, but regained his footing as Brown managed to get to one knee before being tackled into a snow pile.

Using McCully's momentum against him, the deputy threw the potential investor over him, but McCully scrambled back quickly to grasp the deputy's arm. He now saw that Brown was reaching for a shotgun, which caused him to wonder why the man needed any weaponry to search for his father.

As he grabbed Brown's arm, the man threw up an elbow, hitting McCully squarely enough in the nose that he saw a white flash as though someone had taken his picture from a foot away. The sharp pain in his nose told him it might be broken, or at least cut open, but he kicked toward Brown, catching the shotgun as the deputy went to raise it.

Without giving his next move much thought, he charged Brown, sending them both falling into a snow drift. Buried in snow, and unable to see through the millions of flakes around and on top of him, McCully grasped in desperation until his hands wrapped themselves around Brown's throat.

He noticed his self-preservation instincts taking over his rational thought, perhaps because his nose hurt so badly. A few seconds later, he realized the shotgun was far enough away that neither could readily grab it, and Brown was beginning to resist less and less.

McCully released the stranglehold before he killed the man, falling back to a seated position in the snow. As much as his breathing seemed to come in heaves from the excitement, and his injury, Brown's sounded worse as the man coughed to regain normal breaths.

"You're the killer, aren't you?" McCully accused the man between chilled inhales that felt like nitrogen gas entering his lungs.

"You're insane," Brown spat in reply. "I don't know what you're hiding, but I'm going to find out."

"I'm not hiding anything. I came up here to keep you from harming my friends."

McCully rubbed the side of his nose, feeling blood where the skin had split open. It continued to throb, and if it wasn't broken, he would be surprised.

"I'm looking for my father," Brown insisted.

"And we're looking for our missing friend. We can either duke it out, or we can walk in there together like civilized human beings."

The look on Brown's face indicated he did not trust McCully, so it was no surprise when he lurched for the gun once again. McCully tried to block this attempt, but slipped momentarily in the snow, allowing the deputy to slug him with the shotgun's stock. Though a glancing blow, it knocked McCully to the ground, allowing Brown to hammer him in the head with the gun's butt, bringing about a calming darkness.

*   *   *

Jana looked at Keith's discarded belongings lying on one of the industrial metal cooking tables. She sensed their search, or at least Keith's trail, grew cold in the very spot where she stood, but saw no sign of any other exits.

"What is this place?" Duncan asked. "The Clue Mansion?"

"I'm waiting to find the secret passageway that takes us to the entertainment room," she replied, playing along.

"And I'm waiting to find out if it was Colonel Mustard with the candlestick who dragged Keith away."

Jana remained silent a moment, touching one of the nearby walls as she examined a small indented area that looked wallpapered. A shelving unit sat almost perfectly inside, holding an array of canned goods. She looked on top of one can, noticing a thin dusty coating that indicated the can had been there for some time.

She wondered if the cleaning lady missed certain areas during her rounds, doubting the cooking area was a high priority because guests wouldn't normally travel to the cellar. Strangely, Jana never met the woman in person. Their phone conversation led to Jana faxing over a list of instructions, along with the contact information to send an invoice for payment.

They had not spoken since their initial conversation, but Jana hadn't seen any issues with the housekeeping upstairs.

"Penny for your thoughts," Duncan said, bringing her back to their plight.

"I'm beginning to think there's something secret about this room that we're not seeing, all joking aside. Maybe Keith was right about the third floor we saw from outside."

"You're the hostess. Do you want to tear this place apart and see what we find?"

Jana wasn't worried about damages, thinking the consequences of losing several important clients would be much more detrimental than replacing walls and fixtures. Her concern stemmed from the time, or lack thereof, left to find the missing guests.

"I don't know," she replied. "Keith went through the second floor and didn't find anything helpful."

"But now he's gone," Duncan retorted. "And we were near the only real door in this place the entire time. That doesn't leave a whole lot of places to hide."

It suddenly occurred to her that leaving Oswalt alone probably wasn't the wisest move on their part. Granted, he said he wasn't going anywhere, but Keith, Judith, and Laura all vanished without a trace.

Or one uttered word.

"We need to check on Oswalt," she said with more urgency than she intended.

Duncan read her meaning, leading the way toward the stairs. He took hold of her hand, more as a protective measure, rather than a display of affection. Jana felt reassured because of his protectiveness, but even more so that he understood the danger she sensed around them.

He let go of her hand after his body crumpled against the door atop the stairs. His attempt to open it failed, so Duncan crashed against the door, discovering it was stuck in place.

"Ouch," he said, rubbing his left shoulder.

"What's the matter?"

"I think someone locked us in here."

They exchanged concerned looks, knowing Oswalt was responsible for some dastardly acts, or became another missing person during their absence.

Duncan turned the knob more carefully this time, pushing against the door with his shoulder, yielding no success. He looked to Jana with a distraught look.

"Oh, well," he said before thrusting his shoulder against the door once, then twice, before it finally burst outward.

Jana noticed a thin cutting board splintered along the floor, indicating someone had rigged it to block the door. It seemed a weak attempt at keeping them downstairs, so she wondered if it was a stall tactic.

Duncan walked with a purpose through the kitchen area, reaching the doorway as Jana shuffled her feet to keep pace. They both found no people, and no sound, when they reached the open downstairs area. Jana stole a glance toward the chair where Oswalt last sat, seeing only the blanket draped over the arms as though thrown there hastily.

"Maybe he stepped outside," Duncan suggested, stepping toward the door.

He hesitated when his hand touched the knob, deciding to look out a nearby window before stepping outside. Jana noticed the deadbolt and lock were both secured, so it seemed unlikely, if not impossible, that Oswalt had locked them unless he had a set of keys.

The deadbolt turned internally by hand, meaning only a key could access it from outside, or it needed to be locked from the inside. Duncan had exhibited good judgment thus far, so Jana joined him at the window to peer outside, rather than stepping outside.

"My truck," Duncan said on the verge of exclamation.

As quickly as relief crossed his face, it passed. Jana wondered why his truck would be back without any of its last three occupants knocking on the door. Apparently similar thoughts ran through Duncan's mind.

"We're getting out of here," Duncan said, his voice barely hiding the trepidation they both felt.

"How?" Jana felt compelled to ask, knowing the only reason they remained behind was a lack of reliable transportation.

Duncan reached inside each of his pockets, looking more desperate by the second.

"I have a second set of keys," he told her after coming up empty. "They're upstairs with my stuff. I'm getting them, and we're using my truck to go get help."

Jana wanted to argue, but decided she wanted to leave. His truck had apparently made the trip down the hill and back, but she hated the idea of them being separated, even momentarily.

"Be careful," she said quickly, returning her gaze to the window as he headed for the stairs, walking briskly, barely able to maintain his composure.

Thinking she saw a shadow outside, Jana started to follow Duncan's path upstairs, but decided to wait for him instead. Until someone knocked on the door, or attempted to break their way inside, she could simply hope for the best.

A minute or so passed with no activity, and not even the slightest of noises, worrying her. She looked to the door, staring intently at the knob a moment, then hesitantly began ascending the stairway to find Duncan. Every breath came with a sense of dread attached to it, but Jana fought to maintain her composure, wondering deep down if she was the sole survivor of someone's murderous plan.

She recalled how vague Clouse had been concerning the hotel's past, but she knew enough, even though the television news and newspapers provided stories with sketchy details. Murders had occurred at the hotel, and not the poisoned sipping tea kind, either. Bloodshed and gore were symbolic of the grizzly murders at the West Baden Springs Hotel several years prior, and only now did she begin to wonder who might have enough inside information to orchestrate such a fiendish scheme.

"Dan?" she called, waiting several seconds for an answer that never came.

A shiver ran from head to toe as she grasped the railing for support, her hand trembling from fear of the unknown. Taking a deep breath, she took another step forward, beginning to wonder what sights awaited her on the second level.

27

McCully somehow knew he had sunken into a strange level of unconsciousness that transported him once again to a different time, but not a different place.

He couldn't tell the year, because the mansion appeared very much the same. Now able to stand up, he found no snow around him. In fact, the climate looked like an early morning in the spring or fall because fog banks lingered in the nearby hilly fields. Several partly turned leaves were scattered across the yard, indicating it was probably late fall.

Most of the grass appeared a healthy green, covered lightly in moisture as though a giant wet hand grazed the tops of the stout blades. No cars cluttered the driveway to his right, and for a moment it seemed he stood completely alone. The crunch of leaves closer to the mansion drew his attention to two men standing beside one of the twelve stone carvings.

One of the men had his back completely turned to McCully, but the other gentleman seemed older, almost decrepit, the native Tennessean thought. Based on their attire, he guessed this conversation somewhat recent, certainly within the past decade.

Clothing from his childhood certainly had a different look, and he readily recognized such outfits as those he hated from his school photographs. Their clothes looked nowhere near that dated, and McCully thought they looked fairly expensive, like designer brands.

"I take it you've called me here for a reason," the man with his back to McCully stated.

"I've called you here because I'm dying, and I have a need for a man of your talents before my time comes."

"You know I don't come cheap, but I suppose that doesn't much matter to you."

The older man let a grin emerge from behind the wrinkles in his face. McCully felt certain this was a sinister grin, which seemed out of place based on the conversation so far.

"I've saved enough back that I can still adequately cover your fee."

Who was this old man? He spoke softly, eloquently, like a scholar.

A thought suddenly occurred to McCully about who owned the mansion, and the hotel, at one time. He felt reasonably certain he was staring at Doctor Martin Smith, but he couldn't guarantee it unless they spoke one another's names.

"I've taken measures to *prolong* my life, if you will. But I'm not certain how my master plan will unfold."

"Considering the nosedive you almost took off your hotel, I'd say you're lucky to be having this conversation."

Nosedive? McCully wondered. He remembered something about Smith allegedly being murdered when he was thrown from the hotel's roof. It also seemed his death was later disputed by several news agencies. Some of the news made national headlines, and McCully had made a point to do some online research before leaving Tennessee.

"Again, that was part of my plan," the old man said easily. "I'm now able to move about undetected without fear of interference from Clouse or his friends."

McCully didn't recognize the voice of the man conspiring with the older man, but he had some notions about where the conversation was headed. If this man was the one behind all of the disappearances and murders it made sense, but he couldn't see the man's face or recognize the voice. His vision had taken the liberty of planting him in one spot for the duration once he drew this close to the men.

"Move about?" the man questioned. "You're the richest man in the state. No one's going to touch you unless you allow them to."

Again, the old man let a thin smile slip, but this time it bore a look of understanding toward the man's ignorance.

"If my plan works as I hope, I will have no need for your services, but if I should fail, and Clouse or his comrades kill me, I will need you to bring me back."

The man shook his head from one side to the other several times, not comprehending what the doctor had told him. McCully wondered if the mystery man was also a doctor, or possibly a paramedic, based on the older man's words.

"You see, my good man, what I plan on doing is not moral, nor is it legal. And I have it on good authority that you are a man who gets things done for people, no matter what."

"Obviously you know who I am, and what I do, so I wonder if I'm allowed to ask a few questions before you get to the meat of the conversation."

"Feel free."

"Why would you go after Clouse? I thought he was like a son to you."

"Let's just say he took something very precious from me. What he took left a terrible void in my heart that can never be replaced. I had intended to leave him out of my terrible future doings, but what he did cannot be forgiven."

The man nodded in understanding, though McCully still felt confused about what Clouse had done to the man. From what Jana and the media told, he was a pretty upstanding guy.

"Very well then, Doc. I'm not a medical expert, but I have a suspicion you're going to have a hard time enacting revenge against Clouse in your condition. Is that part of why I'm here?"

"Not at all. The next time you see me, my good man, I'll appear younger by twenty years or more, and be completely healthy."

McCully couldn't see the man's expression, but his body language told enough, because he stiffened in surprise.

"You're shittin' me, right?"

"Not at all. The one thing money can't buy is life, but I've found a way to cheat death for as long as I choose. And when I'm finished with Mr. Clouse, I'll have everything I want."

"So if I'm not here to help you against *him*, what exactly am I here for?"

Now the man sounded a bit uncertain, as though he thought the elderly man might make him the next victim in some kind of bizarre plot.

"As I've stated, you are here in case I fail. In case I need to be resurrected to finish my work."

An uncomfortable silence filled the air momentarily. McCully understood the mystery man's position, because he felt utterly confused as well.

"You see, with the same forces that will make me younger the next time I see you, I can be brought back from the dead."

The man remained silent a few more seconds before speaking again.

"I take it you aren't talking about Catholic sanctioned practices here."

"Not quite," the older man answered, holding up his forefinger. "But I think you have an idea about what I speak of."

"I do, but I'm not sure I buy into black magic or witchcraft."

"You needn't buy into it. When we meet again, you'll have your proof."

"And if you're right, what's to keep me from using this miracle cure for myself?"

"A general lack of knowledge on the subject, and the vast amount of money I plan to pay for your services."

Now the man crossed his arms, intently listening. McCully sensed the man was certainly no fool, and his elder had obviously planned this meeting quite thoroughly. The man he believed was Smith seemed to have the answer for any and every question.

"In the unfortunate event of my death, I need you to carry out a certain ritual that will, in theory, bring me back to this world."

McCully realized if this was true, money and the right thugs certainly could buy eternal life. But at what price? In lore, vampires murdered others to maintain their livelihood, so he wondered if sacrifices were necessary to keep Smith young, healthy, and alive.

"See these carvings?" the old man asked, pointing to one of the biblical tales carved in the mansion's stone. "There are twelve in all, and they weren't put here for their symbolism or beauty. They are part of a ritual that must be carried out."

"What ritual?"

"First, should I die, my body must be buried at the hotel grounds for no less than twenty-four hours. Then, it should be transported to this very building with some of the soil from the hotel accompanying it. You see, these twelve pieces of art have numbers, which are significant dates in the history of my hotel down the road."

"You're going a little fast, Doc. Isn't there some elder scroll or something I'm supposed to follow?"

"You would be wise to hold your tongue, young man. Mocking me is not something I pay good money for."

The mystery man cleared his throat uncomfortably.

"No disrespect, Doc, but this doesn't sound like my kind of work."

"Your 'kind of work'?" the reply came with a raised eyebrow. "I think theft, deceit, and murder are right up your alley. Beyond that, the ritual is putting everything into place and pushing a button. I've arranged absolutely everything to keep this simple and foolproof."

A few seconds of silence passed.

"You see," the older man said, "if I die, I don't want to leave my *Easter Sunday* to chance. There is half a million dollars for you right now, to keep you interested in my affairs, and another five-million, if and when the time comes for you to do the deed. You collect a dozen specific people, you hook them up to the contraption I have inside this building, and you walk away. It's not even murder, really. It's more of an assisted suicide, if that eases your conscience. Of course, you'd have to stay in the area and create a cover identity for yourself. Think of it as being the spider spinning the perfect web with which to lure your prey."

The man simply rubbed the back of his neck in thought momentarily.

"Five-million is enough for most men to retire on for the rest of their lives," the old man prodded. "Even a man of your talent and tastes could surely make that last several years."

"I don't suppose it would count if I killed you and brought you back?" the man said, making bad humor that his companion simply scoffed at.

"Your pay would be substantially less, my boy. Now, would you care to have a look inside at the device, or is this where we part ways and never speak of this conversation to anyone again?"

McCully already knew the forthcoming answer, wishing he were back in real time to do something about the tragic events he now understood something about.

"After you," the man said, outstretching his arm toward the front door.

*   *   *

Jana debated whether or not she really wanted to search for Duncan alone on the second floor. Something told her she was already too late if he had been abducted, or worse, so she stood midway up the stairwell for a moment.

"Dan?" she called again, trying not to sound meek or mild in case she found him safe and sound.

She hated appearing weak in front of men, but this time Jana had legitimate reasons to be worried. Her entire life, beginning with her father, she had been subliminally taught that women were inferior. It wasn't until her parents divorced that her mother finally had some talks with her. Going to college for several years put Jana in touch with roommates who were anything but shy, helping her blossom into the independent woman she always wanted to be.

The same drive that brought her success in business now prodded her to take another step upward, then another. She reached the top step a moment later, seeing no evidence of Duncan, or anyone else.

Six rooms to either side of her all had their doors closed. One looked damaged around one side of its frame, indicating it had been kicked inward. What, if anything, lurked behind each of them required her to open them. It occurred to her that Duncan had no reason to shut his door if he simply planned on grabbing keys and a warm coat. She examined the tags on each door, frantically trying to recall which room she assigned him to.

When she found it, Jana walked briskly to the door, then listened, trying to decipher if there was any activity inside. She heard nothing, so she slowly opened the door, hoping perhaps to find Duncan packing a suitcase, or desperately searching for his keys.

It emitted a long, almost painful creak as it swung inward, revealing a strange sight to Jana, barely visible in the low lighting. She stepped inside, putting a hand to her mouth, suppressing a gasp.

Only the desk lamp illuminated the room, throwing strange shadows everywhere. What appeared to be a long, shiny serpent taking up half of the room began to take shape when she dared draw closer.

A crinkling noise entered her ears as the serpentine form jiggled back and forth, sounding somewhat like a cat playing inside a plastic bag. She then heard grunting, like someone struggling to finish a task.

Or break free.

"Oh my God," she said under her breath, seeing the true form before her for the first time.

A person she assumed had to be Duncan appeared trapped inside some sort of long, clear plastic trap that not only ensnared him, but seemed to be dragging him toward the opposite side of the room. The only details she found were the shimmering black from beneath the clear coating that could only be Duncan's motorcycle jacket. She stepped closer, finding his blond hair at the end of the trap, though he seemed completely unaware of her presence.

"Dan!" she shouted to gain his attention. "I'm here."

Only muffled cries returned, so she knew the trap had fiercely taken hold of him.

She reached forward, touching the plastic like someone might test a hot stove, fearing it might have some sort of stickiness or other device to pull her in as well. Getting herself trapped did neither of them any good.

On the surface, the plastic felt somewhat like a thick painter's tarp, but some sort of substance lurked just beneath the surface, likely acting as some sort of flytrap to keep Duncan from breaking free. It felt about as thick as bubble wrap used to package shipping items, but legitimately solid all the way through.

Duncan grunted and groaned a few more times, then sort of whimpered, as though giving up hope.

When the device moved several feet away from her, toward the closet, she pounced on the end just below Duncan's feet, preventing it from moving further. Peering around the room, Jana's eyes came to rest at the desk, spying some scissors, pens, and a letter opener jutting from a desk organizer.

She leapt from atop the trap to snatch the scissors, allowing the mysterious force from within the closet to reel in the plastic like a fish. Duncan thumped along the floor several times, beginning to fight once more to free himself.

Having no idea whether the man consciously knew she was helping him or not, she patted the plastic until she found his feet, immediately diving into the plastic with the scissors. The edges seemed too worn to have much effect on the trap, but some of it split open, revealing a sticky inner liner.

Jana shrieked inadvertently when her fingers rubbed against the substance, immediately believing she was another fly stuck in the web. She pulled free, but decided the scissors put her in harm's way. Something larger, like a garden tool, felt more appropriate for such a task. Time, however, didn't allow for any trips outside to explore the garage.

"Damn it," she said to herself, searching for a way to stop the trap from completely drawing Duncan into its clutches.

She knew if he disappeared into the closet, he would certainly be lost to the inner sanctum of the house none of the guests had found. Keith had been right, and if someone had believed in him sooner, none of them would be in such grave danger.

Duncan struggled against the covering as she sat atop a non-sticky portion of the snare, trying to slow it down. Jana wondered how the man could breathe at all, because the plastic seemed to wrap itself tightly against his body, like a latex glove over a hand.

Though she felt a tug from beneath her, the tarp failed to move any closer to the closet. Now engaged in a losing battle, Jana needed to decide whether to seek a way to cut Duncan free, or simply keep him from being swallowed by the closet, and ultimately, the mansion itself.

Another problem presented itself when the room's main door creaked once again, revealing a shadowy figure standing in the threshold. The low lighting prevented Jana from identifying the person, but the way in which he stood silently made her suspect he wasn't someone friendly.

Making the situation more ominous, it appeared his right hand clutched a shotgun.

After giving him a few seconds to speak, Jana wondered if he was stunned, taking in this strange sight, rather than admiring an evil plan coming together.

"Either tell me who you are, and what you want, or get over here and help me," she demanded, wanting answers.

A few silent seconds passed.

"What the fuck is that?" a male voice with just a hint of a drawl asked.

"I don't know, but it's trying to drag my friend into the closet."

Since the man inquired about the device restraining Duncan, Jana assumed he was friendly, or at least not the cause of her problems.

"I need something to cut him out of this. Can you get a kitchen knife, or something larger, if you can find it?"

Instead of complying or answering, the man stepped forward, finally kneeling down beside the synthetic material. He touched it, giving Jana an opportunity to examine him a bit more closely. He set the gun to his side, which set some of her fears at ease.

In essence, he didn't look much different than the guests from the investment group, wearing cowboy boots and a thick duster. He appeared rugged, but not unkept or unclean. She guessed he might be a local to the West Baden area, but didn't recognize him. A strange smell she couldn't place crossed her nostrils, then it came to her.

He smelled a little bit like the inside of a barn, which she recalled from visits to her uncle's farm as a child.

His curious blue eyes surveyed the trap, then looked to Jana with a degree of uncertainty, as though wondering how far his trust extended.

Looking to his right, the stranger seemed to examine the device restraining the great-grandson of a prominent businessman.

"Where does it lead?" he asked with a bit more emotion than before.

"I don't know," Jana said. "Into that closet, and probably into some secret room. We don't have time to wait, or it'll take him."

Duncan grunted once more, disrupting the break in their conversation. They both had unanswered questions lingering between them, but Jana felt certain Duncan couldn't last much longer in a suffocating elongated bag.

However the device was constructed, it was meant to conduct its business quickly, and without interruption. Perhaps the house itself was haunted, or evil, but she couldn't let it obtain Duncan without a fight. She took the scissors up, then carefully felt his face through the plastic, slitting holes in the substance so he could breathe.

An immediate sigh of relief came from Duncan's mouth as he took in fresh air. Though he seemed unable to formulate words, the entire ordeal appeared to convince the new stranger that something unusual had taken hold of the guests.

"I'll see what I can find downstairs," the stranger finally said of Jana's request for a larger tool with which to cut the plastic, taking up the shotgun. "I've only got two shells for this, and they probably wouldn't want me tearing holes in their new floor."

"At this point, I don't care," Jana replied.

"Give me a minute. I'll find you a big knife, or we'll use this if we have to," he said, holding up the shotgun.

"There are two kitchen areas," she informed him. "The bigger one is actually in the cellar."

"Okay," he said with a nod.

With that, he headed out the door, his footsteps growing less audible as he headed for the stairs.

Jana returned to a seated position on the plastic, feeling it strain as it was tugged with their combined weight upon it. She worried about someone else coming up the stairs, still not completely convinced the new stranger was a friend, rather than a foe.

28

Red continued to walk along the road toward the hotel, wondering how much further he had left to travel. Going downhill in the truck seemed so much faster, especially when he wondered if his life might be taken at any moment.

He worried about Keith and the others, wishing there were some way to simply call and talk to them. The freakish storm had knocked out their cellular phones, and without the benefit of land lines at the mansion or hotel, they were basically stranded. Sheer luck had left power intact at both places, and with the snowfall decreasing, he hoped help might arrive sooner than the next morning.

Looking at his watch, he found it was just past ten o'clock. Though a few hours removed from the witching hour, but he felt exhausted enough to crawl into bed and sleep until noon the next day.

If only the strange events wouldn't plague his mind while he rested.

Red trudged uphill, hoping Jennings had better luck in town. He didn't recall where the town or county police stations were located, but he knew they had to be in the heart of the town, likely in French Lick. If that was so, Jennings had nearly a mile to walk, even after he reached the highway.

Enough snow covered the ground that it looked like early dawn all around him. Even with the cloud cover the night revealed most everything to him, like a movie shot with a bad filter that didn't quite give it a nighttime effect. He saw barren trees, open fields, and the remains of broken fences on both sides of the road.

Now that he trusted Jennings, Red needed to reevaluate his trust within the investment group. He began wondering if someone had brought them to Indiana for malicious reasons as a whole, or if they had fallen prey to a local maniac. Duncan was the person bent on bringing them to see the hotel, but Red saw no reason how the man would benefit from injuring or killing others.

Duncan needed funding from the group if he wanted the hotel. Of course, being a sole survivor and suing the hotel's current owner might bring about wealth enough to attain the property in a settlement.

Red shook off the negative notion, dismissing Duncan as a real suspect. Snow began chilling the lower parts of his legs, where he had no protection from the elements. Years of working ranches with Keith, and driving big rigs, had taken a toll on his knees. They felt more brittle and achy than usual, reminding him why he enjoyed living south of Kentucky.

He distracted himself again by thinking of the people in his group, and his opinions of them.

There was McCully, the young singer who had come from an already famous family. Despite moderate success, the man remained modest, even introverted some of the time. Red recalled seeing a documentary covering the history of bluegrass music where one already successful female singer made a bold statement.

Red grumbled the words, or at least a close rendition, to himself in recollection.

"Everyone who knew anything about bluegrass wanted to be a McCully."

Why Dave McCully had avoided settling down like everyone else in his family eluded Red, but he supposed the man had his reasons. He wasn't one to sleep around with groupies, or throw his money around in public, but something about him wasn't completely normal either.

His thoughts took a right turn, thinking about Oswalt. The music agent wasn't at all shy, and he had been married and divorced several times, as though he just wanted the title of husband for conversation's sake. When there was business to be conducted, he was one of the shrewdest men Red had ever met, but he changed faster than Superman when the time to celebrate arrived.

Oswalt occasionally got slobbering drunk, but always found his way home, or to some woman's apartment for the night. It amazed Red the man's wallet had never been stolen during one of his rendezvous.

Of course he trusted Keith. Not only was the man his older brother, and the one who helped raise him more than his parents at times, but he had no incentive to plan murder or abduction. Above all else, Keith possessed morals and a fear of God that kept him in place before he ever let his emotions lead him into trouble.

Realizing his legs were drenched below the knees, Red began to slow from the uphill journey, feeling sluggish and cold. He needed warmth, and soon, or the snow might swallow him whole. Though it wasn't extremely cold or windy at the moment, the combination of the long hike and the cold wetness creeping up his body gave him concern.

Think of the names, he chastised himself, trying to keep his mind off his troubles. Laura and Turner were missing, which gave them opportunity without being suspected or seen. No, no, he thought.

Jana? He hardly pictured her able to subdue Turner, and she hadn't left the mansion, meaning she could not have killed the retired trooper.

Judith's alibi seemed very similar. Though sometimes a cold fish, Judith was above any illegal activity. She came from nothing, earning everything she had in life on her own terms, none of which meant stepping on other people or taking shortcuts.

Red's thoughts came screeching to a halt when headlights appeared ahead of him, over the hill. They came his way, bobbing up and down, and at a greater speed than he suspected any sane person might drive.

He wondered if joyriding teenagers might be sloshing through the snow and ice recklessly, not daring to stand in the road to flag the driver down. Standing at the side instead, he waited until the car, a little Buick of some sort, came into view before throwing his hands into the air. He crossed his arms back and forth like a plane handler with glow sticks along an airport runway, signaling for help, hoping the driver might be sympathetic.

As though the driver never saw him, the car continued to speed ahead, flying over one short bump, changing its direction just enough that Red felt certain it was going to clip him. He dove to the side of the road as the car continued onward without so much as a tap on the brakes.

Red landed in the ditch, absolutely soaking himself to the core as he looked back. He wondered if the driver even noticed that he almost struck a man, not daring to stop for fear of Red's wrath. Perhaps the driver was drunk, never even seeing the pedestrian at the road's edge.

At this point Red didn't care. He felt certain if the driver had stopped, he still might have been inclined to plant a kiss on him or her for helping him. Any anger would have been tossed aside like dirty water out the back door on a farm.

For a moment, Red remained on all fours, water dripping from his chin, and off his jacket. Every inch of both legs now felt cold and wet as a shiver shot through the length of his body.

He propped himself up to a kneeling position, realizing he now had little time to reach the mansion, or find shelter, before his body completely failed him. Regaining his feet, he plodded up the hill, wishing McCully would return for him, or Jennings might find him any moment with help from the town. He felt both scenarios were unrealistic, which drove him forward, desperate to check on his brother with the deadly new circumstances surrounding the group.

*   *   *

Arlan Brown couldn't believe the events unfolding before his eyes. Had he been drunk beyond belief, or under the influence of some illegal substance, everything might have looked more plausible.

He found himself in the mansion's kitchen, looking for a long knife of some sort, when he really just wanted answers about his father. Pulling out several drawers, he found nothing useful, wondering if the men he found at the hotel were being truthful.

Seeing someone trapped in what he considered an industrial, lengthy garbage bag upstairs unnerved him, but he now believed something very wrong had occurred at the hotel, and this property. And his father was somehow trapped by it as well.

Finding a knife set at the counter's far end, Brown discovered only the smaller knives remained fastened to their holder. He wondered if some conspiracy had enveloped within the mansion, and if his father had found himself in the wrong place at the wrong time.

He took the largest knife possible from the set, thinking scissors were probably a better alternative. Refusing to give up, he opened several more drawers, pawing through them for anything useful. He discovered everything from cheese graters to rolling pins, but nothing with a better, sharper blade.

"Shit," he mumbled as a slight creaking noise entered his ears from behind him.

His shotgun was a few feet from him, but within reach as he spun around, finding the cellar door Jana had mentioned slightly ajar. He debated how much time he realistically had to save the man wrapped inside the plastic before he was pulled inside the closet, or suffocated from the sticky inner liner.

He decided a trip downstairs couldn't take long, so he scooped up the gun, using it to prop open the door long enough for him to slide past. A quick descent of the stairs led him directly to the very industrial kitchen, which obviously served as the heart and soul of any cooking activities.

Brown recognized the room as a kitchen, but barely. It appeared as though a tornado had swept through the room, recklessly reorganizing everything in its path. Pots, pans, and utensils were strewn across the counter tops and floors, immediately causing him to regret the trek downstairs.

When he turned to leave, the ding of an elevator door stopped him cold. Brown slowly turned, wondering where in the room an elevator might be. He dared not waste valuable time, but he wanted to see if the elevator doors were readily visible before heading back.

He cautiously moved from his safe spot toward the area where the ding originated, cranking his neck forward to see around a small corner to his left. After seeing the bizarre scene upstairs, Brown had no desire to be wrapped in plastic or abducted in some other way. Of course he had his trusty shotgun with him, so he felt a bit more at ease.

A shotgun shell possessed the ability to shred almost any object into Swiss cheese at close range. Brown held it in a ready position, hearing a ding, followed by the sound of an elevator door opening.

Unfortunately, Brown had no visual to go with the sound because a strange pantry filled with canned goods stood before a papered wall. Standing momentarily in confusion, he allowed the gun to complacently fall limp in his right hand. He looked at the covering behind the woven metal rack, observing too late that the covering was little more than cardboard doctored up with wallpaper to hide the truth.

Before Brown could contemplate his next move, the false partition and everything in front of it tumbled toward him, knocking him to the ground. He found himself sprawled out and pinned beneath the metal rack with heavy cans of food falling across his body. Several cans injured him, but one in particular struck the side of his head with more than a glancing blow.

The deputy had no time to nurse his wounds because a dark figure gracefully climbed through the tangled mess with dexterity, carrying a large knife. Brown understood now why there had been no large knives around, scanning the area with his eyes for his shotgun while his right hand reached out like an antenna.

He felt only debris with his hand, quickly diverting his attention to the man who seemed intent on attacking him. Both of the deputy's hands thrust upward to stop the knife from plunging into his heart. Still pinned by the shelving, which had become awkwardly propped into the elevator area, Brown had only his arms with which to defend himself.

His assailant rammed the back of his skull into the concrete floor, stunning him momentarily, but not enough to disable him. Brown launched a fist into the figure's face, kicking fiercely with his legs to free himself from the entanglement of shelving and cans.

Again the assailant thrust downward with the knife, but Brown brushed the attack aside with a sweep of his arms. He glanced once more, unable to see his shotgun, which had slid somewhere under the preparation tables. Ensured he had a few seconds without the threat of more assaults, he threw the shelving unit up enough to slide his legs free.

He stood up, finding himself staring into the vacant hood of whom he assumed was the newest killer in a line of people obsessed with the West Baden Springs Hotel. Though Brown didn't know all of the facts about the earlier murders, he knew the motivation stemmed as far back as the 1930s when the Jesuits took possession of the place.

Police detectives from Bloomington, along with the state police, headed the earlier investigations, virtually shutting his father's county police force out entirely. He recalled his father griping about how uncooperative the other agencies were in teaming with him, since he was a new sheriff.

Like his fellow county officers, Brown was shut out of the investigation as well, particularly after one of their own officers was butchered.

Considering he didn't have a weapon in-hand, Brown found himself at a slight disadvantage, but at least he had a vertical base, and an ample opportunity to defend himself. He plucked a rolling pin from the table beside him, somewhat surprised it didn't roll off to strike him in the head like everything else.

Boring a stare into the masked assailant, he flinched forward, faking an attack.

Falling for it, the figure took a half step back, allowing Brown to charge him and swing the rolling pin toward his head. The figure ducked, taking the blow in the shoulder blade instead, but Brown swung again, finding his arm slashed by the knife before the rolling pin left a mark. Instead, it dropped to the ground, rolling away from both combatants.

The wound stung, dripping blood immediately, but Brown clasped the man's knife hand with both of his, swinging the assailant into the wall. He felt relatively certain the cut hit a blood vessel of some sort, but he had no time to assess the wound.

Brown kneed the figure in the groin, trying to gain advantage any way he could. The attack proved effective, hunching the man forward with an audible groan. Brown picked up the rolling pin once more, striking the man in the side of the head with a weakened blow. His injured arm writhed with pain, as though a thousand wasps had stung him at once. His grip on the pin had been weak, indicating his muscles were also injured during the attack.

Basically, his right arm had become useless to him. He crossed the figure's face with a left hook, trying to buy some time. Though he shot a gun right-handed, Brown was in fact a southpaw. As the figure slumped against the wall, apparently nearing unconsciousness, Brown scurried toward the elevator in search of his shotgun.

He reached the debris field in front of the elevator, dropping to his knees to look for his shotgun, which he discovered closer to the other side of the table. With his injured hand, the weapon was certainly out of reach, because he now had trouble grasping objects. The knife had apparently done nerve or tendon damage as well.

Hearing a noise behind him, Brown kicked outward like a mule with one leg, catching the assailant squarely in the abdomen. He then made his way around the table, since it was too low for him to roll beneath. Quickly locating the shotgun, Brown reached with his good hand to pluck it from the cold ground when the figure leapt onto the narrow side of the table, sliding along it like some barroom brawl scene from a movie.

It all happened so fast that Brown couldn't avoid being tackled to the ground. He never grasped his weapon, so the deputy was again forced to use only his hands, one of which was virtually disabled.

He immediately went for the figure's throat, trying to find it beneath the folds of black cloth. His plan immediately went south as the figure produced his knife once again, aiming it toward Brown's chest. Blocking the attempt with both hands, Brown left himself exposed in other areas, and this time it was the attacker who kneed him in the groin.

Pain shot through his crotch, but he continued to block the other attack until he thrust himself away from the figure.

Brown dashed toward his shotgun before standing up completely, looking like a monkey on all fours as he struggled to maintain his balance. He reached the gun, clasped it with both hands, then turned to confront the figure before accomplishing a ready position.

When he turned, he found his assailant already beside him, clasping the shotgun with both hands as well. Brown's injured arm provided about as much strength as a small child might muster, so when the figure thrust the cold metal into his nose, there was virtually no resistence. It busted his nose open, at the bridge, allowing blood to readily cascade down his face.

Several droplets landed in his eyes, blinding him long enough for the figure to ram the shotgun into his nose again, doubling the pain as his eyesight went from a blinding white to a strange black circles like solar eclipses. His fingers lost their grip on the weapon, allowing the figure to steal it away. When Brown recovered enough to look up again, the shotgun's stock had already taken a path leading directly toward the back of his head.

Unimaginable pain shot through his skull within a fraction of a second, then everything went black.

29

McCully found himself napping in a snowbank near the mansion's front wall where Brown had apparently left him. His head ached, but he managed to regain his footing, bracing an arm against the stone wall for support.

He had yet to digest the wealth of information presented to him in the vision, but now understood why his colleagues were so important. They were the fuel for some sort of machine meant to bring a now dead man back to life.

Based on his interpretation of the vision, McCully assumed his hypothesis was correct, and that was why he saw *that* particular set of events during his unconscious state.

Stumbling along toward the front door, he felt certain any passers by would deem him drunk off his ass as he stiff-armed the wall. He felt cold all over, but considered himself lucky Brown didn't bind him, or bury him in the snow. Perhaps the deputy wasn't blinded by rage, or a deranged killer, but McCully now wondered if the man might be a victim.

His feet felt numb, likely a combination of awkward positioning and snow packed around them like ice packs. They began painfully tingling, causing McCully to wish for all of the feeling back, sooner than later.

Shaking each leg as he supported himself against the front door's threshold, he hesitated a moment before touching the door-knob. Entering through the front door might be obvious and just plain stupid if things weren't safe inside.

He had no idea what had transpired in his absence, so he decided to look around the building before walking inside. His hand wrapped around the doorknob, though only to test it, finding it locked. Grunting to himself, he cautiously walked around the corner, finding much more feeling returning to his extremities.

Though the mansion's side had only a few windows, McCully found enough light outside emanating from the snow to guide him. As he rounded the corner, he spied a glass shard of some sort in the snow, immediately wondering how it sat atop a foot of the fluffy substance. He crouched down, plucking it carefully between his thumb and forefinger, examining it closely without cutting himself.

Green in color, it appeared to be about an inch long, and straight, letting him know it wasn't from a discarded bottle. It felt smooth, not like the ruffled glass used in making stained glass. McCully stared at it momentarily, then ran his thumb across the surface, planning to toss it aside afterward.

He missed the opportunity to interact further with the shard when his mind was transported to another time and place once again.

This time he found himself centered in the sunken garden of the West Baden Springs Hotel. It occurred to him that many of the images associated with negativity stemmed from the grounds, but he supposed the place did have a vast amount of history to it.

Looking around, he saw nothing of interest, and only a few people milling through the summertime blossoms surrounding the hotel. He saw a robed figure near the hotel, immediately indicating the time frame. Several feet to one side, a priest worked at planting several colorful plants within the garden, surprising him a bit, since the Jesuits upheld a life of poverty.

Perhaps everyone was entitled to add some beauty to his life, McCully decided, taking a few steps forward.

On the hill, the cemetery was immediately visible, but far fewer tombstones lined the lush, green grass surrounding them.

He saw a boy playing on the hill, near the edge of the tree line. Sensing the boy was the reason for him being there, McCully walked toward the hill as the boy began walking further from the garden, toward the edge of the grounds. Apparently back in the day, the hotel had no fences or enforced boundaries to speak of. Still, the boy didn't seem like a townie just there to play.

Something told McCully he was a permanent fixture around the hotel grounds, though he had no idea why a boy might live within a seminary filled with priests and brothers in training. The boy appeared carefree, jumping, skipping, and picking flowers near the road. The road McCully had nearly killed himself on just an hour or so prior looked like little more than a worn horse trail.

Blacktop and pavement were a wave of future during the early years of the Jesuit stay at West Baden. Strangely, McCully noticed sounds were scarce everywhere around him. Even the boy didn't make a single utterance. No singing, no talking to himself, and certainly no talking to an imaginary friend.

He didn't even whistle.

A car crept up the road from what he knew as Highway 56, likely a brand new car in the day, adorned with polished chrome, shined black tires, and a beautiful black paint job. By no means a car expert, McCully knew the car was a Cadillac, but he questioned the year. He thought 1937 sounded like a fair guess, partly because he knew the Jesuits inhabited the hotel during that decade.

He noticed a single person in the driver's seat without companionship.

McCully never quite got over seeing historical events in real time. It felt like standing on the set of a Hollywood film, but he knew better.

As the car drew to little more than a crawl, he began wondering if the man driving the car wanted directions. Back then, kids were regarded as adults somewhat early in life, but this boy was still very young. It occurred to him that perhaps the man had more evil intentions for the boy, so he strolled that way.

He hated being a passive participant in the visions, especially when things went wrong, but as the man drew his car to a stop, McCully felt dread fill his veins when the man stepped out.

"Williams," he said to himself as the man stiffly straightened his suit jacket with a tug on the front flaps.

From what little bit McCully had seen of the man, loathing didn't quite cover the span of emotions he felt toward the murderous son-of-a-bitch. He had witnessed the man's power and influence when Andrew Duncan last met him at the train station. Now he was by himself, apparently showing off his riches in the valley.

McCully felt somewhat surprised the man remained in the area, but perhaps he felt safer there, and maybe people didn't know about his fiendish ways.

Or perhaps they did, and they simply lived in fear of him.

Either way, the boy didn't seem phased by his arrival. An odd moment of silence passed before Williams addressed the boy, apparently recognizing him from somewhere.

"Do you live here, boy?" he inquired.

The boy nodded, saying nothing aloud.

"Aren't you the boy the papers talked about? The one the brothers adopted from the streets?"

Again the boy nodded, but this time his discomfort began to show. McCully assumed the boy was homeless by Williams' meaning, taken in by the priests.

He stepped forward defensively, remembering he couldn't do a thing, even if he wanted to.

"I need someone to show me a couple places around town," Williams said. "There's an ice-cream cone in it for you if you want to be my guide. Double scoop."

"Liar," McCully said the unheard words in a growl.

As though sensing the same thing, the boy slowly shook his head, beginning to back away.

McCully wondered if Williams was some sort of deranged child molester. Such things were unheard of in the day, not because they didn't happen, but because they weren't publicized. Fetishes were bizarre occurrences swept under the carpet by families and the media.

A lightbulb switched on in the recesses of his mind, reminding him that Williams had discovered some sort of fountain of youth. The very reason he murdered his best friend now, more than likely, had him targeting a young boy he figured no one would miss.

Although the boy might not know any of Williams' secrets, he might be a useful sacrifice because he wouldn't be missed.

Even the brotherhood might simply suspect he went back to the streets to live, or found a better deal somewhere else.

"What do you say, kid?" Williams prompted for an answer, fighting back his impatience.

"Tell him to fuck off," McCully said to himself, finding no reason to state his answer any louder.

No one would hear anyway.

Looking behind him, perhaps for assistance that was too far away, the boy had already made up his mind. He didn't want to go with Williams, but the man wasn't going to simply let him go after this encounter.

A silent, awkward moment passed between them, with neither moving or saying a word. The boy looked from the man to the grounds, then to the grass at his feet, as though about to give in.

"Don't do it," McCully pleaded to the boy who couldn't hear him.

Left with little other option, the boy broke into a sprint along the edge of the property, heading up the hill as he followed the road.

Unlike modern times, the hill behind the hotel had a golf course during its heyday, rather than a dense woods. McCully watched Williams jump into his car, starting it with the strange winding noise vehicles in the day always made, taking chase. He wasn't about to let the boy get away from him to ruin his reputation and expose his secrets.

While the boy darted up the hill, full of youthful energy, Williams struggled to get his car motivated. McCully followed the action, wondering which direction the boy might take. If he stayed by the roadside, he would be easy prey for Williams, and if he broke to the right, he might find help on the old golf course.

Reaching the area first before the child, McCully saw no one near the course. In fact, it displayed the first offspring of what would become the dense woods behind the hotel. The priests had intentionally neglected the area, letting the vegetation, trees, and shrubs overtake the old course. No longer did lawn mowers trim the grass, or players chase little white balls toward flag markers.

And this is precisely why the boy chose to cut across the field, rather than stay near the road. McCully suspected he wanted to double back to the hotel to find help.

By now, Williams had left his vehicle by the road to pursue the boy on foot. Strategically, this made sense because it was quieter, created less distraction, and Williams could navigate the terrain. Though obviously a bit older than when McCully last saw him, Williams remained in excellent physical condition, quickly catching up to the boy.

A trail of rocks and larger smooth stones slowed the boy's run, but Williams moved over them as easily as he might a sidewalk. The boy remained silent, never calling for help, grunting, panting, or emitting any other sort of noise. Williams closed in dangerously upon the boy, causing McCully to lurch forward with a natural reaction that amounted to nothing.

McCully had no physical impact on the world around him, particularly since the events transpired decades before he was conceived.

He stopped short of trying to touch either person before him, partly because he knew his involvement was a moot point, but more importantly because someone else had seen the same events unfolding.

Just as Williams came upon the boy, grabbing him harshly with both hands, McCully noticed one of the priests dashing up the path from the hotel toward the edge of the property. At first he appeared to be searching for the boy, but quickly zeroed in upon the attempted abduction. Now a race ensued with the priest attempting to catch Williams before the man reached his car with the boy.

By no means a passive victim, the boy bit and clawed at his abductor's arms, trying to free himself as he kicked wildly.

His actions allowed the priest to catch up with them quickly, so McCully stood in place, watching the action unfold before him.

"Stop, you!" the priest shouted, apparently realizing there was no sense reasoning with the man.

Or perhaps he knew Williams by reputation.

McCully always pictured priests and pastors as passive, peaceful people, but what happened next changed his perception. Perhaps the priest had a particular attachment to the boy, or simply saw no other way to deal with the situation, but he turned Williams toward him, striking the man across the jaw with a closed fist.

Williams released the boy from his grasp to deal with the interference. The boy fell hard, but quickly regained enough composure to dart several feet away for a safe vantage point.

"Run, Henry!" the priest ordered, but the boy remained frozen with terror.

Not for himself, but for the man defending him, putting his life on the line.

McCully immediately sensed a deep connection between the two. If Williams had known, he might never have targeted young Henry as a sacrifice to benefit himself. Why a man in such good physical condition needed a sacrifice for any reason eluded McCully, because he recalled Williams telling his best friend something about an object that cured or healed with an appropriate sacrifice.

While his experience with the paranormal centered mainly around his own abilities, McCully knew a little something about cursed objects from documentaries and movies. They offered a benefit to an owner, but at the expense of human suffering or death.

He watched as the priest and the wealthy kingpin struggled over the path of rocks, which were now seated about five feet below them as Williams had run slightly uphill in his escape attempt. They grappled like professional wrestlers a moment, each trying to cast the other into the dangerous rock pile below.

Williams broke free, swinging wildly at the priest, but the man ducked, thrusting a fist into the wealthy man's gut. Williams doubled over, receiving a brutal knee to his face. McCully stood in shock, though not because of the violence. Modern television and film had long since conditioned him to brutal, bloody battles. He never envisioned a man of the cloth directing such anger toward another human being.

He supposed even priests had normal lives at one time, and it was human nature to revert to what one knew.

"Don't you know who I am?" Williams spat the words from his knees.

"Yes, and I don't care," the priest answered somewhat coldly. "You don't lay your hands on any child, especially not one in my care."

Williams growled, announcing his next attack before he dove for the priest. The older man dodged the attack, plucking Williams from the ground by the shirt. McCully sensed the man hesitated, unsure of what to do with his attacker because Williams certainly had opportunity to break off the skirmish several times.

McCully doubted anyone would pursue him if Williams chose to retreat to his car, but the priest showed little fear. A call to the authorities would certainly be the next scene in this drama if that were to happen.

"Leave now, or I won't be responsible for what happens next," the priest informed Williams. "Your tyranny has gone far enough."

Williams definitely had a reputation that preceded him.

"I've donated to you people, and this is how you repay me?" Williams stammered with a sneer.

"You think you can simply buy people? You can pay your thugs to protect you and bully the people in this valley, but you aren't taking this boy."

McCully saw Williams reach behind him, thinking he might have a revolver tucked into his belt, but he produced a knife instead.

His hand immediately thrust toward the robed priest, but the man already knew, perhaps even sensing the attack. Simply stepping aside, he twisted Williams' arm in one motion, thrusting the man's own arm toward his abdomen with the sharp end of the knife. Perhaps he expected Williams to drop the knife, or simply didn't care either way, but the attacker stuck the knife deep into his own guts with guidance from the brother.

Somehow McCully wondered if God Himself had intervened when he saw the shocked look on Williams' face before the priest tossed him to the rocks below. Williams landed face down, already dead upon impact. It appeared purely accidental, perhaps even suicidal by some standards back then. McCully suspected no one would give much of a fuss about Williams dying, wondering if the authorities might quickly dismiss the death as a suicide and lose no sleep over it.

Henry, who had remained nearby the entire time, appeared quite shaken until the priest called him over. Kneeling down, the man embraced him so closely that it appeared his robe devoured the boy. For the first time the boy made noise, softly crying against the man's chest, showing he wasn't completely incapable of sound.

After a few minutes, the man held Henry at an arm's length to gain the boy's attention, though he did so softly and with genuine concern.

"What happened here wasn't your fault," the man stated. "This man was an evil predator who made his fortune by hurting others. I don't know what he wanted from you, but I know it wasn't anything good. And you knew that too, didn't you?"

Henry nodded affirmatively, and adamantly, the way kids often do. Reddish pools formed around his eyes from all of the crying. The whites of his eyes, still misty, began looking pink from so many tears, and from rubbing them away.

"I know it isn't right, but I'm going to tell the authorities, and the brothers, that we found this man dead out here. If I tell them the truth, they might take you away. We don't want that, do we?"

Henry shook his head negatively this time.

"Good."

When the priest stood up, something near or on the body caught his attention, because he climbed down the rocks for a closer look, risking his own cover story by lingering at the scene.

He picked up a wooden crucifix that had fallen from Williams' sport coat. It looked somewhat plain to McCully, but a strange red cube toward the bottom of the main stake caught his attention as well. He wondered if this might be what Williams was obsessed over, and how such a curious object might be of any use to him.

The priest tucked it under his robe, placed his arm around Henry, and began walking toward the converted hotel to report the story to the others. McCully realized the close bond between the priest and the boy was strictly plutonic, like brothers, or perhaps an uncle to a close nephew. This was going to be a secret both of them took to the grave, because neither wished to risk their bond being destroyed needlessly.

When he finally emerged from the vision, McCully dropped the glass shard into the snow, wondering if it might be some of the old stained glass from the hotel after all. The Jesuits had added it during their tenure.

He stood up, looked around, and began wondering what the appropriate next move might be.

30

Jana remained perfectly still on the trap holding Duncan on the floor, hoping the stranger might return with something useful. Minutes passed while her hopes fleeted from the lack of sound or the sight of a saving grace.

Duncan continued to struggle against the plastic restraints to no avail. He made sounds that barely escaped the trap, but seemed able to breathe just fine. Whatever tugged at the other end of the trap didn't cease tugging for one second. It wanted Duncan the way a fisherman might fight a tuna for an hour or more to claim his prize.

She had gotten to know the device a little better, realizing even a sharp knife might not easily cut the thick substance. Though it felt like plastic, it had a virtually unending thickness to it. And now it began to pull closer to the closet, ignoring the additional weight she added to its body.

"No," she said under her breath, frantically looking around for any way to slow it, or find a cutting device she might have missed earlier.

When she moved slightly off the plastic, it moved much more quickly than the slow, inching process of before. Shrieking lightly to herself, Jana grabbed onto the snare, pulling for Duncan's life with no success. It began dragging her along as Duncan's muffled cries for help reached her ears.

"I'm trying," she said, doubting it comforted him one bit.

Duncan was the last confirmed person remaining in the mansion. To lose him meant losing any security Jana felt around her, even if he was in a helpless position. Being alone, knowing the events surrounding the valley the past five years, would make even the most courageous person wonder what to do.

At the moment Jana felt anything but courageous. She fought to keep her attention on saving Duncan, rather than worrying about how to save herself if everyone around her went missing.

Picking up the letter opener with newfound determination, she began tearing and cutting into the plastic the best she could, injuring her hand in the process. Though the task seemed pointless because the snare refused to be defeated, she continued, even as Duncan neared the closet door.

If he disappeared into the closet, all hope was lost.

Jana continued slashing at the plastic, seeing it shred in several areas, but even her added weight made little difference to whatever device pulled the plastic from the other end.

A single glance toward the main door changed everything when Jana noticed a cloaked figure standing there ominously, staring at her through a blank, black mask recessed beneath a hood. She gasped, absently removing herself from the trap as she backed away from the figure when she noticed a knife in his right hand.

She suppressed a concerned moan when Duncan disappeared into the closet, lost to her like everyone else who came to the mansion under her supervision. Now in fear for her own life beyond everything else, Jana backed toward a wall, debating how to elude the person behind all of her troubles.

If elusion was even possible.

"Who are you?" she asked when the figure took a step forward.

He stopped as though ready to answer, then raised the knife and began a slow, purposeful walk directly toward her.

Now completely alone, and realizing that simple fact, Jana didn't want to be cornered, so she kept hold of the letter opener, picking up a nearby lamp before tossing it against the figure's head when he drew close enough. He made a pained noise, putting his hands up to block the lamp's shattering pieces. Jana used the opportunity to stab him in the shoulder with the letter opener, drawing another pained cry as the opener's plastic handle cut another slit along her palm.

She ignored the pain as best she could, dashing for the door.

A sense of reserved relief came to her with the safety the open upstairs provided. She quickly weighed the options of hiding in another room, or running downstairs. All of the doors were closed, meaning she might waste too much time checking to see if they were unlocked. Already the figure was recovering, now stiffly walking toward her.

Jana took to the stairs, quickly descending them until she reached the front door. She quickly undid the lock on the knob, tugging on the door to no avail. Someone had snapped off the deadbolt lock above it, meaning it was stuck in a locked position. Short of finding a pair of pliers, she had no way of opening it.

"Shit," she muttered, glancing back to see him descending the stairs one step at a time, apparently in no hurry to apprehend or kill his quarry.

Purely cat and mouse, just like the slasher movies.

She started toward the entertainment room, then remembered it led to a dead end. Deciding to look for a weapon, despite the risk, she ran into the room, finding little else aside from hulking furniture and electronics.

"Knife," she murmured, deciding to make her way to the kitchen if possible.

It made sense to her that this man might be the stranger she met upstairs, but why would he bother to leave the room, just to put on a disguise? Her thoughts quickly turned to self-preservation again as she picked up a walking stick from beside the door, hiding behind the doorway until the dark figure passed by.

With a solid swing using both hands, she struck the figure across the head with the walking stick, flooring him. She had never been so glad her parents encouraged her to participate in high school softball.

Jana whacked the figure in the head several more times like a child attempting to bust open a pinata, despite him lying motionless on the floor. Each time his body convulsed a bit, indicating he remained alive, and able to feel pain on some level.

Standing over him just a few seconds gave her the idea of pulling off his mask, but she decided to find a way out instead. Knowing his identity did little good if she was stuck inside the mansion with him, unable to summon help from the police.

Quickly crossing the lower level, Jana made her way into the dining room where a terrible surprise awaited her. Clasping both of her hands over her mouth, she suppressed a gasp at the sight set across the table before her. One of her arms swung out to catch herself from falling as her hand clutched the doorway, allowing her to steady herself.

Atop the table, Judith Parks was laid out like some sort of strange Roman sacrifice, streaks of blood trailing down her throat from where it had been slit. Her eyes remained open, glazed in a death trance that eerily stared Jana's way. Both of her arms were laid out to either side, palms facing upward, while her legs were crossed atop one another, the knees slightly buckled. To Jana it appeared almost like the way Christ was often portrayed on the crucifix.

Though she kept herself from screaming, Jana held back several muffled sobs, realizing for certain she was certainly not in the middle of some joke. For some reason, the West Baden Springs Murders had begun once again.

Regaining her wits, Jana darted toward the upper kitchen area, hoping to find a knife or better means of defending herself. She saw a mess atop the counter and preparation areas, spotting only a few tiny knives. Seeing the door to the downstairs, she decided not to access it because the last thing she wanted was to enter an enclosed room.

Instead, she hurried to the pantry door, jiggling the handle a few times to swing it outward. The open door produced another body that spilled outward, forcing a shriek from Jana that she quickly regretted. Laura Compton fell face-down on the floor, obviously dead from the amount of blood soaked into her clothes. Jana reeled, taking a step back to regain her senses. She stared at the corpse, wondering if everyone around her was dead, and how in the world she could escape this mansion of death.

She wanted to touch the body, to see how Laura had died, but she knew it didn't matter. If Jana wasted too much time, she would be the next body someone stumbled upon unwittingly. Instinct told her to check the room's main door, to ensure she was safe another minute or so. She stumbled toward the door, feeling numbed by the death surrounding her, wondering how she ever let herself get talked into taking on such a controversial project. Because the first two visiting investment groups didn't have an ounce of trouble, she allowed herself to be lulled into a false sense of security.

A quick check at the doorway revealed the figure was up and moving, but he was searching an area across the hall, knife in hand. Since he failed to see her, Jana quietly moved to the door for the lower kitchen level where knives would surely be in abundance.

As the door swung open, another body revealed itself, but this one remained in the doorway, blocking her egress. She stifled any cries with her hands, taking an absent step back.

Hands strung above his head, a man she thought she recognized from somewhere simply twirled a few inches in each direction. His head slumped downward with no blood, causing Jana to wonder if he was even dead. She carefully reached forward, touching his face.

No reaction.

His skin felt warm, rather than cold and clammy, but she had no time to further evaluate his status as a fresh corpse or unconscious victim.

She checked the door again, but this time the figure spotted her, immediately charging toward the kitchen. Slamming the door just short of his face, Jana used a sliding lock, doubting it would hold. She grabbed a nearby wooden chair, jamming it under the door-knob to buy some time.

Keeping close watch on the door, Jana saw the knob jiggle as someone tried to open it from the other side. It made a clacking noise, adding to the intensity of the situation. Jana backed away, trying to remain silent while keeping her composure. Banging, then slamming sounds boomed throughout the room as one side of the door threatened to give way.

Jana backed away from the door, debating her next move, overwhelmed by the thought of dying in such a horrific way.

A rapping sound from behind her startled her, because her mind immediately thought someone else might be coming through the window for her.

Whirling around, she found McCully tapping the exterior window with his knuckles. He looked concerned, but not nearly to the extent she felt. Jana knew he wasn't the figure chasing her around the mansion, so she tossed aside her trust issues, hurrying toward the window.

She went to throw it upward, realizing the locks kept it in place. The two latches faced opposite directions, so she twisted one to its other side as the thumping behind her at the door grew louder.

The figure was about to break through the lock, and the chair began twisting awkwardly, indicating it might break any second. Jana desperately tried to lift the window once more, finding she had turned the lock the wrong way. She fumbled with the locks once more as McCully watched helplessly from the other side. If the killer got inside, Jana would have no defense, and no one else to help her fend off his attack.

Her fingers felt as stiff and immobile as tree limbs when they tried to switch the locks to the opposite position.

"Other way," McCully encouraged from the outside, his eyes dancing between her dilemma and the door, which now had a knife plunging through its wooden frame.

Jana finally threw both locks into the other direction, lifting the window hard enough that it shuddered within its frame. McCully had already removed the screen, now putting up his arms to help her down as the door burst open behind her.

Letting out a brief shriek as she dove through the window into McCully's arms, Jana landed atop her new hero as the figure emerged at the window, staring down ominously before dashing toward the mansion's front.

"What the hell?" McCully asked of the situation in general.

"Everyone's dead," Jana managed to state as they both stood from the cold ground. "We've got to get out of here and get help."

McCully stared at her a moment, as though unable to comprehend everyone in his group might actually be dead, then fished inside his front pocket for keys.

"Dan's truck is out front. We can get into town with it."

Taking her by the hand, McCully led the way toward the front of the house, around the front corner. From nowhere, the figure tackled McCully to the ground as the two began battling for position. The truck keys flew clear of their skirmish, landing in a pile of snow. Though concerned for McCully's safety, she immediately began searching for the keys, hoping to retrieve them for a speedy exit if necessary.

"Get out of here!" McCully managed to bark between punches from the killer to his face.

"But-" Jana began to argue.

"Go!"

She ran toward the truck, turning only once to see the killer getting the best of the bluegrass musician. The keyless remote gained her quick access to the truck, and once inside, Jana immediately started the engine. It purred to life instantly as she switched on the headlights, looking back to find the distance between her and the mansion too great to witness the battle between McCully and the figure.

Everything between her and the mansion had been engulfed by shadows.

She sat a moment inside the truck, waiting to see if McCully might appear. As a precaution, Jana locked the doors, then put the truck into reverse for a quick escape.

Taking her by surprise, the killer popped both of his hands against her side window, knife grasped in one of them. He pulled that particular hand back, as though he planned to smash the window with it, but Jana stomped on the accelerator, throwing the truck back hard enough that it smashed one of the other vehicles. She quickly shifted into forward, starting toward the road as the truck began to fishtail in the snow.

A look in the rearview mirror revealed the figure stalking the truck as far as the road, then standing in the center of the street with knife in hand, simply staring forward. Jana quickly diverted her attention to her driving, mainly because the truck's grip on the pavement quickly diminished.

"Whoa," Jana said to herself, trying to keep the truck from sliding into either ditch.

Despite slightly warmer air temperatures, the roads seemed extremely slick because of thawing and secondary freezing. Jana nearly had the truck under control when someone jumped out from the side of the road, frantically waving his arms.

Without much thought, Jana stepped on the brakes, quickly finding the truck violently swerving back and forth once again. The back end clipped whomever had stepped onto the road, thumping him haplessly into the ditch as Jana fought the steering wheel for control. Her mind barely comprehended the fact that she likely struck Red Sanders, because he seemed to recognize the truck, as she veered dangerously toward the opposite ditch.

Accidentally correcting the truck too much, she sent it into a skid that dumped it front-first into the ditch, thrusting her against the wheel as the airbag deployed. She felt as though her face had just been struck by a boxing glove the size of a beach ball, but Jana rubbed her forehead, moaning to herself.

Thankfully she hadn't lost consciousness, but a wave of terrible thoughts ran through her mind. McCully had likely given his life to protect her, she may have just killed Red in a hit-and-run type accident, and the police were nowhere to be found.

Realizing she might be the only person left to find help and bring the killer to justice, she tried the door, finding it stuck against the side of the ditch. In the distance she heard a motor start, sounding slightly like a chainsaw, then spied a single headlight peering over the hill from above.

A snowmobile?

"Damn it," she cursed, feeling unwavering resolve to survive this terrible ordeal around her.

Since the passenger side appeared wedged against the opposite side of the ditch, Jana looked behind her, realizing the rear window had shifted position during the crash. The truck's frame and upper molding had been compromised, leaving the rear window on the verge of falling out.

Undoing her seatbelt, Jana turned around, kicking at the window twice before it fell into the truck's bed. She climbed out through the back, using every ounce of strength and willpower within her to clear the cab. She might as well have been a contortionist the way she maneuvered her arms and legs like a spider to drag herself out.

As she reached fresh air and a stiff breeze once more, she saw the headlight of the snowmobile or a four-wheeler bob over the hilltop, realizing she had mere seconds to move before the figure found her once again.

31

McCully found himself embedded in the cold ground once more, wondering if the same man had bested him twice in the same evening. He sometimes wished he had grown up more scrappy like his father, but extended hard labor and fistfights were among the list of things he never experienced growing up.

He rubbed the side of his head, wondering where everyone had gone, and why he was still alive. The last thing he remembered was the cloaked figure ramming his head against a nearby rock.

Apparently the man decided to chase Jana, rather than finish the job at hand.

Seeing the truck now gone, he hoped she had made it to safety. Plucking his cellular phone from his side, he checked for a signal. One bar of signal strength presented itself, but as soon as he dialed 911 for assistance, the phone cut out, leaving him alone in the world.

McCully decided to go inside for warmth, and perhaps some answers about the strange events surrounding him. The front door, now slightly ajar, allowed him to easily slide by, revealing an eerie scene of a well-lit mansion with no sounds, and no one else nearby.

Curious, he immediately turned his attention to the upper kitchen area, where he had rescued Jana through the window. Though difficult to see from outside, McCully felt reasonably certain he saw the lifeless bodies of several investment group members.

Drifting carefully to the right of the main entrance, McCully spied the body of Judith Parks lying across a table. He stopped short of the doorway, having no reason to doubt she was dead, and not wanting to disturb evidence for the police.

"Dear Christ," he said to himself, leaning an arm against the doorway for support.

He suddenly felt wary of his surroundings, wondering if the killer had definitely left the premises. It made sense for him to chase Jana before she found help, but it would take mere seconds to kill McCully himself if he wasn't suspecting an attack.

Turning to look around, he heard no footsteps, and saw no one else inside the mansion.

Proceeding to the next doorway, he stopped short once again, seeing Laura Compton slumped awkwardly along the floor. He told himself she had to be dead, even though he didn't want to believe it. It humbled him to think he had narrowly survived an encounter with the person who murdered part of his group.

Not knowing who the man swaying in the doorway might be, he cautiously stepped over, using a nearby paper towel to first turn the man one way, then pluck his wallet from his pants. McCully flipped it open, instantly seeing a golden badge inside with five tips. A certain portion of the wallet was dedicated to carrying business cards, which informed the bluegrass singer the man before him was indeed the local sheriff.

"Holy shit," he muttered, taking another look at the body, which seemed full of color for a corpse.

McCully began studying the man, who hung from a doorway via tied hands. He swung slightly to and fro, especially after being turned to retrieve the wallet. The examination came to a screeching halt when a drawn out creak came from behind McCully.

Someone had entered the front door.

He quickly rushed out of the room, half expecting to confront the killer right there in the foyer. With no one in sight, he quickly panned the large room, seeing no one once again. He returned his attention to the door, seeing it had swung open, despite McCully believing he closed it tightly.

A stiff breeze broke up the otherwise warm confines of the mansion, chilling McCully enough to send shivers through his muscles. He convulsed slightly, then headed toward the door to shut it, stopped in his tracks when someone stepped in front of it. The person passed across the doorway outside, stumbling in McCully's opinion, until he or she fell out of sight.

As though someone stole his ability to breathe, McCully froze like a statue, unblinking as he waited to see another glimpse of whomever had fallen across the doorway. He remained near the bottom of the stairs, possessing no weapon with which to defend himself.

After several tense seconds passed, he slowly made his way toward the door, leery of the person just outside. Fearing a knife or some other weapon might lunge at him from outside, he took to the opposite side of the door, trying to examine his surroundings before moving any closer.

For all he knew, this was the killer trying to lure him in for the kill. Perhaps the figure had an accomplice, allowing them to double their efforts in abducting and murdering the investment group. The possibility also existed that someone might need his help, which reminded him of what happened when he assisted Jana.

He felt nervous, though in control of his emotions as he pulled near the door's frame. Peering around the side revealed nothing at first, then McCully tensed when someone fell directly before him on the short concrete landing.

"Red?" he questioned, kneeling down to examine his colleague, seeing the man clutch his leg around the knee. "What the hell happened?"

"I got clipped by a truck. I think the son-of-a-bitch was trying to finish me off, but I hobbled and crawled here along the side of the road."

"Is it broken?" McCully inquired, noticing he clutched the leg right beneath the knee.

By no means a medical expert, McCully recalled two separate bones comprising the human leg below the knee. Both were fairly thin, and easily broken by a hard collision.

"I heard a snap," Red reported. "I can't put any weight on it."

He wondered if the killer had somehow commandeered a vehicle to pursue Jana, and if so, McCully hoped against all odds she was alive and well.

Carefully helping Red to his feet, he heard a noise in the distance that sounded like a small motorized vehicle revving up to full speed.

"Let's get you inside," McCully said, putting forth a braver front than he felt.

The night's events had taken a toll on him, and until help arrived, relief would be a distant hope.

*   *   *

Jana jumped clear of the truck as a four-wheeler came over the hill with a cloaked figure steering it directly toward the wreck. Looking like some kind of hokey horror movie spoof toy, the sight of the figure mounting an off-road vehicle might have seemed humorous if not for the dire circumstances.

She darted behind several nearby shrubs as he jumped off the four-wheeler, desperately, even angrily searching the area. He ran to the window, fighting off the snow at his feet, still holding a knife in his right hand. Seeing nothing there, he began circling the truck.

Jana looked from the truck to her trail, realizing her footprints led to the exact spot where she crouched behind the bushes. A mere second after her realization, he discovered the flawless footprint trail left in the snow.

The chase was on.

Jana took off further into the wooded area behind the wreck, hoping the four-wheeler couldn't cross the large ditch and navigate the terrain. Barely audible over the sounds of her own heavy breathing, Jana heard the four-wheeler start, move forward over the course of a few seconds, then stop again.

She suspected he had quickly abandoned his mode of transportation, but wasn't about to stop for verification. Branches smacked her in the head as she passed, realizing she was actually heading toward the mansion, deviating from her original plan to find help.

At this point, preserving her own life became Jana's number one priority.

Weaponless, and not exactly what she considered dressed for winter, Jana stumbled through the snow as best she could. Though she had dressed warm when Duncan originally wanted to leave the mansion, her attire still lacked appropriate layers for snow and windy conditions.

Bad planning?

No. She fully expected to return home after the tour and dinner, never anticipating the sky would dump two feet of snow on the valley.

Bad luck?

Perhaps. The snow, combined with an individual, or two, sabotaging any means of communication and travel had allowed for the entire investment group to be systematically picked off.

Jana tripped over a branch, barely keeping her feet under her to avoid the cliche helpless female in the horror movie routine where she would fall on her face. The group members were unsuspecting victims, while Jana planned to outlast and outwit the man pursuing her.

But how?

Surely the killer knew the area, and the mansion, very well. She had grown up in the area, but that meant nothing in the middle of the night surrounded by trees and shrubs. She might as well have been wearing a black light to lure the killer closer.

That's it, she thought, beginning to realize she made herself easier to track if she remained mobile.

Now far enough ahead of him, she doubled back along her own tracks nearly a bus length. Jana created a new path that led into a small tree grove where the leaves, water droplets, and fallen branches from above broke up the snow-covered ground. Without wasting much time, she stomped around the area a little bit to add to the mess, then took a large leap out of the grove, taking a completely different direction than before.

While her direction loosely aimed her toward the mansion, her route now became more roundabout, taking her further into the woods. Though dangerous territory for a stranger to the land, she figured the killer would believe she took the route easiest to navigate, and return to the road.

Realizing the noise from her running and heavy breathing might be enough to draw the killer her way, Jana stopped momentarily behind a tree. There, she rested as she caught her breath, listening for approaching footsteps. Hearing none, she took off once more, beginning to veer her course toward the road after another hundred yards.

While the road afforded her less cover, its snowy covering wasn't deep enough to leave footprints as traceable evidence. She jumped over the ditch when she reached it, landing on the road with enough balance that she quickly crouched down, judging her distance from the totaled truck down the hill.

Feeling relatively safe, she began running up the hill toward the mansion, hoping the eerie nighttime light cast by the snow didn't make her an easy target.

She stayed on the opposite edge of the road from the wreck, wondering how long it would take the killer to discover her ruse. When he did, even the mansion wouldn't provide a safe haven from his wrath.

Though it wasn't yet in sight, the mansion materialized in her mind, perhaps because she so desperately wanted to be out of the elements and harm's way. As the hill's angle grew more steep, Jana struggled to keep her footing. She nearly tripped and fell, but caught herself once again.

A moment later, the mansion's gate came into view as the sound of a motor echoed behind her, driving her forward. One glance behind her showed a headlight gleaming like the Northern Star in the distance, fragmented by the misty air. He was already heading her way, either giving up on finding her, or realizing the truth about her deception.

Jana jumped into the ditch, figuring he hadn't seen her. She waited until the headlight drew near, feeling as though someone was standing on her insides. Sucking in her last breath, Jana expected the four-wheeler to stop, the man to jump off, and the chase to begin all over again. At this point, she felt she had little resistance left. Her mind and body felt numb, as though conspiring against her.

Apparently they had decided death sounded better than the strenuous effort of running for dear life.

Jana hadn't.

Her concerns drifted away with the passing of the off-road vehicle, leaving her several alternatives, none of which felt too safe. Venturing through the woods could get her lost, while staying near the road might get her killed.

She stood up, seeing a pair of tracks along the road, pointed toward the mansion. They looked like cowboy boot tracks, and they seemed awkwardly staggered, like someone had walked with a limp.

"Red."

Even if she didn't rush inside to his aid, Jana decided she wanted to assess the situation and help him if she found the injured man. Drawing closer to the front gate, Jana realized she didn't hear the sound of the four-wheeler, as though it had stopped short of the mansion. Sensing grave danger, she remained at the gate's first corner, waiting to see someone, anyone, before making her next move.

32

Inside the mansion, McCully had also heard the sound of a motor outside. With Red now inside, and the both of them toward the back of the mansion, he suppressed his curiosity. For all he knew, Jennings might have returned with help, or the killer was now mobile.

"This is ridiculous," Red complained as McCully adjusted his position inside a fairly spacious utility closet within the entertainment room.

"You're going to be safer in here with that leg than you will running around with me."

"Was that supposed to be funny? 'Running'?"

"No. Any sense of humor I might have had abandoned me when Laura disappeared."

McCully set Red with his back against the closet's far wall, enabling him to fire upon any unwanted visitors with the weapon he took from the deputy at the hotel.

"Don't you be getting antsy and trying to get out of here," McCully warned. "I'll be back for you as soon as I can."

"I hate being cooped up. It's bad enough your new girlfriend tried to run me down."

McCully had accidentally spilled the beans about Jana driving Duncan's truck.

"I only said I thought she got into it. Hell, the killer might have chased her away and stole it for all I know."

"The only thing I know is that it crashed after clipping me, so I suspect she was driving."

McCully wondered if that might be a disparaging remark about female drivers, opting not to press the issue. He handed Red a flashlight he found after a brief trip to the first floor kitchen, thinking the man might need extra light while cooped up in such a tiny space.

"Where are you going?" Red asked, since they hadn't discussed much of a game plan.

"To town if I have to, but I'm going to find some help."

"The hunter already went that way, and he's not back yet."

Shaking his head, McCully decided he wasn't leaving anything to chance.

"For all we know, the man went home, or the killer got to him. There's still an outside chance he's not on our side, too."

"Who the fuck can we trust?"

It took a moment for McCully to answer, because he really didn't trust anyone at the moment, although he felt compelled to believe Red and Jana were certainly innocent.

"I don't know. But I'm not waiting around here to become another victim. I'll get some help, then I'll come back for you."

He started to back out of the closet door when Red motioned for him to wait.

"What?"

"I want a code."

"A *what*?"

"Some kind of signal or knock so I don't blow you away when you come back. You know, like they do on commercial flights for cockpit access."

Sighing aloud, McCully knocked on the door three times, then once more after a brief pause.

"Three, then one. Okay?"

Red readily nodded in agreement. It seemed as though he really didn't like the idea of being left alone, and McCully couldn't blame him. If the roles were reversed, he would probably take a chance and hobble as far as he could from the mansion.

"I'll be back," he promised, shutting the door behind him before Red could protest.

He decided to check on the noise he heard earlier from the front yard before going anywhere. Instinct told him to be cautious, but he felt an obligation to assist anyone else who had eluded capture or a worse fate.

Peering out the large living room's first window, he saw nothing aside from the disabled vehicles. Beside him, a pair of pliers sat atop a small table, which had likely turned the broken deadbolt lock.

He dared open the front door, finding nothing noteworthy except for a pair of tracks that looked like they were made from a four-wheeler. He saw no middle track, and the treads were too large to be that of a snowmobile.

He remembered seeing snowmobile tracks on a vacation trip to Wyoming with his family. The treads on the side made a small indentation in snow, while the snowmobile's rear typically made a solid streak, as though someone had dragged a lunch box across the snow's surface.

The realization he had no reliable or quick method of transportation dawned on him, so he decided to check out one last area before making his departure. He felt guilty for stuffing Red into a closet without carrying through on his promise immediately, but knew they were both safer without the threat of his limp making them easy targets.

Leaving the security of the open foyer, McCully moved toward the upper kitchen, ignoring the ghastly scene in the dining area when he passed by. He found it difficult to believe dinner was the last time anyone in his group felt remotely comfortable and safe. Putting the memory to rest, he cautiously moved toward the kitchen, finding it strewn with litter, but something missing.

While Laura's body remained on the opposite end of the room, the man bound at the doorway was now gone. McCully froze in his tracks, slowly turning to look behind him. He almost expected someone to be standing there with a knife, or a corpse he somehow missed lying near the stairs.

Neither of his dreaded thoughts proved real, so he returned his attention to the room, stepping inside as he peered behind the door to ensure no one was lying in wait. Finding himself safe once more, he let his blue eyes wander to the door that led downstairs.

Taking a moment to consider the possibilities, he wondered if the bound man might have somehow escaped the mansion, or possibly been the killer using a clever ruse. After all, who would suspect a sheriff, or someone *posing* as a lawman?

He also considered the possibility that the killer simply moved the body elsewhere.

Feeling both tense and more than a little frightened, McCully stepped trepidly toward the door. Already open enough for him to see down the stairwell and behind the door, he took a deep breath to calm himself as he peered downstairs. Flipping the light switch just beyond the doorway, McCully watched the fluorescent lights below slowly flicker to life as he took the first step down.

He stepped slowly, careful to prevent his feet from making noise enough to alert anyone to his current position. Able to see the entire length of the stairwell, McCully found visibility equally good across the length of the downstairs kitchen.

Much like the upstairs kitchen, this one looked as though someone had ransacked it. One of the tables, and some shelving, were lying across the floor as though knocked down during a skirmish. Adding proof to his fresh theory, McCully found speckles of blood along the floor beside the shelving, and even more near the discarded table.

He scooped up a large droplet, rubbing it between his fingers and thumb before wiping it on a nearby towel.

Now he felt even less optimistic about the survival of his fellow group members. He saw Keith's hat and sport coat nearby, then he spied something that changed everything about his search.

An elevator.

"What the hell?" he asked, standing to investigate this strange new development, wondering what awaited him at the elevator's upmost stop.

*   *   *

Jana decided she had waited long enough for events to unfold at the mansion. She stood outside, looking up at the strange third level that couldn't be explained. Red's tracks led to the mansion, so Jana figured he had returned, wondering exactly where he might have gone.

She approached the front door, turning the knob slowly. With the foyer completely in view, Jana stepped inside, quietly closing the door behind her. Feeling as though she had somehow betrayed Duncan by letting him get swallowed by the trap upstairs, she wanted to see if he was indeed gone.

If so, she wanted to know how the device worked, and if any chance to save him remained.

With a clear path ahead of her, Jana made her way up the stairs sensing no one around. To call out would obviously be foolhardy, so she walked silently, finding the door to Duncan's room still slightly ajar.

Her memory flashed back to what seemed like moments prior, when the killer chased her out of the house. Only McCully's intervention saved her, and now he couldn't be found.

Having absolutely no desire to search the mansion for Red and McCully, she worried about finding the one person she didn't care to see. As she drew near Duncan's room, she felt somewhat apprehensive until she peered inside, discovering an empty room with no visible threats.

She stepped inside, flipped on the lights, and began examining the strange closet, which showed absolutely no signs it had swallowed a human being whole, less than an hour prior. In fact, it looked solid, indicating no sliding doors, trick walls, or imprisoning devices of any sort. It simply looked like any normal closet.

Frustrated, Jana felt around the walls, careful not to trigger anything too suddenly, which might deliver her to wherever Duncan had been dragged. It dawned on her, as she searched, that each of the guests had a specified room. *She* had not picked the room, which also got her thinking the entire mansion stay was an orchestrated event, used to fulfil someone's devious plan.

It suddenly dawned on her as she exited the closet, unable to believe her own analysis of who had coldly murdered at least two verified people. The very man who hired her.

As the door slowly swung open, she saw the dark figure once more, but there was no visible knife this time, and she felt far less fear confronting him.

"Why?" she demanded in an exasperated tone. "Why would you do any of this?"

"I'm simply following orders," the figure replied, pulling the hood back from his head, revealing his face for the first time.

Indeed Bryan Bell, the man who hired her to sell investment property, stood before her, now producing a knife from a sheath located at his side.

Several years older than Jana, Bell always had a professional air about him. He never hit on her, or made any kind of sexual jokes or comments around her. He maintained a steady flow of business throughout his agency, and drew the attention of young ladies everywhere in Bloomington.

Jana supposed his picture perfect lifestyle provided the ideal cover for his evil deeds, though his motive continued to elude her.

"You don't seem surprised," he commented, giving her an eerie grin.

"No, because I finally realized who created this environment, who wanted this group here, and who ordered me to change things at the last minute. The only thing I don't know is why, but I'm sure you'll tell me."

"It's quite a long story. Where would you like me to begin?"

Jana's eyes searched the room for something to use against him if he drew closer, but she needed to stall if she hoped to find any useful tools or weapons.

"From the beginning."

*   *   *

McCully discovered the elevator serviced only two floors, namely the basement level, and an upper level he assumed was hidden away from anyone inside the conventional portions of the mansion.

Already inside the car, he pushed the up button, watched the doors close, then felt a steady pressure as the elevator moved upward. It lacked a floor indicator, but he tried to reason the number of floors it passed during its ascent, figuring he was on the third level when the car gently stopped.

Strangely absent were the dings that accompanied most commercial elevators when the door opened. He found that odd, considering it made a noise on the basement level, almost like a Venus Flytrap luring its prey.

When the door finally opened, McCully found a dark horror before him like nothing he had ever imagined, or visualized subconsciously. Nearly the size of a basketball court, he found the room encompassed by darkness with only small, subtle lights lined up in rows along the floor. It took his eyes a moment to adjust to the lit areas, but when they did, he found something that looked like a scene from some alien abduction movie.

Two sounds reached his ears as he remained perfectly still.

A constant low hum overtook the entire room, likely from some machine performing a task associated with the light at each of the twelve stations he found on the third floor. Each light was placed at the base of a slab just larger than the human being each one held. Barely enough light to see by, McCully thought the devices looked like a museum after hours, allowing someone to navigate the room.

The other rhythmic noise came from in and out breaths of the people attached to some form of restraining devices beside each light. He took a step forward, finding his footstep echo throughout the room over the ambient sounds.

When he approached the first victim, he discovered the deputy from the hotel strapped to some sort of flat, black board. The device stood almost vertically, inclined just slightly back so its captive's feet barely left the ground. McCully doubted the tilting was for added comfort because it seemed painfully obvious the man was in some sort of unconscious or semi-conscious state.

He breathed in and out, but two tubes ran from his left arm, disappearing into the machine that kept him in place. McCully saw liquids flow through each of the tubes, having no idea what purpose they served. With his eyes now growing accustomed to the darkness, he found most of the devices held someone in their clutches, each alive and in some comatose state.

"No wonder he killed only two of them," he muttered, reflecting upon the vision where Smith talked of extended life.

Someone had plans to use the people strapped to the tables as sacrifices to carry out some sort of ritual.

McCully moved to the closest wall, finding unusual inventions along each block where a person was stationed, beginning to piece together a likely scenario. Though each device appeared different in make and design, they served a common purpose. Each sat atop a mobile pedestal that traveled downward into each guest's room with the intent of luring and ensnaring.

Had McCully not left the hotel with Red and Jennings, he too might have suffered a fate like those of Laura and Judith. It seemed they were expendable in the plan, but why? One table remained open on the opposite side of the room.

"Birthdays," he recalled one of the guests saying about the stone carvings outside.

Stone carvings that almost certainly aligned perfectly with the traps he now looked upon.

While the mansion served as Smith's home for years, it harbored a deeper, darker purpose. McCully realized the building was constructed for the sole purpose of this particular day.

"A three-story human sacrifice," he said to himself, returning to the deputy's side.

He looked at the tubes entering his arm, then looked at a strange needle looming above the man's chest. Attached to a spring, it looked much like it was designed to plunge downward. Based on the tube attached to its hind end, he believed it would stab into the heart, drawing vast amounts of blood to a centralized location.

His eyes followed the tube in question to the floor, then along several beams to the centerpiece he had missed earlier, because it had no illumination surrounding it. Though the size of a coffin, it lacked the intricate design and carved patterns one might find when attending calling hours at a funeral home.

In fact, it looked homemade, like something placed in a yard around Halloween. Painted completely black, some of the brush strokes remained visible, even in the dim lighting.

McCully didn't suppose it needed to look fancy. This was hardly Frankenstein's castle or a movie set, so details mattered very little. What concerned McCully were the twelve tubes running into the box, and even more so, the bizarre green cube set in its own specially carved area atop the box so it didn't come loose.

Since the box's cover seemed loose, he dared move it aside, wondering if he was the bumbling idiot who unknowingly opened Dracula's coffin, receiving certain death as a reward.

Made of lightweight wood, the cover slid easily to one side, revealing a sight McCully truly didn't expect. All twelve tubes ran through the sides of the box, then inside where they ended at a needle. This didn't surprise or shock him, but what the needles were lodged into gave McCully the creeps.

He sucked in a breath and held it, anticipating a terrible odor that never wafted his way.

Somewhere between mummified and petrified, an unrecognizable corpse had been placed into the makeshift casket. Each of the twelve needles found a home, embedded within the dried skin, causing McCully to wonder how long the body had been removed from its earthy covering. Looking far from restful, the corpse seemed quite worn for someone allegedly dead for only two years.

Rotting teeth showed past the decaying skin, which looked flaky on the surface. McCully reached toward the body to see how the skin felt, then thought better of it. Even the suit looked tattered, as though worms had been eating through it. A man of Smith's position surely had a huge funeral, complete with the best of caskets and burial plots. Something about McCully's original theory didn't feel right after seeing the recipient of the potential human sacrifice.

He replaced the casket's top to keep from giving away his activities, then backed away from the coffin, feeling extremely uneasy. Whether or not the human sacrifice would work was irrelevant in his eyes. The fact that someone would even attempt to take a dozen lives to resurrect one disturbed him greatly.

Relief came in the fact that the eleven people surrounding him were still alive, but he suspected their condition was temporary if the twelfth person was caught. He didn't know where to begin if he wanted to release them from the snares. There could be booby-traps on each one, or he might kill one of the victims by pulling out the wrong needle. The situation laid before him was best left to the police and medical personnel.

Making rounds, he began to see familiar faces, careful not to touch any of the devices keeping them in place. In addition to the deputy, he found Keith, Oswalt, Turner, and Duncan among the ensnared people, raising his desire to find help.

And quickly.

Each of them appeared in good health, still breathing, though none of them noticed his presence. They remained in an unconscious state, whether drug induced or by some other means, closer to death than any of them possibly knew.

Many of the people were strangers to him, some looking very thin and pale, like comatose patients lying around in a hospital without the benefit of movement or company. Thinking a bit deeper on the subject, McCully realized several had unkept hair and nails, the way nursing home patients were sometimes neglected when they had no real motor functions, or little brain activity.

These people were kept alive, but at minimum expense and effort. McCully's group had provided the last of the crop for the killer, but he wondered who the twelfth victim might be. Only a few of them remained, including himself, which caused him to wonder if the killer had left him alive for a reason.

"Jana," he said to himself, remembering how the killer desperately chased after her.

At first, McCully had reasoned she was a dangerous witness, capable of getting police and foiling the killer's plan. Now, he believe she might have been the final intended target. Either way, he needed her in place before he carried out whatever the now dead doctor's final instructions might have been.

Knowing he could simply lie in wait for the killer to arrive with Jana, McCully decided passiveness served little purpose. Red was trapped inside a closet with no physical means of escape, while Jennings or other visitors might stumble into the mansion, unaware of the danger.

No, he decided, walking toward the elevator. Waiting around for the killer to arrive might cause more spilled blood, and he wanted no part of anyone else dying.

McCully pushed the button, ready to find the killer and confront him before anyone else was hurt. He now knew the truth, and this began and ended with one person's evil dream. If he had his way, the dream would be buried forever inside the mansion.

33

Jana couldn't shake the feeling she was dreaming, about to wake up when daylight streamed through her window. She felt exhausted, her mind wandering to all sorts of bizarre scenarios, even as her boss stood before her with a knife.

Ex-boss, she decided immediately.

"I'm in no hurry to drag you downstairs," Bell confessed, "so I'm going to tell you everything before the longest day of my life comes to an end."

Jana waved her hand across her front like a game show hostess, indicating he could begin any time.

"You're just hoping the extra few minutes you get while I tell this tale will bring some savior through the front door, don't you?" he teased, running his fingers across the knife's flat side. "But I want you to know exactly what your sacrifice will mean to its recipient, and to me."

"Then just get on with it," Jana stated, knowing Bell had a surprise coming if he thought she was just going to cordially walk downstairs with him in a few minutes.

"As you wish," Bell replied, a strange, sinister grin crossing his face.

Jana began to realize he wasn't going to kill her outright with the knife. She had only seen two bodies, while everyone else had disappeared. Her mind scrambled to decipher what he meant by sacrifice, suspecting he needed her alive and intact long enough to carry out some kind of ritual in the basement, or the secret third level.

"I wasn't always a real estate baron," Bell confessed. "In fact, until two years ago, I never thought of it as any kind of career option for me. In some circuits I was known as a mercenary, an enforcer perhaps. Some called me a con artist, but they didn't realize my talents for what they were. Well, one dying man recognized my talents, and he asked me to do something for him I'd never done before."

Bell paused.

"Kill."

He loosely waved the knife with one hand as he began entering a comfort zone while his tale unfolded.

"It took me awhile, weighing the whole heaven and hell, does God really exist thing, but in the end I thought 'fuck it' because we're only on this planet once, and we might as well live a good life while we're here. And don't get me wrong, I don't like having to kill people, which is why I'm so glad the whole sacrifice process is self-inclusive. Getting messy isn't my thing, either, so I'll just wait to see what happens, then take my cut."

"You're not making any sense," Jana told him. "There are a few gaping holes in your story."

"Such as?"

"Such as who hired you, and how this process of yours works without you."

"I was getting there," Bell replied with a snappy tone. "It'll be better for me to *show* you how the process works, but as for who hired me, let's just say Dr. Martin Smith didn't want to rest in peace after all."

Jana felt floored. Utter insanity entered her ears, but her brain wasn't able to process it correctly. Her mind recalled the ambiguity with which the media covered his "second" death a few years earlier, partially because they lacked evidence of his involvement. The word was that the man faked his death the first time, tried to kill Clouse and the man's family, then died for real. The story had more holes than Swiss cheese, but the public seemed to buy it without very much hoopla.

Perhaps because Smith had no family to speak of, no one really cared if his name was slandered, or maybe it wasn't slandered at all.

Only one person probably knew the whole truth, and Clouse wasn't around to explain anything to her. Damn him for getting her into this whole mess, she thought. Clouse hired Bell, who in turn hired her, creating this catastrophic chain of events she found herself centered within.

"How did you get Clouse to hire you, being so new to property sales?" she asked her former boss.

"He trusts people far too easily. For someone with lots of money, he doesn't have the brains or experience to go along with it. I knew he was going to unload the property eventually, so I dropped a bug in his ear with an e-mail about a year ago. I simply gave my name and contact information, then let him know we would find the property some ownership with integrity, that would keep the hotel historically accurate, and keep his name out of the press."

"Everything he wanted to hear," Jana said, thinking of Clouse as less of a guilty party.

He simply wanted things right for everyone, and now he was partly responsible for another string of abductions and murders, as well as all of the negative repercussions sure to follow. Lawsuits and negative press were on the coattails of this evening, Jana thought, still trying to find a monkeywrench that could stop Bell's plan.

"There are a lot of other things you need to know," Bell admitted, continuing to block the room's only realistic escape route. "Like why this group, why not the first two?"

"Sure. Why?"

"Because their birthdays are important to making the process work."

"Process? You make this sound like slaughtering mindless cattle, not taking human lives."

Bell feigned a hurt expression.

"Funny you should make that analogy, considering half these people are country folk. But what's most important about them is their birthdays. Well, a few of them anyway."

"Why their birthdays? Does it tie into the carvings outside?"

"Oh, it does *much* more than that," Bell said, a nearly orgasmic look crossing his face, proving he believed in what he was doing. "See, the birthdays are intricately tied into the grounds Dr. Smith fought to keep. The same grounds his son was murdered on, in fact. Where he witnessed murders as a child, and where the deep secret of several very special cubes was revealed to him one fine day."

Little of this explanation made sense to Jana, but she believed Bell was telling the truth, at least as Smith had told it to him. Perhaps Smith had taken Bell under his wing, as only a father could, to replace the loss of his own son. Convincing Bell his experiment was ill-conceived seemed unlikely, leading her to wonder if Smith grasped at straws near the end of his life, or he believed in dark magic himself.

"How do you have any idea if this works or not?" Jana asked, trying to interject some reason into his inconceivable plan.

"Because I met a man near death, and the next time I saw him, he was my age. He had reversed his age and the condition killing him from the inside."

"But at what cost?" Jana asked, infuriated that anyone could be so selfish.

She had been raised around the church all her life with her mother and grandmother, understanding the careful balance between life and death, right and wrong. She believed in a spiritual world, doing right in her one earthly life to attain the right to enter the gates of heaven. To take human life for one's own benefit was worse than personal conquest in her eyes.

"Obviously at the cost of human life, my dear," Bell scoffed as though she had asked him a rhetorical question. "And to think I had such high hopes for you when I brought you into the firm."

"And why did you set me up for this? Why me?"

"Isn't it obvious? You're the last person I need before this little experiment goes live."

Jana wanted the complete answer, and Bell seemed to detect this by the way she stared a hole through him.

"In the year 1966, Mr. and Mrs. Whiting from Michigan bought the hotel at auction for less than half its original value. This particular purchase changed history and saved what would have been a doomed West Baden Springs Hotel. Therefore, it is one of the most important dates in the hotel's storied past. And like the eleven other people awaiting your presence, who share important dates from the hotel's past, you fit into the puzzle because of the day you were born."

"November 2," she murmured.

"Bingo. It takes extremely powerful spiritual presences to make this shit work," Bell stated. "Dates, times, people," he said with an airy wave, "all make the magic work. You can think I'm disillusioned or just after the money, and you'd be partly right. Smith offered me a lot of cash to finish the job I started."

"And how do you know he won't just murder you to cover his tracks, even if this insane plan of yours actually works?"

"I've taken all kinds of precautionary measures. The old man might have had this mansion built to suit his own purposes, but I made a few modifications in his absence in case he tries anything crazy."

Bell held the knife up, forcing a complimentary smile.

"Now I think I've told you everything you needed to hear. I'm sorry you won't be around to see the end result, but you'll go out knowing you served a greater purpose."

"Your bank account?"

"Oh, you're taking this so badly, Jana," he said, acting emotionally torn once again. "I realize you thought I hired you for your brains, or your good looks, so this must be quite a letdown for you. But you'll have to forgive me. I've had a very rough day after several of your clients and a certain deputy sheriff roughed me up, so I'm going to ask you to just make this easy and walk downstairs with me."

Jana needed a few more minutes, hoping someone remained to help her. If not, she felt mentally prepared to engineer her own escape.

"Why kill Laura and Judith if you can't stand taking lives, as you say?"

"They both caught me preparing the traps for the other guests. You see, each of these closets has a device used to lure and ensnare unsuspecting guests into them. It's ingenious really. I can't *wait* to show you when we get to the main room. I'm sure you noticed I kept the sheriff alive, Jana. I needed him until his lackey son came after him, but I didn't have the heart to kill him. Doc can decide what to do with him when he comes back to the land of the living. I've never had much use for peace officers myself, but killing a sheriff does draw a lot of unwanted attention I'm sure Dr. Smith won't want."

"You'll send the good doctor my condolences?" Jana remarked sarcastically.

Bell seemed to enjoy the comment, his expression lightening considerably.

"Now that's what I'm going to miss about you. Your wit and charm."

"And I'm going to miss my paycheck," she said, walking toward him since she had yet to find a suitable weapon. "But we all have to move on, don't we?"

Bell openly didn't like her walking toward him, but his threat with the knife seemed halfhearted, giving her an opening to launch her right foot toward his groin. Bell tried to block it with one hand, allowing Jana time to grab a lamp off a nearby end table, which she smashed over his head.

And the chase was on once again.

34

Jana thought she had safely cleared the room's main door when Bell's hand grasped her ankle, tripping her enough that she toppled to the ground. She saw another pair of feet appear before her, thinking Bell had a partner and her life was at a certain end. She looked up to see McCully deck Bell before the man could launch another attack.

"Come on," McCully said, hurriedly helping her up by one arm.

He took her hand, leading her toward the stairs, as she looked back to see an infuriated Bell pursuing them, knife in hand.

"Who is he?" McCully asked when they reached the bottom step, rushing directly toward the front door.

"My boss," Jana answered, drawing a perplexed look from McCully as he tried opening the front door, only to find it locked and jammed once more.

"Fuck."

Taking Jana by the hand, he led her toward the kitchen area, narrowly missing having a knife stuck in the side of his head when Bell lodged it into the front door instead. Unlike Jana, McCully served no useful purpose to Bell if he remained alive.

"You're both dead," Bell called behind them angrily. "You're going to die slow and painful-like, country boy."

McCully took Jana as far as the upper kitchen area, then blocked the doorway.

"Get out of here," he told her.

"No!" Jana yelled her reply, partly because she didn't want McCully getting killed, and partly because Bell was closing in.

Jana felt cold air rushing inside from the open window she had used before. Escape was so close, and so easy, but where would she go? Where would she find help? The sheriff and one of his deputies were already prisoners inside the mansion.

She snatched a glass pitcher from the kitchen counter, and as McCully engaged Bell, he immediately fought to keep the knife from plunging into his side. Jana seized the opportunity, smashing the pitcher over Bell's head, buying them a few moments of time to rethink their strategy. Bell fell to the ground, by no means unconscious, but in no condition to pursue them immediately.

"Come on," McCully said, leading her toward the stairwell once again.

"There's no way out that way," Jana said, looking back to see Bell remaining stunned on the ground.

"Yes, there is," McCully countered. "Come on."

Refusing to release her hand, even for a second, McCully charged up the stairway. When they reached the top step, he let go of her hand to dash into the closest bedroom. He returned with a bed sheet in hand, then repeated his efforts in the next room. When he emerged from the room, he glanced downstairs to check on Bell as he began tying the sheets together.

"You're not serious," Jana said, beginning to comprehend the plan inside his mind.

"Unfortunately, I am."

"He'll just follow us," Jana insisted.

"Maybe. But you still have the truck keys, right?"

She nodded, feeling comforted by his confidence, but lacking time enough to reveal the truck's condition to him.

"Open up the balcony doors," he requested as he finished tying the sheets together, now spiraling them so they formed a shape that resembled a thick rope.

Jana did so, finding herself constantly looking behind her toward the stairway. A burst of cold air rushed inside the warm confines of the mansion as McCully finished a makeshift braiding of the sheets.

He took one end of the sheets, tying it tightly around the balcony railing as Jana dared to look down at the snow-covered ground. It almost looked safe enough to jump upon, but she knew better.

"Get ready," McCully said, cinching the knot as tight as the cloth allowed.

Jana wondered if he had Boy Scouts or military training, because he seemed much more calm than she felt.

She wanted to ask if he expected her to climb down bed sheets to safety, but decided she already knew the answer. Watching him test the knot with a solid tug, Jana forgot all about Bell until the man surprised them both by rushing through the open balcony doors, knife held high by both hands.

McCully whirled too late to save himself from injury, though he deflected the knife upward. It sunk into his right shoulder, forcing a pained cry, as his other elbow clipped Bell in the chin. Jana stepped back, preparing for the worst-case-scenario, which came almost immediately.

Bell recovered quickly, clasping McCully's foot, then throwing him over the balcony in one motion because the man only had one useful arm. She saw his hand flail, grasping for dear life at the balcony railing, then fall out of sight after the rest of him.

Jana now found herself completely on her own.

"No!" she shrieked, looking over the railing to see her one remaining source of help lying awkwardly on the ground, either dead or unconscious.

A small blood pool formed in the snow beside him from the shoulder wound, continuing to grow until Jana felt two strong arms wrap themselves around her. Though she kicked, fought, and screamed bloody murder into the surrounding woods, Bell inevitably dragged her into the mansion.

Her head struck the doorway, probably from Bell's intentional doing, and the world around her whirled like a typhoon before going black.

35

When Jana next awoke, she found herself inside a large dark room that felt strangely cold to her.

In more ways than one.

Though the temperature felt somewhat chilly, the room contained devices with various people strapped into them. They breathed systematically, like coma patients, unaware of their surroundings, or their impending fate.

Lying on the ground, Jana tried to stand, but quickly realized her hands were bound behind her. Her head ached, but not too badly. Obviously she hadn't been out very long, indicating the bump that knocked her out was minimal.

"Don't struggle," Bell said from behind her. "It'll be easier in the end."

She managed to swing her body around, finding him readying a device for use.

"There's still time to stop this," Jana insisted, trying to reason with him. "These people are alive. You can still save them."

"Save them?" Bell scoffed. "I'm the one who put them here."

"But you don't have to do this. You don't know for certain it'll work. And if it doesn't, you've just wasted twelve lives, and ruined all of their families."

"You don't think I've reasoned this out?" Bell said, adjusting a leather strap meant to restrain a victim into place. "You can give me all the spiritual mumbo jumbo you want, but you're not going to sway me. I've come too far to just give up."

Realizing her bonds were braided rope, Jana twisted her hands, rubbing them up and down against one another as she tried loosening the bonds. She needed to keep Bell talking, but he seemed content to work on the device.

"How exactly does that work?" she asked, hoping to find a way to counter it if she failed to undo her restraints.

"Yours will work a little bit differently," Bell confessed. "Some of these people have been here for weeks, so they have nutrient tubes to keep their bodies satiated. *You* won't have to worry about any of that. The other tube you see is to keep them sedated. If it makes you feel better, I can put you out before the process begins. It's really the least I can do."

"How kind of you," Jana said, her words dripping with sarcasm.

Bell chuckled as she checked over the needles and tubes surrounding the restraining device.

"I suppose I should have done this sooner," he commented, "but it's just been such a busy night. You wouldn't believe the planning and timing that goes into pulling something like this off."

Jana wanted to stand up and smack him, but she continued working on the ropes. Not only did he lack a conscience, but his sense of humor stunk.

"Oh, the cleaning lady you hired is over there," he said, pointing across the room to an unconscious woman tied down to a tilted slab. "She probably regrets ever taking this job."

"You were the one who recommended her," Jana said, feeling defeat within her voice. "I should have figured it out sooner that you were behind this."

"Don't be so hard on yourself, dear. Your blind devotion to your job made this far too easy for me. Most employers love your qualities in their workers, whereas I just cared about the date of your birth. After tonight, I'm retiring, but I'll take time before my trip to the Bahamas to place some nice flowers on your grave."

Jana seethed with anger toward him, wishing she could break free just to give him a few swift kicks, if nothing else. Then she felt a small strand of the rope break apart. Feeling it with her fingers, she discovered it had all kinds of loose strands on the outside, meaning the rope was an old utility rope, disintegrating from years of being used in the elements.

"This last needle, though, is the one you've gotta watch out for," Bell continued, oblivious to Jana's progress.

He held up the last tube and needle contraption so she could see it, but to her it looked exactly the same.

"All twelve of you will have this plunged directly into your hearts simultaneously, killing each of you instantly, and bringing the life juices to the good doctor over there."

Jana noticed a box centered in the room for the first time where twelve tubes fed directly into the sides. She dreaded the thought of dying, but detested the idea of helping bring back someone who obviously held very little regard for human life even more.

Some doctor, she thought.

"Doc was kind enough to teach me everything I needed to know before his tragic passing a few years ago," Bell continued. "There wasn't very much fanfare surrounding his second funeral, but I guess the cops thought silence was the best thing for everyone involved. It just made my job that much easier."

Bell continued to double-check every last connection on the leather straps, the needles, and the tubes while Jana broke several more strands on the rope. She refused to simply lie back and be a victim. Not only could she save her own life, but eleven others who didn't deserve any of the torture Bell had put them through.

"Everything will change tonight with the simple flip of a switch," Bell added with an air of vanity that his entire plan came together so nicely.

"Where?"

"'Where' what?"

"Where is the switch you're talking about?"

Bell nodded toward the large box centered in the room.

"Beside it. Once all of you are sedated and I'm certain the needles are in their correct positions, it'll be a matter of seconds before Dr. Smith is awakened and I get paid my stipend."

Jana thought back to her October tour. She wondered if the grave disturbance had been related to Bell digging up the body. Considering Smith had two funerals, it sounded reasonable, but burying such a man with the Jesuit priests sounded entirely blasphemous. She recalled Clouse stating something about losing a court case, forced to bury Smith within the property he loved.

After two years, the man's body had to be deteriorated in some regards. If he was embalmed, there would be no blood within him, so how could he function? The entire plan sounded incredibly far-fetched to Jana as she snapped another two outer strands away from the rope.

"Well, it looks as though we're ready," Bell said, turning from the device to confront Jana, who had yet to free herself.

He started reaching toward her when the elevator doors opened from across the room, drawing their attention.

36

When the elevator door slid open, no one emerged from inside, causing Jana to wonder if some glitch had caused the movement. Several of the devices blocked the view of the elevator's lower half for both her and Bell, so her captor cautiously moved toward the only entrance in the third level.

"Your boyfriend isn't going to like finding me here," Bell said, giving a hardened stare at Jana before taking another step toward the elevator.

He searched the area momentarily, discovering no one around or inside the car, so he returned, determined to end his task without delay.

"I'm going to get you strapped in, then I'm going to throw that switch," he proclaimed. "After that, I'll deal with any stragglers left around this place, including your new boyfriend."

Jana resented the remark, partly because his accusation was simply false, and because Bell talked about McCully as though he were a piece of ground chuck.

From the looks of the device, Bell needed to untie her before restraining her with the leather straps, both around her wrists, and around her body. He reached down, plucking her off the floor with a hard jerk that allowed her to break the last few remaining strands around her wrist. She launched a knee into his groin, connecting entirely this time, then used the length of rope that once bound her wrists, to slash him across the face.

Bell yelled in agony as he fell to the floor, allowing Jana time to run for the elevator. She hated to leave the others behind, but without her, Bell couldn't throw the switch, meaning they were in no real danger.

Jana hit a slick spot along the floor that tripped her up. She hit the floor hard, sliding against the side of the elevator as Bell regained his footing. Jana scrambled to her feet, virtually launching herself into the elevator as she fumbled for the down button. Bell reached the elevator as the door began closing, causing her to kick toward him, which immediately reversed the door's movement.

Thinking she had attempted her last escape, Jana prepared to fend off Bell's next attack when someone streaked across the open door, tackling Bell to the ground. Jana stepped forward to observe her latest savior when a noise from above captured her attention.

She looked up, spinning defensively, finding Craig Jennings climbing down from the elevator's emergency hatch. Fearing the worst, she wondered if Jennings had teamed with Bell long before the visitors ever reached the mansion, but he jumped down, gave her a reassuring nod, and stepped forward. She realized he was looking for the skirmish at hand, so Jana also left the elevator car, finding Bell getting the best of McCully until Jennings grabbed him from behind.

For his trouble, the hunter received a knife to the side of his right calve muscle, flooring him as he hollered in pain. Jana realized the two men had formulated a quick plan to ride the elevator up. One of them had apparently observed the third level earlier, knowing Bell would instantly be aware of their presence when the elevator opened.

Fighting like a cornered badger, Bell seemed to handle both of his injured attackers with ferocity and intensity unlike anything Jana had ever witnessed. He threw McCully against a nearby wall, where the bluegrass singer hit back-first, then slumped to the ground in a heap. Bell then turned on Jennings, who had been distracted by his new injury.

The hunter looked up when Bell closed in, unable to prevent the killer from stomping on the injured leg. Jennings screamed again, but Bell's close proximity allowed the hunter to buck with his good leg, kicking Bell in the kneecap. Though Jana didn't hear a crack to indicate any broken bones, the blow crumpled Bell to the floor, temporarily giving the three men even footing.

Jana decided to cripple Bell the best way possible as her eyes surveyed the room.

She ran over to the closest victim, who happened to be Oswalt, then began pulling the needles from where they entered his skin. Held in place by bandage tabs, the needles easily slid outward, then dropped to the floor when Jana let go. Knowing what purpose the tubes served, she let go of any fear that she might hurt the victims. She assumed Bell had told her the truth, because he seemed so confident his plan was about to end perfectly.

Fighting activity resumed nearby, but Jana paid minimal attention to it as she went cot to cot, freeing each of the victims from their feeding tubes and whatever form of anesthesia kept them sedated. Hearing a yelp of pain, she looked up to find Bell hurling Jennings into the elevator car, pushing a button inside before the doors closed.

For the moment, Jennings was removed from the battle against Bell, who now turned his attention toward Jana.

Infuriated by her actions, he clenched his fists before stomping toward her. With six of the victims now freed from their tubes and bonds, Jana stared directly at Bell while she undid the restraints on Keith's cot. The needles dropped to the floor as Bell reached the cot, but she had already sought shelter behind the next slab.

"You bitch," Bell stammered, his fury quite obvious.

If he were a cartoon character, steam would blow out the sides of his ears. And in a cartoon, the knife clutched in his right hand probably wouldn't seem nearly as ominous.

She didn't consider herself untouchable, but felt it necessary to make a statement that she wasn't going to cower before him. Undoing Keith's restraints while looking at him got her point across, but now Jana found herself without assistance, and few places to run.

"This time I'm going to choke you out before I put you on that slab," Bell sneered. "Then I'm going to gut every one of your little helpers."

"Thought you didn't like getting your hands dirty," Jana retorted, trying to stall once again.

"I'll make an exception for you, sweetie."

Bell waited behind one of the filled slabs, trying to time when Jana would run. She tested the waters by pretending to dart one way, then pulling herself back to the safety of the slab. Bell didn't fall for it, poising himself for whichever way she chose to run. When she finally dashed out, like a rabbit cornered by a coyote, he dove and missed her feet by inches.

Making her way to the next restraining cot, Jana released a stranger from the confines of the straps and the tubes. She had only three people left to free, but Bell was already on his feet, pursuing her once again.

Despite his injuries, McCully made another valiant effort to stop Bell. From out of nowhere, he rammed Bell from the side, knocking them both to the floor. This time Jana got a closer look at his shoulder wound, which continued to bleed, based on the shiny liquid pooling atop his clothes. She suspected he was in great pain, and likely on the verge of losing consciousness after losing so much blood.

The elevator door opened, panning more light into the room once more. Jennings stepped out, looked around hurriedly, and found Bell beginning to get the better of McCully. He tried intervening once, found himself thrown back for his efforts, then scrambled to pull Bell away from McCully a second time.

Jana took advantage of the distraction, quickly undoing the tubing and bonds from another captive. She looked over, finding McCully receiving a vicious punch from Bell before Jennings struck him from behind. Barely phased, Bell turned on the hunter, kicking his wounded leg again. Jennings reached for the injured appendage, allowing Bell to shove him away.

Hearing a thunderous crash from Jennings falling over a pile of discarded clothing, Jana returned to the task of freeing the two remaining prisoners. She heard several painful grunts, looking up to see Bell repeated kicking and stomping Jennings in the area of his stomach and ribs.

Refusing to be distracted, she continued her work, hoping their efforts to distract Bell weren't in vain.

While undoing the leather straps holding the final stranger, she heard a clanking noise across the room, thinking perhaps a knife had hit the wall, or perhaps been dropped to the floor.

She dropped the final set of tubes to the floor with a wave of relief crossing her mind.

With all of the captives out of immediate danger, she looked for something to use against Bell, who had once again gotten the better of his two assailants. McCully and Jennings had bravely confronted him, but he had a size and strength advantage, as well as bladed weapons.

In the center of the room, she spied the switch Bell had referred to at the base of the large makeshift coffin. Though she didn't have time to study it further, Jana decided it looked very simplistic. One simple push forward likely activated the spring loaded joints meant to plunge the last needle into every prisoner's heart.

Jana had removed all of the tubes, and in most cases, snapped the killing needles from their deadly mechanisms. If Bell wanted to kill them all tonight, he would be spending countless hours putting the contraptions back together.

After a quick but fruitless search, Jana looked up, seeing Bell standing over both McCully and Jennings with no weapon in hand. She immediately looked for it, thinking it might be lodged somewhere in one of the men, but saw no knife handle. Hearing a groan from along the floor, she saw both of them move slightly, indicating they were alive, but in bad condition.

"I never would have hired you, had I thought you were so disobedient," Bell said, taking an ominous step toward her.

"You must have missed the part where I turned in my two-weeks notice," Jana countered, bringing a sinister grin to his face.

"That's okay. I'm going to give you a severance package you won't soon forget."

Jana began backing away from him, knowing she was truly on her own this time. Weaponless, she ducked behind one of the slabs for cover, simply prolonging the inevitable. In nearly complete darkness she managed to elude the shrewd eyes of a predator she once called her boss.

"You can't get away," Bell chided as she crawled from one device to another, hoping the low lighting didn't give her away. "Even if you make it to the elevator, you won't get the doors closed."

He continued to search for her, apparently unable to see her, or any shadows she made while crawling. Grasping around one of the cots, he missed her, because she was now three slabs away from him, looking up at Dan Duncan's unconscious form, thinking back to the last time she saw him wrapped in plastic.

His jacket and jeans contained sticky residue, as did his face. The plastic wrap had acted as a thick spider web of sorts, containing him until Bell subdued and unwrapped him. He looked peaceful, breathing in and out, but Jana refused to be mesmerized by the sight. She also refused to give up hope on Duncan and the other prisoners.

She needed a way out of this situation, away from Bell to buy some time.

The closet traps, she thought suddenly. A fleeting and hopeless thought, she decided quickly was using a trap from one of the twelve rooms to assist her. She had no idea how they worked, or how to open them, so Jana quickly moved on to simple preservation.

She made her way over to her injured protectors, finding McCully first. He didn't seem aware of her presence, but she couldn't do much for him without being noticed.

"Dave?" she whispered to him. "Dave, it's Jana. Can you hear me?"

His eyes remained closed, so she ran her hand up his back to detect his condition, and whether or not he was breathing. From beside her, Jennings groaned lightly, distracting her before she could analyze McCully.

She saw the hunter's eyes flutter open, then look beyond her. At first she thought he might be looking toward the pearly white gates in a death trance, then his lips moved.

"Behind you."

Jana whirled around, catching Bell by the right arm, but he forced her to the floor without hesitation or the least bit of trouble. Hitting hard, Jana injured her left wrist, but backpedaled away from Bell until she struck the narrow side of the coffin.

She hit headfirst, nearly knocking her senseless.

Bell took advantage of the opportunity, wrapping his hands around her throat, immediately cutting off the air to her lungs. Gasping for air, Jana heard a strange croak emit from her throat she'd never heard before. Before she was too far gone, she dug her nails into his forearms, scratching a trail from his hands to his elbows before he released his grip.

"That does it," he spat angrily, reaching again for her throat.

Jana had spotted a set of fully intact needles and tubes on the ground beside her, so instead of defending herself, she plucked them from the ground. As Bell lurched forward to strangle her, Jana plunged the needles with all her might into what she believed was his heart, using both hands.

A stunned look crossed Bell's face, almost paralyzing Jana with fear because he didn't fall over dead. Instead, he looked from the needles to her in obvious pain and utter shock. She recovered her senses enough to reach behind her, flipping the switch beside the coffin. Hoping the needles and tubes had enough kick to finish the job, she wriggled her way free from under him, then used both hands to give the needles one last shove into his chest.

The tube meant to plunge into the heart of its intended victims had already begun drawing fluids, and she now knew Bell had been mortally wounded. His eyelids fluttered momentarily, then stopped. A death trance crossed his face as he crashed to the floor. His eyes remained open, despite his head landing hard against the bare floor, his mouth partly agape.

Bell's death stare looked anything but peaceful.

Jana thought once of verifying his death, but decided to check on McCully and Jennings first.

Standing up, she heard only the sound of her footsteps as she crossed the room. When she reached the two injured men, she found Jennings attempting to sit up, clutching his ribs as he did so.

"You okay?" she inquired.

"I think so," he said, beginning to test his ribs by rubbing them. "I don't think any of them are broke."

Jana gently rolled McCully onto his back, trying to assess what Bell had done to him. He seemed to be breathing, but his chest rose and receded in a very shallow pattern. She detected no other open wounds aside from the shoulder, so she decided to test his consciousness.

"Just nod if you can hear me," she said in a soft voice, her face mere inches from his.

"I'm not deaf," he murmured in reply. "And I must say you still smell really nice for what you've been through."

He opened his eyes painfully, wincing when he tried sitting up.

"I hope you two didn't fake unconsciousness so I'd save you," Jana said, trying to break any remaining tension.

"There was no faking," Jennings said, still rubbing his side. "He put an ass-whoopin' on us."

Jana heard the suction of the tubes from behind her, so she stood to turn off the device, realizing quite a bit of Bell's bodily fluids had already been drained. She found a rag draped over one of the slabs, so she snagged it to apply pressure on McCully's wound. He didn't make a sound when she covered his wound, indicating some form of shock had overtaken part of his mind.

"We have to get Red," he stated, though not moving.

"Where is he?" Jana asked, thankful to hear he was alive.

"I left him in a closet downstairs with a gun."

Jana wondered why Red wouldn't have helped overpower Bell.

"Why didn't he come up with you?"

"His leg is broken. I put him in there for his own safety, thinking the killer might come after him."

Realizing she had most certainly struck Red with the truck, Jana felt bad, wondering if perhaps she had saved him in a roundabout way.

"How did you get back here?" she asked Jennings.

"I got to town and couldn't find any help, so I doubled back through the woods and found Dave downstairs. He told me what this place looked like, so we used the elevator and hid out to fool the bad guy."

"My boss," Jana revealed, drawing stares somewhere between mystified and deeply concerned from both men. "Well, ex-boss."

All three chuckled momentarily, too tired to find help, leave the room, or even get up from the floor.

37

By early morning, everyone inside the third level had recovered to the point they were awake and able to be moved downstairs. Like refugees, they sat or stood throughout the downstairs. Most were covered with blankets, refusing to stray very far from the safety of other people.

Jana noticed a variety of emotions and expressions from the survivors. Some appeared shocked, while others cried. Some simply sat quietly, while others found comfort in conversation.

McCully and Jennings found the sheriff in the basement kitchen area lying against the far wall. He seemed quite irritated, but in excellent health. Bell had indeed left him alive, though sedated and bound. The two men freed him, then explained the situation as best they could.

Brown listened, only after verifying his son was among the living, though he seemed dismayed about Bell's crazy plan. Jana felt better knowing the best local legal authority knew the real story before anyone else, so they didn't all sound crazy when the time for questions came later.

As the storm front passed through Southern Indiana, Red finally got a signal from his cellular phone, allowing him to call the authorities. Jana tried keeping everyone away from the grizzly death scene in the dining area and upper kitchen, but Keith refused to be denied. He grieved Laura in his own way, though he didn't actually touch the body thanks to advice from his brother.

"He's taking it hard," she commented to Red.

He simply nodded, supporting himself on a doorframe as they waited for the police and ambulances to arrive.

"You really should sit down," Jana told him.

"It's okay. I guess tonight made me realize how important friends and family are. I'm just really glad I didn't lose *him*."

His blue eyes continued to stare at Keith, although his older brother seemed frustrated, angry, and saddened all at the same time. Perhaps he held himself partly responsible, but Bryan Bell wouldn't want to share his credit, or the money he might have received for his services.

Keith seemed to be holding back his emotions, and possibly some tears, but he paced the foyer, occasionally punching a wall as his head drooped toward the floor. For the first time Jana had seen the man without his hat and sport coat. He didn't appear nearly as distinguished, looking disheveled after losing his temper, and some self-control.

"I'm not sure I understand all of this," Red told Jana.

"Me neither," she answered. "I keep thinking this is some weird dream and I'm going to wake up from it any minute."

She looked around, finding the mansion far more peaceful, like the aftermath of a weathered hurricane. A few of the long-term prisoners appeared weak, pale, and dreadfully thin. Jana wished she could cook them up a quick meal, or at least serve them a hot drink, but going into the kitchen wasn't an option.

McCully had said a few things to her that indicated he knew quite a bit about how the device upstairs worked, and how Bell and Smith knew one another. She didn't press for information, because she still felt thoroughly confused about the situation. What the hell was she going to tell the police?

Placing the blame on Bell's insanity, or at least the insanity of his plan, seemed appropriate, but no one could verify her story. Jana only knew she wanted to speak with the police, because it would surely be mandatory. After that she could go home to a hot bath.

She found McCully waiting by the front door, so she walked over to him, gently putting a hand across his back. Staring out the same glass trim, she noticed the snow had began melting outside as a warm front moved into the area.

Despite his injuries, McCully refused to rest until the others were freed. Jana nursed his wounds the best she could, applying fresh towels to the stab wound in his shoulder. She also found bandages for his busted nose, knowing it would require stitches to heal correctly.

Staring at the snow banks, she knew it might take a few days for the snow to completely disappear, but depressions along the tops of the snow piles indicated warmer air was already moving through. A dark purple horizon appeared over the tree line, indicating dawn was inevitable.

"Easy come, easy go," McCully said, his eyes still fixed beyond the window. "I can't believe we were trapped here all night, and now the weather clears up. It's almost like your boss had custom ordered it."

"No," Jana replied evenly. "The blizzard splitting us up might have been the only thing that saved us."

"Tell that to Laura and Judith."

Having no reply to such a comment, Jana simply took hold of his nearest arm, trying to pat it reassuringly. McCully didn't resist, so she assumed he still wanted company.

"This house might have been built for the wrong reasons, but the weather was a saving grace," she added a moment later. "Things could have been a lot worse."

Blue and red lights appeared like beacons in the distance, looking something like blinking Christmas lights against the snow outside. At last the authorities had made their way up the hill, now nearing the mansion.

"The cavalry," McCully said with absolutely no enthusiasm.

A moment passed as they waited for the police cars to make their way up the treacherous road, then park as close as they could to the mansion.

"Where do you go from here?" McCully asked Jana, as though realizing he had been absorbed in his own thoughts all evening.

"I guess I'll be searching for a new job," Jana said in a light-hearted voice, though knowing she spoke the truth. "Maybe Mr. Clouse needs an executive assistant."

"He'll be needing something, alright. After tonight, I doubt his empire will be the same."

McCully paused momentarily, thinking about something.

"Smith really hated him."

"How do you *know* that?" Jana inquired, suspecting McCully told the truth, though unsure where he attained such information.

"I just do. He thought Clouse caused his son's death, and I guess I can relate to a father and son bond. Just makes me wonder what the truth really is."

Jana counted three police cars in the driveway, hearing more sirens in the distance. Two county officers and one town marshal from West Baden made their way toward the mansion as she and McCully stepped aside to let them through.

All three men stepped inside, saying nothing momentarily as they surveyed the walking wounded with confused stares.

"Who called this in?" one the county officers finally asked, despite Roland and Arlan Brown sitting near everyone else.

"I did," Red claimed, hobbling on his good leg toward the officers. "You're going to need a few ambulances and a couple of thick notepads, boys."

*   *   *

It felt like forever as the group waited for medical attention while the officers took their statements. Everyone wanted to go home, or at least escape the confines of the mansion.

McCully had already given his statement to an officer, or at least the parts of it he felt comfortable speaking about. One word about psychic visions would instantly discredit him as a viable witness, so he kept quiet about the insider details.

One officer taped off the area surrounding the two bodies downstairs, leaving the lower level entry door free for travel. The officers seemed hesitant about going near the bodies, mainly because the coroner had informed them he was en route.

McCully currently sat by himself in the large living room, looking at the survivors around him. Most of them he didn't know, but Oswalt and Duncan made their way toward him once the police finished with them.

It seemed the authorities deemed it necessary to interview everyone right away to preserve evidence, as though some of them might change their stories or forget details.

"How are you two?" McCully asked, truly wondering what each of them had experienced.

Jana had informed him about Duncan's struggle with a certain plastic trap.

"Better," Duncan admitted, still trying to peel some of the sticky substance from his clothing.

The residue spots along his jacket and jeans looked as though someone had taken a paintbrush and dotted him intermittently with rubber cement.

Jana had given him a wet cloth to wipe the residue from his hands and face. She had no idea what the substance might have been, but it held a stout man in check without fail. Smith had planned the sacrifice perfectly, using his medical expertise and some creative inventions.

"I'll never get this shit off my jacket," Duncan complained, trying to wash it off with the wet rag.

"And I thought my last divorce settlement was the worst day of my life," Oswalt said, indicating his wry sense of humor had already returned.

"Jana isn't saying much," Duncan stated, "so can you tell me what the hell just happened up there, and why?"

McCully sat a moment, thinking of exactly how he wanted to craft his words.

"Seems to me someone wanted to bring a warped, rich old man back to life. You guys were the sacrificial lambs."

"I gathered that," Duncan said stiffly. "I guess my real question is would the thing have worked?"

McCully believed with all of his heart the device actually would have succeeded. He doubted Dr. Smith was a fool, or a man who wasted valuable time and energy on anything lacking merit.

"You know, I've experienced some weird things in my life," McCully admitted, "so I wouldn't doubt the thing might have worked. I guess it's a good thing we didn't find out."

Oswalt sat pensively a moment, probably reflecting on the night, and how close to death he truly came. He sniffled as he breathed in, though McCully couldn't tell if he had a cold, or emotions had overwhelmed him. The agent rubbed his cheeks momentarily before burying his entire face within his palms.

A moment later, he looked up with a more resolved appearance.

"For what it's worth, thanks for everything you did up there," he finally said to McCully.

"Jana did most of it, but you're welcome."

Both men seemed reluctant to give Jana any credit, despite her efforts to save Duncan from his earlier predicament.

"If it wasn't for her, we wouldn't have been here," Oswalt commented.

"No," Duncan stated very sternly. "If not for *me*, you wouldn't have been here. I was the one who got us into this mess. I let my devotion toward this place and my grandfather blind me."

McCully didn't feel like placing blame. Simply happy to be alive, he didn't want to think about touring with his father, or investing in property. He wanted to lay his head on a pillow inside some well-secured hotel room and forget about the past twenty-four hours.

"Don't blame yourself," he told Duncan. "There's no way we could've known this was all a trap."

He then turned to his agent.

"And don't blame Jana. She was duped like the rest of us, and if Bell had gotten her strapped in that thing upstairs, you all would have been dead."

Oswalt gave a genuine nod that he understood. Everyone had survived a major ordeal, so emotions ran unchecked as they recalled the experience. McCully stood, placing an understanding hand on Oswalt's shoulder.

"You going to be okay?"

"I'll be fine."

"Good. It's all over, so don't sweat it, Frank."

Oswalt nodded once more, though his eyes seemed to drift to a faraway place.

When the coroner arrived a few minutes later, more questions ensued. He spoke mainly with the police officers, then talked to Red, who simply shrugged at most of the questions. McCully imagined he was inquiring about any witnesses to the deaths of Laura and Judith, but of course no one had seen either incident.

The mansion had a way of hiding its events.

The coroner retreated to the outdoors, then returned with his camera momentarily. With a police officer keeping close watch on the door, he began snapping photographs of the death scenes. McCully thought it somewhat odd the coroner worried about interference from people who had no desire to see their dead colleague a second time.

McCully found himself watching the business of the coroner and the police, to satisfy personal curiosity more than anything, from the foyer. He left Oswalt and Duncan to talk amongst themselves, but no words seemed to express their true feelings after surviving such an ordeal.

The town marshal returned from the lower kitchen with an exasperated look on his face. Though no lip reader, McCully thought he recognized the word "body" from the man's lips. He subconsciously began stepping closer, wondering what the fuss was about, because the officer's expression seemed unusually concerned.

All morning the officers had secretly exchanged smirks and jokes when they thought none of the guests were looking, but McCully noticed. He drew as close as he could to the door without looking like he was eavesdropping, then remained perfectly still.

"They said there were two bodies on the third level," the officer reported to the county officer in charge, and the coroner. "I only found one."

All three exchanged worried looks.

"Talk to some of the guests again," the county officer said, wanting verification. "I'm sure they said there were two."

McCully watched him ask a few of the guests who had been ushered from the third level hurriedly to keep them from seeing the bodies. They simply shrugged, saying they had no idea how many bodies were upstairs.

For a moment, he wondered if they didn't count the shriveled corpse as a body, thinking there were supposed to be two fresh corpses. He doubted the marshal would be so naive, nor would he return without checking the entire upstairs thoroughly.

McCully motioned for Jana and Jennings to join him as the marshal made his way toward them. He wanted the two people who could confirm what he knew to be the truth with him when the question was asked. Both had snuck a peek at Smith's corpse while they waited for the other prisoners to revive.

"What's wrong?" Jennings questioned.

"You're about to find out."

Holding his hat in his hands, the marshal made his way over to them, looking uneasy. McCully sensed the man hated to bother them, especially since everyone else had said they knew nothing about bodies upstairs.

"Folks, I hate to bother you, but I have to ask a question."

He hesitated until he received the full attention of all three people. Jana had continued looking to McCully for answers, but he simply nodded toward the marshal, hoping she would do the same.

"How many bodies were there upstairs?"

"Two," Jennings answered immediately, his answer confirmed by nods from Jana and McCully.

Now he appeared even more discontent about their conversation.

"You're positive?"

"Absolutely," McCully said. "One was the killer who masterminded the whole thing, and there was another one inside that coffin thing in the middle of the room."

Simply nodding, the marshal turned to report back to the county officer.

In his heart, McCully already knew the answer to the new mystery, but Jana took a step forward, grasping the marshal's arm.

"What's wrong?" she virtually demanded. "Bryan was dead. I'm sure of it."

Now caught by his own actions, the marshal swallowed hard, forced to reveal something about the new development.

"Ma'am, he was up there. It was the other body we couldn't find."

Jana's grasp released the officer's arm, her hands falling away like wilting vines from a fence post. She turned to McCully with a look of disbelief and horror, asking what in the hell happened upstairs without uttering one word.

Jennings appeared equally stunned, but he immediately shook his head in disbelief aimed at the cops, rather than the impossible possibility all three initially questioned.

"They're covering it up again," he stammered angrily. "I can see the writing on the wall."

Jana looked confused, then bought into his theory because it seemed so much more realistic, and easier for the mind to digest. McCully pulled her into an embrace as her world crumbled around her, believing differently than his two companions. He had seen the look on the marshal's face when he emerged from the kitchen stairway.

Like Jennings and Jana at first, his face displayed total disbelief. Though McCully thought it impossible through conventional wisdom and simple logic, he wondered if Bryan Bell had indeed given life to the dead through his *own* sacrifice.

Counting himself lucky to be alive, McCully didn't dare pose questions he couldn't answer. Something told him if this mystery wasn't finished, his mind would let him know it in due time.

He watched the exasperated marshal explaining the situation to the county officer and the coroner, his arms doing some of the talking for him. McCully kept his arms wrapped around Jana while Jennings continued to fume over what he considered a police scandal. Local people had been given a raw deal by the press and police before, so his thought process seemed logical.

Taking in a deep breath, McCully created his own vision, placing himself sleeping the rest of the day before heading home to Tennessee. Perhaps one day he would write a song based on the tragic experience at West Baden, but right now he felt content just being alive.

The arch near Highway 56 at the hotel's grand entrance has taken on several names over the years.

A snowy scene along the brick path leading toward the West Baden Springs Hotel. The same scene used on the cover (credit Amy Burke for photo).

The opposite view of the brick path during springtime. A look from the hotel's entrance toward the highway and arch.

One of the two remaining springs, Apollo stands near the entrance of the sunken garden. The Jesuits capped it with rocks and concrete, so it no longer functions as a working spring.

The fountain is centered in the sunken garden, reconstructed from old photos by the Cooks and Historic Landmarks during the restoration.

The Jesuit cemetery remains on the hotel grounds. The Jesuits have always maintained the garden, even when the rest of the property was overgrown with weeds and shrubs.

The Hygeia Spring was fully restored during renovation of the grounds. Attempts to restore it to a working spring failed, so it remains capped, offering beauty through its stained-glass windows and trellises.

To keep his guests on the grounds as much as possible, Sinclair built a Catholic church behind the hotel. Named Our Lady of Lourdes, the church was torn down in 1934 due to structural instability.

The entrance to West Baden Springs Hotel provides a different view than years past. Large trees were left intact during the restoration, providing shade around the veranda.

During the hotel's heyday, the veranda often provided guests a spot to converse, or simply sit in rocking chairs. The lobby doors were often opened for ventilation before the days of air-conditioning.

The Sinclair coat of arms was built into the veranda during the 1917 renovation
of West Baden Springs.

A rear view of the hotel shot near the observatory.

A view of the hotel's grand atrium. Five levels of rooms loom over the 1st Floor, providing guests with a view over the atrium.

At one end of the atrium is a fireplace large enough to hold a handful of adults at one time. The imp known as Sprudel can be seen on the right.

The upper portion of the lobby, which the Jesuits converted to a chapel because the atrium was too large for their needs. Many of the intricate details shown here were redone by hand during the restoration.

A view of the old barbershop taken from beside an atrium doorway. The room also housed an area for shoe shines.

Highlighted is Andrew Duncan with a number of associates and hotel guests
before the renovation of 1917.

Dave McCully (top left): Bluegrass singer from Nashville, Tennessee.

Jana Privett (top right): Agent hoping to sell the West Baden Springs Hotel for Paul Clouse.

Dan Duncan (bottom left): Investor and avid motorcyclist who hopes to purchase the hotel with his group. Has ties to the Salem, Indiana area.

Craig Jennings (bottom right): Hunter who shows up where the investors are staying when everything seems to be going wrong.

Frank Oswalt (top left): Music agent from Nashville, Tennessee who works for Dave McCully and the singer's father.

Red Sanders (top right): Owns a trucking business. Started the Lone Star Investment group with his older brother.

Arlan Brown (bottom left): Deputy who goes searching for his missing father and discovers more than he hopes for.

Keith Sanders (bottom right): The leader and founder of Lone Star Investments. Made his millions through cattle ranching in Texas.

About the Author

Author Patrick J. O'Brian works as a firefighter in Muncie, Indiana. A theme park and roller coaster enthusiast, he writes during his spare time. Patrick also enjoys photography and traveling to carry out his research. This is his tenth book in print.

978-0-595-42136-7
0-595-42136-9

Printed in the United States
65441LVS00004B/271-309

9 780595 421367